MIDDLE UNEARTHED
THE BEST FANTASY
SHORT STORIES
1800–1849

ANDREW BARGER

BOTTLETREE BOOKS LLC
UNITED STATES OF AMERICA

#BESTFANTASYSHORTSTORIES

Again to Maeve,
whose mind never ceases to amaze, and gaze never
ceases to find room for improvement in my draft
manuscripts.

Up spoke the moody Elfin King,
Who won'd within the hill,—
Like wind in the porch of a ruin'd church,
His voice was ghostly shrill.

1810 "Lady of the Lake"
Sir Walter Scott

CONTENTS

MIDDLE UNEARTHED

Before there were lovable green ogres called Shrek and fury-footed hobbits named Frodo, there were these stories, which are perhaps the ten best fantasy short stories written in the first half of the nineteenth century. In a sense they are the "middle earth" of fantasy stories; published in a time before our modern tales that have become so popular they have put these characters of the genre onto T-shirts and lunchboxes, and had action figures and animated movies created in their likeness. Yet the fantasy stories in this collection were penned after the very early folktales and dramas and poetry that spawned many of these characters in the first place. The stories rest somewhere on the loamy soil between these two states of the fantasy genre.

Elves. Gnomes. Sprites. Fairies. Trolls. Wizards. Sylphs. Kelpies. Mermaids. Witches. Brownies. Number-nips. Goblins. Dwarves. Ogres. These popular fantasy characters were all known and their stories were being developed during the fifty year period between 1800 and 1849. Unlike werewolf and vampire stories, which were fledgling genres at the time, most other parts of the fantasy genre were quite robust; thanks, primarily, to European storytellers who towered over this space and transformed legend and folktales into exciting fantasy tales.

The Brothers' Grimm were two of the most popular German writers during this time and published the enduring children fantasy stories "Little Red Riding Hood," "The Frog and the Prince," "Rumpelstiltskin," "Cinderella," "Snow White," "Hansel and Gretel," and many others. Ernst Raupach, German author of one of the earliest vampire stories in the English language, "Wake Not the Dead," included a wizard who resurrected a corpse in his most famous shorts story. The venerable Sir Walter Scott thought so highly of the genre that he published *The Black Dwarf* in 1816 as part of his popular series of Waverly Novels. Two years later, James Hogg, another well-known Scott writing in the fantasy genre, penned *The Brownie Bodsbeck* that was well received and was, perhaps, the first novel about those mischievous brownie creatures who were rumored to take up residence in the homes of the unwary.

For the most part, the American literati shied away from the fantasy genre during this fifty year period. This may be a result of the European dominance in this space or because they simply felt a need to establish themselves in more serious ways. The fantasy legends that had been bubbling up over the centuries were, after all, not American. America, the country, did not even exist before 1776. With little surprise, it was Edgar Allan Poe who wrote the most American fantasy stories during the fifty year period in question. For the most part, however, they are lackluster efforts that failed to rise to the level of the stories in this collection given their lack of character development. The fantasy genre is unlike the horror genre where Poe rose over all other writers (regardless of their native land) in both scope and depth of stories. Washington Irving and Nathaniel Hawthorne wrote a couple of fantasy stories, too. But neither included any traditional fantasy characters in them such as fairies or gnomes.

This is not to say that a story must contain a troll or dwarf or fairy to be considered a fantasy tale. Fantasy is a catch-all genre of sorts. Many stories that lack description of how a thing is done or operates, fall out of the science fiction genre and are snared by the wide net of fantasy. Stories with magic potions and disappearing protagonists come to mind. The first half of the nineteenth century was also a time when the term "fairy tales" actually meant stories about *fairies* instead of the common definition that is so often used loosely today to encompass *any* type of fantasy story aimed at children.

In the late sixteenth century we have dancing fairies in *A Midsummer Night's Dream* by William Shakespeare. But fantasy characters were known as far back as the thirteenth century when Thomas Learmonth penned "Thomas the Rhymer" that had the protagonist being taken to Elfland in the poem. Sir Walter Scott translated and expanded the ballad in 1804 to include a sequel where Thomas returns to Elfland in "middle earth," referencing a place on earth (or rather a place under the earth's surface); a habitation inside its deep caves, many of which had yet to be explored.

Middle earth.
A more traditional meaning of the term was laid out by Shakespeare, two hundred years before Sir Walter Scott's definition. Shakespeare had the fairies referring to middle earth as a place on the surface of the earth in his comedy, *The Merry Wives of Windsor.*

> And twenty glow-worms shall our lanterns be,
> To guide our measure round about the tree.
> But, stay; I smell a man of middle earth!

And we find this definition in the footnotes of *The Merry Wives of Windsor* contained in "The Plays of William Shakespeare with Notes by Johnson and Steevens," Vol. III, dated 1805:

"Spirits are supposed to inhabit the ethereal regions, and fairies to dwell underground; men therefore are in a middle station. *Johnson.*

"So, in the ancient metrical romance of *Syr Guy of Warwick* bl. I. no date:
'And Win the fayrest mayde of *middle erde.*'

"Again, in Gower, *De confessions Amantis*, fol. 26:
'Adam, for pride lost his price
'In *mydell erth.*"

"Again, in the MSS. called *William and the Werwolf*, in the library of King's College, Cambridge, p. 15:
'And saide God that madest man, and all *middel erthe.*'

"Ruddiman, the learned compiler of the Glossary to Gawin Douglas's Translation of the □*neid*, affords the following illustration of this contested phrase: 'It is yet in use in the North of Scotland among old people, by which they understand *this earth in which we live, in opposition to the grave:* Thus they say, *There's no man in middle erd is able to do it, i.e. no man alive, or on this earth,* and so it is used by our author. But the reason is not so easy to come by; perhaps it is because they look upon this life as a *middle state* (as it is) between Heaven and Hell; which last is frequently taken for the grave. Or that life is as it were a *middle* betwixt non-entity, before we are born, and death, when we go hence and are no more seen; as life is called a coming into the world, and death a going out of it.'—— Again among the Addenda to the Glossary aforesaid, '*Myddil erd* is borrowed from the A. S. MIDDAN-EARD, MIDDANGEARD, *mundus*, MIDDANEARDLICE, *mundanus*, SE LAESA MIDDANEARD, *microcosmus*.' *Steevens*.

"The author of *The Remarks* says the phrase signifies, neither more nor less, than the *earth* or *world*, from its imaginary situation in the *midst* or *middle* of the Ptolemaic system, and has not the least reference to either spirits or fairies."

From the surface of the earth to somewhere below its surface was the traditional meaning of middle earth until J.R.R. Tolkien came along. He took a different approach in the twentieth century; or perhaps misinterpreted the traditional meaning of middle earth. He admitted that he did not invent the term and further defined it as a fictional *time period* on earth instead of a location. "Middle-earth is not an imaginary world. The name is the modern form (appearing in the 13th century) of *midden-erd* or *middel-erd*, an ancient name for the oikoumene, the abiding place of Men, the objectively real world, in use specifically opposed to imaginary worlds (as Fairyland) or unseen worlds (as Heaven or Hell). The theatre of my tale is this earth, the one in which we now live, but the historical period is imaginary." (Letters, no. 183)

The first appearance of middle earth in a short story appears to come from the highly acclaimed German author Friedrich La Motte-Fouqué in 1821. In the "Dwarfs of the Nine Mountains of Rambin," he tells of the "realms of middle earth" that are inhabited by dwarfs. This is a reference to middle earth being a location underground, where the dwarfs hold sway; a place somewhere between the center of earth and its surface just as Sir Walter Scott described it in his 1804 translation of "Thomas the Rhymer."

Because of its disjointed storyline, the "Dwarfs of the Nine Mountains of Rambin" did not make the cut for inclusion in this collection because so many great authors—Hall of Fame authors—wrote in the fantasy space. As stated, Edgar Allan Poe and Washington Irving and Nathaniel Hawthorne wrote American fantasy short stories. Despite these heavyweights who wrote in the genre, the rather obscure Joseph Holt Ingraham and Elizabeth Ellet were the only American fantasy writers whose stories rose to the level of this collection. They were both one-hit wonders in that regard. In Germany, Friedrich La Motte-Fouqué and E. T. A. Hoffmann and Wilhelm Hauff wrote ground-breaking stories in the fantasy genre, along with many others.

Britain's Mary Shelley gave us the darkly romantic "Transformation" thirteen years after *Frankenstein; or, the Modern Prometheus*. Her countryman, George Darley, penned "Lilian of the Vale" in 1824, which is the oldest fantasy story in this collection and a cornerstone of character-driven fairy tales in the English language. Five years later, the mystical "Seddik Ben Saad the Magician" was published in the British magazine *The Imperial*. George Soane (one of the most underrated horror and fantasy writers of the early nineteenth century) penned another excellent fairy tale in "The Pale Lady" that is also included in this collection. John MacKay Wilson was another Brit who, like Mary Shelley, gave the world a darkly romantic fantasy story in "The Doom of Soulis." Last but not least is good ole Charles Dickens who published the funny and frightening tale "The Story of the Goblins Who Stole a Sexton," which many view as a precursor to his famous novella "A Christmas Carol."

Enjoy these fantasy short stories from above and below. They are not the first and certainly not the last to whet our literary minds with fantastic creatures. They come from the "middle earth" of the genre.

Andrew Barger
January 25, 2015

Charles Dickens
(1812-1870)

"Charles Dickens was born near Portsmouth, England, February 7, 1812. Early on he developed a fondness for reading, and when only nine years old had read *Don Quixote*, *Gil Bias*, *Robinson Crusoe*, and several of the early English novels.

"When he was ten, his father, who was a clerk in the Navy, lost his employment, and was imprisoned for debt. The boy was placed in a blacking factory, where he pasted labels on the bottles of blacking. After a time his father, released from prison, secured an engagement as reporter on the Morning Herald, and Charles was again sent to school. A few years later he entered a lawyer's office as clerk, but he had no taste for this work, and taught himself shorthand, with the idea of becoming a journalist. At the age of seventeen he became a reporter at Doctors' Commons, a court building of London, and at twenty-two he was employed as a reporter on the staff of the London Morning Chronicle. His work required him to travel all over England, collecting items of news and writing up such incidents as are now telegraphed to the papers daily by local reporters. As there were no railroads at the time, he went by stagecoach from place to place, and in this way he mingled with the people and saw every phase of life. While thus engaged he began to contribute original papers, under the signature "Boz," to the Evening

Chronicle. They were afterwards collected and published separately as "Sketches by Boz." In 1836 the *Pickwick Papers* appeared. These brought him fame and fortune, and he soon became the most popular writer of English fiction.

"The events and surroundings of Dickens's own early life, the people he met, and the places he visited as a reporter, constantly appear in his novels and stories. It was at Camden Town, for instance, while he worked in the blacking factory, that he lived with an old lady who took children to board, and who, he afterwards said, was the original of Mrs. Pipchin in *Dombey and Son.*

"The most striking feature of Dickens as an author is the skill with which he seizes upon some peculiar trait or quality in one of the persons of his story, exaggerates it, and keeps it before his reader until all other traits and qualities are forgotten, and that character becomes the very personification of that one quality. This is called caricaturing, and Dickens was such a master of the art, that the very names of his leading characters have become a part of our language, and stand as synonyms for their respective peculiarities. We can today give no better idea of a miser than to call him a Scrooge, or of a hard master than to call him a Tackleton.

"Nearly all Dickens's novels were written with some distinct good purpose. In *Dombey and Son* the pride and selfishness of old London merchants are depicted; *Oliver Twist* exposed the practice of training boys to commit crime; *Nicholas Nickleby* called attention to the cruel treatment of boys in cheap boarding-schools; *Hard Times* showed the sufferings of the factory hands; *Bleak House* pictured the position of wards in Chancery and the slow process of law in England at that time; *Little Dorrit* showed the horrors of the debtors' prisons. *David Copperfield* is supposed to refer in some parts to his own life.

"Dickens loved to write about children, and of all his child-characters there are none so beautiful, so noble, so affecting as Little Nell, as we see her in *Old Curiosity Shop.* Her gentleness, her kind and loving nature, her devotion to her grandfather, her wonderful patience in her many sufferings—these have excited the admiration of all readers of Dickens. The story of her death, and of the old man's grief and loneliness until he was laid to rest by her side, is perhaps the most pathetic writing in the English language. Few can read it without being moved to tears.

"Dickens visited America first in 1842, and upon his return wrote *American Notes* and *Martin Chuzzlewit*. His sarcasm and the severity with which in these two books he caricatured the people he met excited indignation among Americans. This feeling gradually passed away, however, and in 1868, upon his second visit, he was cordially received in all the larger cities of the United States. He read selections from his own works, and crowds came to hear him.

"In England he was universally popular. The queen offered him a title of nobility, but he declined it, saying that he wished to be remembered by no other name than Charles Dickens. He continued to write until the very day of his death, and left unfinished *The Mystery of Edwin Drood*, which promised to be one of his best novels. He died suddenly on the 8th of June, 1870, and the nation paid him homage by burying him in the Poets' Corner in Westminster Abbey."[1]

It may come as some surprise that "The Story of the Goblins Who Stole a Sexton" is a precursor to *A Christmas Carol*, arguably Charles Dickens's most famous novel and on which countless plays are still acted out during Christmastime to this very day. There are also never-ending movies and animated shows based on the novel. The fantasy story, "The Story of the Goblins Who Stole a Sexton" was published in 1836, seven years before Dickens published *A Christmas Carol* on December 19, 1843.

"The Story of the Goblin Who Stole a Sexton" was published as the tenth installment in his serialized collection of short stories—*The Pickwick Papers*—in December of 1836. It has all the trappings of the enduring Dickens's classic. The story happens on Christmas Eve to a crotchety sexton who is visited by very interesting goblins determined to change the sexton's ways. But this is not the story of Ebenezer Scrooge; rather one about "Gabriel Grub! Gabriel Grub!"

---

[1] "The Story of Little Nell from Old Curiosity Shop," Introduction, 1897

THE STORY OF THE GOBLINS WHO STOLE A SEXTON
1836

IN AN OLD abbey town, down in this part of the country, a long, long while ago—so long, that the story must be a true one, because our great grandfathers implicitly believed it—there officiated as sexton and grave-digger in the churchyard, one Gabriel Grub. It by no means follows that because a man is a sexton, and constantly surrounded by emblems of mortality, therefore, he should be a morose and melancholy man. Your undertakers are the merriest fellows in the world, and I once had the honor of being on intimate terms with a mute, who, in private life, and off duty, was as comical and jocose a little fellow as ever chirped out a devil-may-care song without a hitch in his memory or drained off a good stiff glass of grog without stopping for breath.

But notwithstanding these precedents to the contrary, Gabriel Grub was an ill-conditioned, cross-grained, surly fellow—a morose and lonely man, who consorted with nobody but himself, and an old wicker bottle which fitted into his large deep waistcoat pocket; and who eyed each merry face as it passed him by, with such a deep scowl of malice and ill-humor, as it was difficult to meet without feeling something the worse for.

A little before twilight one Christmas Eve, Gabriel shouldered his spade, lighted his lantern, and took himself towards the old churchyard, for he had a grave to finish by next morning, and feeling very low, he thought it might raise his spirits, perhaps, if he went on with his work at once.

As he wended his way, up the ancient street, he saw the cheerful light of the blazing fires gleam through the old casements, and heard the loud laugh and the cheerful shouts of those who were assembled around them. He marked the bustling preparations for the next day's good cheer and smelt the numerous savory odors consequent thereupon, as they steamed up from the kitchen window in clouds. All this was gall and wormwood to the heart of

Gabriel Grub; and, as groups of children bounded out of the houses, tripped across the road, and were met, before they could knock at the opposite door, by half a dozen curly-headed little rascals, who crowded round them as they knocked up stairs to spend the evening in their Christmas games, Gabriel smiled grimly, and clutched the handle of his spade with a firmer grasp, as he thought of measles, scarlet-fever, thrush, hooping-cough, and a good many other sources of consolation beside.

In this happy frame of mind, Gabriel strode along, returning a short, sullen growl to the good-humored greetings of such of his neighbors as now and then passed him, until he turned into the dark lane which led to the churchyard. Now, Gabriel had been looking forward to reaching the dark lane, because it was, generally speaking, a nice gloomy mournful place, into which the townspeople did not much care to go, except in broad daylight, and when the sun was shining. Consequently he was not a little indignant to hear a young urchin roaring out some jolly song about a merry Christmas, in this very sanctuary, which had been called Coffin Lane ever since the days of the old abbey, and the time of the shaven-headed monks.

As Gabriel walked on, and the voice drew nearer, he found it proceeded from a small boy, who was hurrying along, to join one of the little parties in the old street, and who, partly to keep himself company, and partly to prepare himself for the occasion, was shouting out the song at the highest pitch of his lungs. So Gabriel waited till the boy came up, and then dodged him into a corner, and rapped him over the head with his lantern, five or six times, just to teach him to modulate his voice. And as the boy hurried away with his hand to his head, singing quite a different sort of tune, Gabriel Grub chuckled very heartily to himself, and entered the church-yard, locking the gate behind him.

He took off his coat, set down his lantern, and getting into the unfinished grave, worked at it for an hour or so, with right good will. But the earth was hardened with the frost, and it was no very easy matter to break it up, and shovel it out; and although there was a moon, it was a very young one, and shed little light upon the grave, which was in the shadow of the church. At any other time, these obstacles would have made Gabriel Grub very moody and miserable, but he was so well pleased with having stopped the boy's singing, that he took little heed of the scanty progress he had made, and looked down into the grave, when he had finished work for the night, with grim satisfaction, murmuring as he gathered up his things—

> Brave lodgings for one, brave lodgings for one,
> A few feet of cold earth, when life is done;
> A stone at the head, a stone at the feet,
> A rich, juicy meal for the worms to eat;
> Rank grass overhead, and damp clay around,
> Brave lodgings for one, these, in holy ground!

"Ho, ho!" laughed Gabriel Grub, as he sat himself down on a flat tombstone, which was a favorite resting-place of his; and drew forth his wicker bottle. "A coffin at Christmas—a Christmas box. Ho! ho! ho!"

"Ho! ho! ho!" repeated a voice which sounded close behind him.

Gabriel paused in some alarm, in the act of raising the wicker bottle to his lips, and looked around. The bottom of the oldest grave about him was not more still and quiet than the churchyard in the pale moonlight. The cold hoar frost glistened on the tombstones, and sparkled like rows of gems among the stone carvings of the old church. The snow lay hard and crisp on the ground, and spread over the thickly strewn mounds of earth, so white and smooth a cover that it seemed as if corpses lay there, hidden only by their winding sheets. Not the faintest rustle broke the profound tranquility of the solemn scene. Sound itself appeared to be frozen, all was so cold and still.

"It was the echoes," said Gabriel Grub, raising the bottle to his lips again.

"It was not," said a deep voice.

Gabriel started up, and stood rooted to the spot with astonishment and terror; for his eyes rested on a form which made his blood run cold.

Seated on an upright tombstone, close to him, was a strange unearthly figure, whom Gabriel felt at once was no being of this world. His long fantastic legs, which might have reached the ground, were cocked up, and crossed after a quaint, fantastic fashion. His sinewy arms were bare, and his hands rested on his knees. On his short round body he wore a close covering, ornamented with small slashes; and a short cloak dangled at his back. The collar was cut into curious peaks, which served the goblin in lieu of a ruff or neckerchief; and his shoes curled up at the toes into long points. On his head he wore a broad brimmed sugar loaf hat, garnished with a single feather. The hat was covered with the white frost, and the goblin looked as if he had sat on the same tombstone very comfortably, for two or three hundred years. He was sitting perfectly still. His tongue was put out, as if in derision; and he was grinning at Gabriel Grub with such a grin as only a goblin could call up.

"It was not the echoes," said the goblin.

Gabriel Grub was paralyzed, and could make no reply.

"What do you do here on Christmas Eve?" said the Goblin sternly.

"I came to dig a grave, sir," stammered Gabriel Grub.

"What man wanders among graves and churchyards on such a night as this?" said the goblin.

"Gabriel Grub! Gabriel Grub!" screamed a wild chorus of voices that seemed to fill the churchyard. Gabriel looked fearfully round—nothing was to be seen.

"What have you got in that bottle!" said the goblin.

"Hollands,[1] sir," replied the sexton, trembling more than ever; for he had bought it of the smugglers, and he thought that perhaps his questioner might be in the excise department[2] of the goblins.

"Who drinks Hollands alone, and in a churchyard, on such a night as this?" said the goblin.

"Gabriel Grub! Gabriel Grub!" exclaimed the wild voices again.

The goblin leered maliciously at the terrified sexton, and then raising his voice, exclaimed—"And who then, is our fair and lawful prize?"

To this inquiry the invisible chorus replied, in a strain that sounded like the voices of many choristers singing to the mighty swell of the old church organ—a strain that seemed borne to the sexton's ears upon a gentle wind, and to die away as its soft breath passed onward—but the burden of the reply was still the same, "Gabriel Grub! Gabriel Grub!"

---

[1] Dutch gin

[2] Government department that levies sales tax on certain goods

The goblin grinned a broader grin than before, as he said, "Well, Gabriel, what do you say to this?"

The sexton gasped for breath.

"What do you think of this, Gabriel?" said the goblin, kicking up his feet in the air on either side of the tombstone, and looking at the turned up points with as much complacency as if he had been contemplating work, the most fashionable pair of Wellingtons[3] in all Bond Street.[4]

"It's—it's—very curious, sir," said the Sexton, half dead with fright. "Very curious, and very pretty, but I think I'll go back and finish my work, sir, if you please."

"Work!" said the goblin. "What work?"

"The grave, sir, making the grave," stammered the sexton.

"Oh, the grave, eh?" said the goblin. "Who makes graves at a time when all other men are merry, and takes a pleasure in it?"

Again the mysterious voices replied, "Gabriel Grub! Gabriel Grub!"

"I'm afraid my friends want you, Gabriel," said the goblin, thrusting his tongue farther into his cheek than ever—and a most astonishing tongue it was—"I'm afraid my friends want you, Gabriel," said the goblin.

"Under favor, sir," replied the horror-struck sexton, "I don't think they can, sir. They don't know me, sir. I don't think the gentlemen have ever seen me, sir."

"Oh yes, they have," replied the goblin. "We know the man with the sulky face and the grim scowl, that came down the street tonight, throwing his evil looks at the children, and grasping his burying spade the tighter. We know the man that struck the boy in the envious malice of his heart, because the boy could be merry and he could not. We know him, we know him."

Here the goblin gave a loud shrill laugh, that the echoes returned twenty fold, and throwing his legs up in the air, stood upon his head, or rather on the very point of his sugar-loaf hat, on the narrow edge of the tombstone, from whence he threw a somerset with extraordinary

---

[3] Tall leather boot brought into fashion by Arthur Wellesley, the First Duke of Wellington

[4] Fashionable shopping street that runs between Piccadilly and Oxford Streets in London

agility right to the sexton's feet, at which he planted himself in the attitude in which tailors generally sit on the shop-board.[5]

"I—I am afraid I must leave you, sir," said the sexton, making an effort to move.

"Leave us!" said the goblin. "Gabriel Grub going to leave us.—Ho! ho! ho!"

As the goblin laughed, the sexton observed for one instant a brilliant illumination within the windows of the church, as if the whole building were lighted up. It disappeared, the organ pealed forth a lively air, and whole troops of goblins, the very counterpart of the first one, poured into the churchyard and began playing leap-frog with the tombstones—never stopping for an instant to take breath, but overing the highest among them, one after the other, with the most marvelous dexterity. The first goblin was a most astonishing leaper, and none of the others could come near him. Even in the extremity of his terror, the sexton could not help observing, that while his friends were content to leap over the common sized gravestones, the first took the family vaults, iron railings and all, with as much ease as if they had been so many street posts.

At last the game reached a most exciting pitch. The organ played quicker and quicker, and the goblins leaped faster and faster, coiling themselves up, rolling head over heels on the ground, and hounding over the tombstones like footballs. The sexton's brain whirled round with the rapidity of the motion he beheld, and his legs reeled beneath him, as the spirits flew before his eyes, when the goblin king suddenly darting towards him, laid his hand on his collar, and sank with him through the earth.

When Gabriel Grub had had time to fetch his breath, which the rapidity of his descent had for the moment taken away, he found himself in what appeared to be a large cavern, surrounded on all sides by crowds of goblins, ugly and grim. In the center of the room, on an elevated seat, was stationed his friend of the churchyard; and close beside him stood Gabriel Grub himself, without the power of motion.

"Cold tonight," said the king of the goblins, "very cold. A glass of something warm, here."

---

[5] Cross-legged stance

"At this command, half a dozen officious goblins, with a perpetual smile upon their faces, whom Gabriel Grub imagined to be courtiers,[6] on that account, hastily disappeared, and presently returned with a goblet of liquid fire, which they presented to the king.

"Ah!" said the goblin, whose cheeks and throat were quite transparent, as he tossed down the flame, "This warms one, indeed. Bring a bumper of the same for Mr. Grub."

It was in vain for the unfortunate sexton to protest that he was in the habit of taking anything warm at night; for one of the goblins held him while another poured the blazing liquid down his throat, and the whole assembly screeched with laughter as he coughed and choked, and wiped away the tears, which gushed plentifully from his eyes after swallowing the burning draught.

"And now," said the king, fantastically poking the taper corner of his sugar-loaf hat into the sexton's eyes, and thereby occasioning him the most exquisite pain— "And now, show the man of misery and gloom a few of the pictures from our own great storehouse."

As the goblin said this, a thick cloud, which obscured the farther end of the cavern, rolled gradually away, and disclosed, apparently at a great distance, a small and scantily furnished, but neat and clean apartment. A crowd of little children were gathered round a bright fire, clinging to their mother's gown, and gamboling round her chair. The mother occasionally rose, and drew aside the window-curtains as if to look for some expected object. A frugal meal was ready spread upon the table, and an elbow-chair was placed near the fire. A knock was heard at the door. The mother opened it and the children crowded round her and clapped their hands for joy as their father entered. He was wet and weary, and shook the snow from his garments as the children crowded round him, and seizing his cloak, hat, stick,[7] and gloves, with busy zeal, ran with them from the room. Then, as he sat down to his meal before the fire, the children climbed about his knee, and the mother sat by his side, and all seemed happiness and comfort.

---

[6] Advisor to the royal family

[7] Walking cane

But a change came on the view, almost imperceptibly. The scene was altered to a small bedroom, where the fairest and youngest child lay dying. The roses had fled from his cheeks and the light from his eyes; and even as the sexton looked on him with an interest he had never felt or known before, he died. His young brothers and sisters crowded round his little bed, and seized his tiny hand so cold and heavy; but they shrunk back from its touch, and looked with awe on his infant face; for calm and tranquil as it was, and sleeping in rest and peace as the beautiful child seemed to be, they saw that he was dead, and they knew that he was an angel looking down upon, and blessing them, from a bright and happy heaven.

Again the light cloud passed across the picture, and again the subject changed. The father and mother were old and helpless now, and the number of those about them was diminished more than half; but content and cheerfulness sat on every face, and beamed in every eye, as they crowded round the fireside, and told and listened to old stories of earlier and by-gone days. Slowly and peacefully the father sunk into the grave, and, soon after, the sharer of all his cares and troubles followed him to a place of rest and peace.

The few, who yet survived them, knelt by their tomb, and watered the green turf which covered it with their tears; then rose and turned away, sadly and mournfully, but not with bitter cries, or despairing lamentations, for they knew that they should one day meet again; and once more they mixed with the busy world, and their content and cheerfulness were restored. The cloud settled on the picture, and concealed it from the sexton's view.

"What do you think of that?" said the goblin, turning his large face towards Gabriel Grub.

"Gabriel murmured out something about its being very pretty, and looked somewhat ashamed, as the goblin bent his fiery eyes upon him.

"You are a miserable man!" said the goblin in a tone of excessive contempt. "You!" He appeared disposed to add more, but indignation choked his utterance, so he lifted up one of his very pliable legs, and flourishing it above his head a little, to ensure his aim, administered a good sound kick to Gabriel Grub; immediately after which, all the goblins in waiting crowded round the wretched sexton, and kicked him without mercy, according to the established and invariable custom of courtiers upon earth, who kick whom royalty kicks, and hug whom royalty hugs.

"Show him some more," said the king of the goblins.

At these words the cloud was again dispelled, and a rich and beautiful landscape was disclosed to view—there is just such another to this day, within half a mile of the old abbey town. The sun showed from out of the clear blue sky, the water sparkled beneath his rays, and the trees looked greener, and the flowers more gay, beneath his cheering influence. The water rippled on, with a pleasant sound, the trees rustled in the light wind that murmured among their leaves, the birds sung upon the boughs, and the lark caroled on high her welcome to the morning. Yes, it was morning, the bright balmy morning of summer. The minutest leaf, the smallest blade of grass, was instinct with life. The ant crept forth to her daily toil, the butterfly fluttered and basked in the warm rays of the sun. Myriads of insects spread their transparent wings, and reveled in their brief, but happy existence. Man walked forth, elated with the scene; and all was brightness and splendor.

"You a miserable man!" said the king of the goblins, in a more contemptuous tone than before. And again the king of the goblins gave his leg a flourish. Again it descended on the shoulders of the sexton; and again the attendant goblins imitated the example of their chief.

Many a time the cloud went and came, and many a lesson it taught to Gabriel Grub, who, although his shoulders smarted with pain from the frequent applications of the goblin's feet, looked on with an interest which nothing could diminish. He saw that men who worked hard, and earned their scanty bread with lives of labor, were cheerful and happy; and that to the most ignorant, the sweet face of nature was a never-failing source of cheerfulness and joy. He saw those who had been delicately nurtured, and tenderly brought up, cheerful under privations, and superior to suffering, that would have crushed many a rougher grain, because they bore within their own bosoms the materials of happiness, contentment, and peace.

He saw that women, the tenderest and most fragile of all God's creatures, were oftenest superior to sorrow, adversity, and distress; and he saw that it was because they bore in their own hearts an inexhaustible well-spring of affection and devotedness. Above all, he saw that men like himself, who snarled at the mirth and cheerfulness of others, were the foulest weeds on the fair surface of the earth; and setting all the good of the world against the evil, he came to the conclusion that it was a very decent and respectable sort of world after all. No sooner had he formed it, than the cloud which had closed over the last picture, seemed to settle on his senses, and lull him to repose. One by one, the goblins faded from his sight, and as the last one disappeared he sunk to sleep.

The day had broken when Gabriel Grub awoke, and found himself lying at full length on the flat gravestone in the churchyard, with the wicker bottle lying empty by his side, and his coat, spade, and lantern, all well whitened by the last night's frost, scattered on the ground.

The stone on which he had first seen the goblin seated stood bolt upright before him, and the grave at which he had worked the night before, was not far off. At first he began to doubt the reality of his adventures, but the acute pain in his shoulders when he attempted to rise, assured him that the kicking of the goblins was certainly not ideal. He was staggered again, by observing no traces of footsteps in the snow on which the goblins had played leap-frog with the gravestones, but he speedily accounted for this circumstance, when he remembered that being spirits, they would leave no visible impression behind them. So Gabriel Grub got on his feet as well as he could, for the pain in his back; and brushing the frost off his coat, put it on, and turned his face towards the town.

That he was an altered man, and he could not bear the thought of returning to a place where his repentance would be scolded at, and his reformation disbelieved. He hesitated for a few moments; and then turned away to wander where he might, and seek his bread elsewhere.

The lantern, the spade, and the wicker bottle were found that day in the churchyard. There were a great many speculations about the sexton's fate at first, but it was speedily determined that he had been carried away by the goblins; and there were not wanting some very credible witnesses who had distinctly seen him whisked through the air on the back of a chestnut horse blind of one eye, with the hindquarters of a lion, and the tail of a bear.[8] At length all this was devoutly believed; and the new sexton used to exhibit to the curious, for a trifling emolument,[9] a good-sized piece of the church weathercock, which had been accidentally kicked off by the aforesaid horse in his aerial flight, and picked up by himself in the churchyard, a year or two afterward.

Unfortunately these stories were somewhat disturbed by the unlooked-for re-appearance of Gabriel Grub himself, some ten years afterward, a ragged, contented, rheumatic old man. He told his story to the clergyman, and also to the mayor; and in course of time it began to be received as a matter of history, in which form it has continued down to this very day. The believers in the weathercock tale, having misplaced their confidence once, were not easily prevailed upon to part with it again, so they looked as wise as they could, shrugged their shoulders, touched their foreheads, and murmured something about Gabriel Grub's having drunk all the Hollands, and then fallen asleep on the flat tombstone; and they affected to explain what he supposed he had witnessed in the goblin's cavern, by saying that he had seen the work and grown wiser.

But this opinion, which was by no means a popular one at any time, gradually died off; and be the matter how it may, as Gabriel Grub was afflicted with rheumatism to the end of his days, this story has at least one moral, if it teach no better one—and that is, that if a man turns sulky and drinks by himself at Christmastime, he may make up his mind to be not a bit the better for it, let the spirits be ever so good, or let them be even as many degrees beyond proof, as those which Gabriel Grub saw in the goblin's cavern.

---

[8] In Greek mythology, the winged hippogriff had a body of a lion and was created by the union of a horse and a griffin.
[9] Payment

Joseph Holt Ingraham
(1809-1860)

"Ingraham, Joseph Holt (January 25 or 26, 1809 to December 18, 1860), author, Protestant Episcopal clergyman, was born in Portland, Maine, a grandson of one of the city's chief benefactors, for whom he was named, and the son of James Milk and Elizabeth (Thurston) Ingraham.

"His grandfather's shipping interests and his own love of adventure were responsible for his becoming a sailor in his youth. The Bowdoin College records do not bear out the statement sometimes made that he graduated there. He seems, however, to have become a teacher in Jefferson College at Washington, Mississippi (now a military school), which he described in *The South-West, by a Yankee* (2 vols., 1835); and thereafter the title "professor" was used frequently on his numerous publications. His *Lafitte* (2 vols., 1836), the most elaborate of the fictitious chronicles of the *Pirate of the Gulf,* is typical of his work in that it makes of an impossible series of events on which to hang a luxurious fabric of Spanish treasure troves and Byronic ravings. His *Burton; or the Sieges* (2 vols., 1838), inscribed to S. S. Prentiss, the famous Mississippi lawyer for whom his son was named, is a sensational defamation of the early career of Aaron Burr; *The Quadroone; or, St. Michael's Day* (2 vols., 1841), an even more absurd romanticization of history. In *The American Lounger* (1839) Ingraham shows the literary influence of Nathaniel Parker Willis, and in the story "The Kelpie Rock," the effect of

Joseph Rodman Drake's and Washington Irving's pioneer work in putting the Hudson River into legend.

"For a period after the publication of these books Ingraham wrote so rapidly that it is no longer possible to trace all of his works. According to the entry in Longfellow's journal for April 6, 1846, 'In the afternoon Ingraham the novelist called. A young, dark man, with soft voice. He says he has written eighty novels, and of these twenty during the last year; till it has grown to be merely mechanical with him. These novels are published in the newspapers. They pay him something more than three thousand dollars a year.' (Samuel Longfellow, Life of Henry Wadsworth Longfellow, 1886-87, H, 35.)"[1]

Ingraham's fantasy story is about the kelpie, or rather the rock on which the creature was rumored to sit while spying over the body of water in which it lived. The kelpie was derived through Scotland folklore and is a water spirit that takes the form of a horselike creature, but can shapeshift into a human. Kelpies are usually found sitting on large rocks near the water, hence the term "kelpie rock."

In 1839 Joseph Ingraham wrote one of America's first great fantasy stories and it involved a kelpie rock by the Hudson River. The story did not come from the usual suspects named Edgar Allan Poe or Nathaniel Hawthorne or Washington Irving, although all wrote in the genre.

"The Kelpie Rock," as mentioned in the short biography above, routinely cites Joseph Rodman Drake's poem, "The Culprit Fay." Edgar Allan Poe, however, did not hold the poem in as high esteem. "Dr. Drake was employed upon a good subject—at least it is a subject precisely identical with those which Shakespeare was wont so happily to treat, and in which, especially, the author of 'Lilian' has so wonderfully succeeded."[2] The fantasy story also gives plentiful reference to Washington Irving's two volume book of historical fiction: *A History of New York from the Beginning of the World to the End of the Dutch Dynasty.* Ingraham admits as much in his short "Author's Note" at the end of the story.

---

[1] *Dictionary of American Biography*, edited by Dumas Malone, 1932

[2] "Fancy and Imagination," Edgar Allan Poe, *The Works of the Late Edgar Allan Poe*, 1850, p. 377

The first publication of "The Kelpie Rock" appeared in *The American Lounger; or, Tales, Sketches, and Legends Gathered in Sundry Journeying's* that collected Ingraham's short stories and attributed their authorship merely to "the author of *Lafitte*." Ingraham dedicated the anthology to the author, editor, and dramatist, Nathaniel Parker Willis, who assisted the fledgling writing careers of Edgar Allan Poe, William Wadsworth Longfellow and, of course, Joseph Ingraham. In the very same year "The Kelpie Rock" was published, Willis's play "Tortesa or, the Usurer Matched" debuted in Philadelphia and was called by Poe "the best play by an American author."

Ingraham went on to write other tales, but "The Kelpie Rock" would remain his most popular story.

THE KELPIE ROCK
A LEGEND OF THE
HUDSON HIGHLANDS
1839

"Fairy, Fairy, list and mark!
  Thou hast broken thine elfin chain;
Thy flame-wood lamp is quenched and dark,
  And thy wings are dyed with a deadly stain—
Thou hast sullied thine elfin purity
  In the glance of a mortal maiden's eye!"[1]

Thus happily did they pursue their course, until they entered upon those awful defiles, denominated the Highlands, where it would seem that the gigantic Titans had erst waged their impious war with heaven, piling up cliffs on cliffs, and hurling vast masses of rocks in wild confusion.—"The History of New York," by Diedrich Knickerbocker.[2]

SO LONG AS we have the inspired poet who first struck his woodland harp among the Hudson Highlands, and sung of fairy land and the two vast labors of the Culprit Fay[3] so long as we have that veritable historian and authentic chronicler of great sublunary events, the profound and erudite Diedrich Knickerbocker[4]—be his memory thrice honored!—to stand by us in support of our legend, which is not a jot less true than his own veracious history, we do not care a whiff of

---

[1] Quote from "The Culprit Fay," a poem by Joseph Rodman Drake published in 1819

[2] *A History of New York from the Beginning of the World to the End of the Dutch Dynasty*, Washington Irving, a historical satire published in 1809

[3] "The Culprit Fay" by Joseph Rodman Drake

[4] Pseudonym of Washington Irving

tobacco smoke, if the incredulous and the critics believe not one word of it.

We have fortified ourself in the outset, like one when he putteth on his armor for the battle, with a quotation from this sweet poet of fairy land, and another from the pen, dipped in Hybla, of this great man and learned historian, and feel that confidence within, which inspires courage, and that will enable us to hold out stoutly to the last. It was late one August day, after a fruitless hunt for game through the wild ravines and along the heights of "Bull Hill,"[5] is a mountain emerging from a forest of oak and larch, I found myself on the summit of the lofty cliff, which, with a sheer fall of a thousand feet to the verdant plateau beneath, terminates the range of eastern highlands above West Point, to the south. The wide and glorious scenes that burst on my sight, fixed me like a statue.

The Hudson lay at my feet, completely land-locked—a lake sleeping among mountains—looking like a mirror of polished steel. Old Cro'nest[6] lifted his "shaggy breast" from its bosom, and hid his hoary head in a cloud which had lazily rolled half-way down his sides. West Point, with its lovely plain, its snowy tents, its charming villas, seemed like a picture done by a lady's fingers, so delicate was the penciling of each outline, so exquisite the play of lights and shadows.

From the height above, "Old Put,"[7] looked down with a protecting air—with his hoary front and war-worn look—a fine feature in the far and varied scene. At my feet lay the quiet and picturesque village of Cold Spring. Its dusty streets, with a group of children at play, a goodwife with an apron over her head, crossing to a neighbor's; a wagon, with a solitary occupant slowly wending toward his farm; a cow, lounging homeward at her leisure, whisking her long tail, and doubtless chewing her cud in peace and contentment; its little cove sprinkled with boats; a single

---

[5] Also referred to as Mount Taurus, is near the village of Cold Spring along the Hudson River

[6] Another mountain on the Hudson River, also term used in "The Culprit Fay"

[7] Reference to General Israel Putnam (a.k.a. Old Put) who on February 26, 1776, as legend has it, avoided capture by the British by descending down a cliff on his horse

sloop unloading at the wharf, where one or two little urchins are fishing for catfish; its chapel, romantically perched on a rock overhanging the water, all presenting a lively contrast to the dark, solemn majesty of the surrounding highlands.

At the very base of the cliff, and seemingly so near that I could have dropped a St. Nicholas' bon bon down its chimneys,[8] in the center of a wide verdant plateau, sloping to the water, lay, like a map open on my palm. Undercliff, the romantic city with its noble villa, gardens, fountains, pleasant groves and winding avenues, all exposed, as they would be to the eye of a bird in its empyrean flight.

There was not a breath of air to fan a lady's cheek, or stir a child's ringlets. The lake-like Hudson was a mirror, and old Cro'nest threw his "huge, gray form, in a dark-blue cone on the wave below."

A far-extended fleet of vessels was dispersed on the water—their idle sails furled to the slender yards, or drooping gracefully from the masts—waiting the evening breeze. So clear was the element on which they were suspended, that beneath each, another was seen, its ropes, spars, even the sailors moving about, so accurately copied, that it could not be told from its fellows, save that the wrong end was upwards. Occasionally, a light skiff, with a single oarsman, would shoot from the shore and dart along this mirror, leaving a widening wake of tiny waves to sport and glance their little minute in the sunlight. Just before me, in a romantic inlet, called Kelpie Cove, with a vast rock lying solitary on its curving beach, a family of geese, whiter than snow, sailed gracefully along, wheeling about at times, now facing the land, now the open river, as if expecting an attack, and were prepared to meet it.

On looking again toward old Cro'nest, I observed the fleecy cloud which I had seen sluggishly rolling down its sides, gradually to assume a darker hue, and to shoot off from the mountain; and then it slowly sailed through the air towards the cliff on which I stood, and nearly on a level with my eye. Soon other clouds from the hills to the north and west, also came sweeping majestically along, at the same level, and in a few moments the summit of the cliff

---

[8] Reference to Saint Nicholas's gifts of candy to children, a precursor to the Santa Claus legend

was enveloped, and the river, with the rich pictures painted on it, gradually disappeared in a veil of mist, as the scenes on a magic mirror fade before the waving wand of the magician.

For a moment I was as bewildered as if sudden blindness had come upon me. The union of the several masses, which came trooping along as if to a storm gathering, momentarily increased the density of the cloud, which at first was so rare, that I could see twice the length of my gun, whereas I now could touch a tree and not see it. The heavy moisture saturated my garments and ran off the barrel off my fowling piece in a trickling stream.

It occurred to me that I must be in the lowest stratum of the clouds, which, on approaching, did not appear to hang six feet lower than my position. I remembered that, not far off, there was a cleft which with a bold descent, obliquely approached a lower shelf of the cliff. With some difficulty I found it, and cautiously descended. I had advanced thirty feet, and was still within the cloud, which, on touching the mountain, had settled heavily about its summit. When, all at once, it rolled up like a curtain, and the scene below once more burst upon my sight. The under surface of the clouds stretched away to the opposite mountain, discolored with a dark, murky hue, and were rolling and heaving like an inverted sea. They cast over the landscape a somber shade, giving a wild and cheerless aspect to the face of Nature before so smiling. Through an opening in their dark bosom, there suddenly shot a bright, glorious beam of golden sunshine. It fell on the water where a vessel was furling her canvass to encounter the brewing tempest, and gave to the white sails, contrasted with the surrounding gloom, a lustre as if overlaid with burnished gold. Slowly passing off from this solitary object, leaving it, to the eye, almost black from the sudden contrast, it travelled across the water, gilded the roof of the Chapel of the Rock, "Our Lady of Cold Spring,"[9] and then the envious clouds closing up, shut it in, and it disappeared.

The spot on which I now stood was a shelf, about thirty feet lower than the highest part of the cliff, and had the appearance of an excavation made by the falling of a

---

[9] Chapel built in 1834, five years before publication of this short fantasy story

detached fragment. There remained beneath, however, no traces of a fragment one twentieth part large enough to have filled the space. After giving the subject a moment's thought, and saying, half aloud, "By St. Nicholas, I should like to know how this cavity was formed!"[10] I turned to retrace my steps, and gain the delightful shelter of Undercliff, which, although it seemed as if I could lay my hand on its balconies, it would take a good mile's stout walking to reach. The thunder already muttered audibly in the distance, and the clouds threatened every moment to break out into rain. My situation was one of sublimity, and I was at one time tempted to remain and outbreast the storm—companion of the lightning and thunder; but there was no sublimity in a wet jacket, and so I shouldered my gun, and turned to go. My retreat was unexpectedly and strangely intercepted.

On a projecting lap of the rock, and directly in the narrow path by which I had descended, was seated a singular looking being, but evidently of flesh and blood, from the rosy hue of his ample cheeks, and the energy with which he ejected currents of tobacco smoke, now through either orifice of his carbuncled nose, now through both, now from between his lips, which quietly closed over the stem of a fair long pipe, of the days of Peter the Headstrong.[11] Voluminous brown trunk-hose encased his capacious ribs, and Flemish boots were rolled around his ample calves. A green jerkin,[12] of a queer, old-fashioned cut, covered his upper man, and studiously left open in front, displayed a broad Flemish ruff, soiled with tobacco-smoke.

A high, peaked hat, was briskly cocked in front, and surmounted by a rusty plume. He wore it jauntily on one side of his head. One hand rested on an antiquated spyglass, which lay across his knees. He had a cock in his

---

[10] Joke in reference to the candy given out by Saint Nicholas and the cavities they gave children

[11] A history of Peter the Headstrong is contained in Book VI of *A History of New York from the Beginning of the World to the End of the Dutch Dynasty*, Washington Irving, 1809 and is a caricature of Peter Stuyvesant (1612-1672), the last Dutch General of the colony of New Netherland in America, later ceded to England and subsequently called New York.

[12] Sleeveless jacket

left eye, as if he was still spying. I should have mentioned, also, that a brace of enormous pistols, with rusty locks, and barrels, were stuck in his belt, and a whinyard,[13] half a fathom in length,[14] hung by his left thigh. Altogether he was a very formidable and truculent-looking personage, especially, to be encountered in so wild a spot.

He permitted me to survey him from head to foot. While, shutting one eye, he deliberately, with the other, took the same liberty with me. He then distended his cheeks with smoke till they were as round and sleek as a pippin, then emitted it from either corner of his mouth and both nostrils, and, as it seemed to me, also from his ears and eye, so multitudinous were the currents—so dense the volume of smoke that rolled from him. It soon hid his head, and all but the tip of his rusty plume, which I could see nodding at me above it, the twinkling of his gray eye, and the gleam of his fiery proboscis, which I could discern glowing through it like the end of a stout, red-hot poker. He at length spoke, and his voice seemed to come from the mouth of a speaking-trumpet, though it had a tone that was meant to be courteous.

"You vas vish, mynheer, how in der duyvil von rock pe proke vrom de kliff, here, an no pe to de pottom, dere?"[15]

He then puffed away within his cloud, and seemed to await my remarks. I was not altogether at my ease, and was doubtful of my company. I nevertheless spoke confidently, "I merely expressed a passing wish," I said, carelessly; "but, nevertheless, should be glad to have my curiosity gratified. You have the advantage of me with your telescope," I added, wishing to draw him out, and to show him that I was not dashed at his sudden appearance and fierce aspect. "I see you are a judicious rambler. Distant scenery, after the surprise of the first *coup-du-sil*, should always be viewed in detail. For this a spy-glass is most essential. A happy thought in you, sir."

"By St. Nicholas, mynheer, I know every shtone in de Highlants petter nor mine pipe. I hash not put dish shpy-

---

[13] Sword

[14] Three feet or 1.8 meters

[15] You has wished, my dear, how in the devil yon rock be broke from the cliff, here, and not be to the bottom, there?

klass to mine eyes vor more dan two huntret ant vivteen years."[16]

"Two hundred and fifteen years!" I repeated with unmingled astonishment, and a slight degree of alarm, casting, as I took a step backward, a suspicious glance at each of his feet, which, much to my relief and gratification, were, I observed, both well-shaped, and, save being rather broad and large across the toes, as we often see those of fat gentlemen, unexceptionable.

He made no reply to my exclamation, but puffed away in composure and in silence. The sunset gun from the military post, at this instant reverberated among the Highlands, starting a thousand echoes, which grew fainter and fainter as one answered to the other, till they died away far to the north, like the distant growling of thunder. Then the hoarse voice of my companion was heard from the cloud of blue vapor in which his upper man was enveloped.

"Tunder and blickzens! Ven I vaked dese echoesh de first time two huntret and venty years ago, mit de guns of de Halve Mane, more nor ten tousant eaglish vas scared vrom de kliffs! Dere is only dat one left now!"[17] he said, pointing with a jerk of his spy-glass to a noble, white-headed eagle, sailing through the air a hundred feet below us. "Dis gap vas not here den neider. Dat creat rock dere vas den on dis kliff vere ve stant."[18]

He extended the end of his telescope through the smoke, in the direction of an inlet of the river, which gracefully curved towards the foot of the cliff, in the shape of a crescent. Its northern horn terminated in a bold, rocky headland, extending far into the water. Its southern boundary was a low, verdant tongue of land, with a shelving, sandy beach, and terminating in a rude pier-head, crowned by the white parsonage of the village

---

[16] By Saint Nicholas, my dear, I know every stone in the Highlands better than my pipe. I have not put this spy-glass to my eyes for more than two hundred and fifteen years.

[17] Thunder and blitzen! When I heard these echos the first time two hundred and twenty year ago, from the guns of the Halve Mane, more than ten thousand eagles was scared from the cliffs! There is only that one left now!

[18] This gap was not here then neither. That great rock there had been on this cliff where ye stand.

pastor. On the smooth beach, conspicuous and alone, reposed a vast rock, or boulder, of many tons, the same I had before noticed. At lowtides it was many yards from the water, at high-tide the waves flowed around it. Its shape was irregular. It lay far from any other rocks, and a third of a mile from the cliff. Past it wound the road to Fishkill, and the plateau, which here gently inclined to the beach, was verdant. Its position there was evidently accidental. I gazed on the rock several seconds, took its shape in my eye, and turned to apply it mentally to the cavity in which we stood, yet I could arrive at no satisfactory result. He saw my perplexity, and said, coolly:—

"Dat rock was vonce in dis place, mynheer. Ash you vish to know, I vill tell you de storish."[19]

"By all means," I said, forgetting the gathering storm, the thickening twilight, and the mystery hanging about my companion, in my curiosity to hear a veritable legend, from a source seemingly so well entitled to do it justice. Moreover, if I had desired to beat a retreat, the antiquated stranger had so completely monopolized the only avenue of escape with his bulky form, and seemed so quietly to enjoy his seat, that I doubt, if I had made the attempt, it would have succeeded, even if it had been safe, of which I also have my own opinion. I therefore seated myself opposite him, on a fragment of the rock, and prepared to listen.

The elements favored a story of diablerie, as I anticipated this to be. The lightning vividly illuminated the vast fields of clouds, and the thunder bellowed among the opposite mountains, and rumbled through the long ranges of hills in ceaseless reverberations. After one or two prefatory whiffs, he took his pipe from his lips, whereupon the cloud of smoke slowly ascended from below his face, and mingled with the cloud a few feet above our heads, displaying a good-humored physiognomy, with the roistering, devil-me-care look of a merry Dutch skipper, who loves to smoke his pipe, drink schiedam,[20] and tell a long story. Settling himself more at ease on his seat, he then commenced his narration, which I give word for word

---

[19] That rock was once in this place, my dear. As you wish to know, I will tell you the story.

[20] Dutch gin named after the same Dutch city from the libation is distilled

as he related it, saving here and there the substitution of the king's English for his peculiar phraseology.

"That vast and rugged boulder you see in Kelpie Cove, looking so lonely and so out of place, the fair, smooth beach, and springing grass around it, goes by the name of KELPIE ROCK, and, within my memory was a portion of this cliff. You doubtless may have heard that from the oldest time, these highlands were the abode of ogres, kelpies, and other superhuman, yet earthly beings;—that when they dwelt among these mountains, a lake, and not, as now, a river, reflected their huge sides. The lake and highlands, which shut it in, were also the prison house of evil demons, and the dark spirits, who, from time to time, had rebelled against their master. Here were they penned up until the time approached that this new world was to become the inheritance of the children of the old. Then were they all unbound, for the good spirit had designed their vast abodes for mortals; but they murmuring and rebelling at this decree, he bound them in eternal chains, and confined them in horrid dungeons, in that adamantine prison, now called the Palisadoes.[21]

"They are there walled up to the light of heaven, and although above the earth are unable to behold it. There are they doomed to pass their painful years in hideous clamors and howl and yell away their dreadful bondage. The giants, ogres, gnomes, and kelpies, he suffered to remain, yet bound them by certain laws. Then opening the hills that walled it in toward the south, he let the waters of the lake seek the distant sea. Fearful was the roar, and loud the clamor of the imprisoned demons, when, from their gloomy cells, they heard the roar of its wild waters, as in one vast flood the unchained lake rolled thundering past their dark abodes, washing their foundations for many a league.

"Now it was that the titans, the gnomes, the kelpies, the giants, and the ogres, became greatly enraged at the destruction of their secluded lake, and this opening of their fearful haunts to the intrusion of daring mortals. Besides, these malevolent and awful beings, perhaps you may have heard that in the mountain opposite, the queen

---

[21] Palisades, a prison formed by walls of tall stakes

of fairies holds her elfin court.[22] Fairies, who are beings of a gentle nature, and favor mortals, and the genii, who are stern, implacable, and fierce, and hate mankind, are always hostile toward one another, and let no chance escape of showing their ill-will.

"Now, it was, that after the lake was changed into a river, wide and vast, as now it rolls, the Europeans had laid their hands on this continent as a new and bounteous gift from nature, and their ships had entered this river's mouth, that a young fay, called Erlin, a favorite page of the fairy queen,[23] was swiftly flying through the air, his wings glittering like silver, for it was a moonlit night, when he spied a little vessel gliding along between the river shores, with all its canvass spread to the favoring breeze. His curiosity at the novel sight was instantly aroused, for he had never seen a vessel, and thought, at first, it was a large white bird. After surveying it curiously for a time, he folded up his purple wings, and descended like an arrow. He hovered long above it, with mingled wonder, fear, and admiration. At length, having gratified his curiosity, he was about to mount again to the upper regions of the air, when there appeared on the deck a beauteous virgin, her fair head rich with clustering ringlets of glossy brown; a mouth, dimpled over with the play of merry smiles; a cheek, in which the lily and the rose exquisitely were blended; and a form, for sylph-like symmetry and female grace, he thought was every whit as perfect as that of fairy queen. Altogether, he was convinced that she was the most radiant being he had ever seen, and forthwith became enamored of her. He hovered around her, invisible, till he began to fear he should be called to answer for his prolonged stay, for he was bound on diplomatic business to an elfin court, far distant, when the barque[24] of Hendrick Hudson[25] arrested him in his arrowy flight."

---

[22] Reference to "The Culprit Fay" poem by Joseph Rodman Drake published in 1819

[23] The Fay Erlin is the protagonist in "The Culprit Fay" by Joseph Rodman Drake.

[24] Bark

[25] Henry Hudson (1560/70s-1611) was an Englishman who explored the Hudson River area in the seventeenth century.

"Hendrick Hudson!" I exclaimed. "It was then the vessel of this great navigator?"

"It vas, mynheer,"[26] he answered complacently, and nodding with the gratified air of a man who has received a flattering compliment, putting the long stem of his pipe in his mouth, and taking half a dozen quick, short whiffs, to keep the fire in the bowl from going out. "Ant te young laty vas hish taughter."[27]

"I have often heard of Henry Hudson's lovely daughter," I said.

"When the Fay Erlin returned to his mistress," he continued, after having slowly emitted from one corner of his mouth a slender thread of smoke, which curled gracefully upward like a wreath of mist, and mingled with the cloud, "the queen sharply inquired why he had lingered on the way. He invented a ready lie, as pages are used to do, and so for the present, escaped; for you must know either fay or fairy who glances on a mortal with an eye of love, breaks its elfin bond, and is, in a manner, guilty of high treason. The penalty of an offence so dire is weighty, and proportioned to its enormity. The culprit's lamp is extinguished, which is the same thing as the breaking of the criminal's sword by a mortal king; and its purple and silver wings are stained with dark unsightly hues, which is equivalent to the blotting out of the escutcheon[28] of an attainted noble. Besides these marks of degradation, they are also punished by the imposition of severe and ponderous tasks.

"The little vessel continued slowly to ascend, anchoring each night with cautious fear, for it was entering a gloomy region, wild and vast, and all unknown. The Fay Erlin, impatient to behold once more the fair and beauteous mortal, who from his faith and sworn allegiance to his queen, had seduced him, stole from the court, spread his purple wings, and glancing through the moonlight like an arrow shot by Diane,[29] lighted in an instant on this cliff. From it, as you can see, the eye in looking south, takes in the river for many a mile. The white sails of the approaching vessel glimmering in the

---

[26] It was, my dear.

[27] And the young lady was his daughter.

[28] Lighted torch

[29] Goddess of hunting in Roman mythology (Diana in Greek myth)

distance as the moon shone down upon them, caught his eager sight. His little heart bounded wildly with the joy he felt, and opening wide his plumes, he was about to fly towards it, when a low, deep muttering, mingled with horrid sounds, fell upon his ears. He balanced himself on his half-spread wings and listened to the uproar, which seemed to come from the bowels of the cliff. This cliff is hollow, and was then the council chamber where the fearful beings I have before made mention of, held their dark and direful consultations, and planned and plotted mischief against the human race. Erlin bent his ear an instant to the ground, and boding danger from their secret councils to the lovely mortal, he stole softly along, and entering the cave with noiseless step and wing, beheld them to his wonder, all in full assembly.

"There was an ogre with a flaming eye, a horrid aspect, and hideous form, who, in a vast, black cavern under Old Cro'nest made his abode, growling and grumbling if the thunder chanced to break his after dinner nap, and shake his house. There was a gnome, to mortal eyes invisible, but whom Erlin saw in all her fearful power; in whose awful form beauty and hideousness were strangely blended, whose eyes were lamps, whose limbs were writhing serpents, whose wings were like a bat's, whose face and bosom surpassed in loveliness the loveliest of mortals. There is a single grotto beneath the cliff in Kosciusko's garden, now hid from human eye. That was where she lived. There was a kelpie, with a human head, and breast, shaggy and hideous, and clothed with hair. In size he was a leviathan.[30] He haunted the rocks and beach of Kelpie Cove, and lived in caves beneath the water.

"There was a giant, of enormous stature. A long black beard and a fierce mustache, made his wild aspect still more fierce. He leaned on a sapling, torn up by the roots, which served him both for staff and weapon. There were besides, whom also Erlin saw, beings still more wonderful and monstrous both in shape and size. He gathered from their speech and clamors, that the rumor of the coming ship had reached their ears, and that they now were met in council to devise some present means of averting from their heads the impending evil.

---

[30] Giant

"'If,' said the ogre, rolling as he spoke, his only eye, which, set in the middle of his forehead, glared strangely, all over the assembly, and making most hideous grimaces, while his voice rumbled like an earthquake, 'if we permit these blue-eyed mortals to enter our abodes, our power is gone. The fairies opposite are troublesome enough to us. I cannot sleep on moonlight nights for their dancing and capering over my head. There is the queen's page, Erlin, a mere hop-o-my-thumb, who loves mischief as he does moonshine, shoots his sharp steel arrows into my eye when I sleep after sun-up, as if he could find no better mark.'

"'So, ho! grim ogre!' said Erlin to himself. 'I owe you one for that!'

"The gnome then rose, and gleaming with her lamp-like eyes round on each one, rested them on the ogre as he took his seat, and then spoke in tones half hissing, like a serpent, and half articulate, like a sweet female voice.

"'The ogre is right. These mortals must not pass the old barrier which confined the river when a lake. The ogre is again right. The fairies are troublesome. They are always fickle. They may aid the mortals to spite us, whom they hate. There is also an old tradition,

> Ogres, giants, kelpies, gnomes!
>   Fly—fly your ancient homes!
> When an elf shall thrice defend
>   A maid 'gainst whom ye all contend,
> Then, then your power shall end!'

"The giant then rose, shook himself, and in a voice of thunder delivered the following speech:

"'It is my opinion we destroy these mortals without delay, lest the fairies put their finger in, and spoil the pie.'

"The kelpie, in a shrill voice, which sounded like a horse's neigh, save that it was shriller, also rose to say that he acquiesced in the general sentiments of his friends, the honorable members of the council. Just at this moment, a huge, lazy titan, lounging in the entrance of the cavern, said that a strange white bird had landed on the water. 'The Mortals! The mortals!' was the cry. The council broke up in hurry and confusion, and the members made for the outlet, so hastily, that Erlin just escaped, through his great alertness, from being drawn into the vortex of the ogre's mouth as he inhaled an immense draught of fresh air, while rushing from the cave.

"When they gained the summit of the cliff, the adventurous vessel appeared in open view, bravely rounding the west point of yonder headland. It was a fair and novel sight to these gaping, wondering monsters, to see her glide along like a living creature with snow-white wings, flinging the foam about her prow, and leaving a boiling wake stretching far behind. Erlin, impatient to light on her deck, did nevertheless restrain the impulse, and waited unobserved; the motions of the group, himself concealed in the velvet folds of a mullen leaf.

"The gnome proposed flying from the cliff, lifting the vessel in mid-air, and dashing it on the rocks. This was approved unanimously. Erlin gained the bark before her and balanced himself on the mast. The gnome could not raise it an inch, and defeated flew back again enraged. The ogre was for creating a storm. The waves began to roar and the winds to whistle around the lonely bark; but it sailed on unharmed, for the elf was there perched on the yard, protecting his lovely mistress. The giant tore up a vast tree to hurl at it, but could not lift it from the earth, for Erlin sat on it. Great was their rage at these repeated defeats. They knew their foes, the fairies were at work; and the prophetic rhymes the gnome had spoken, made them quake with fear that their time had come. The kelpie, in his fierce and boundless wrath, struck the cliff with a violent blow of his hoof and loosened a huge fragment covered with earth and trees. It was falling, to be dashed in atoms at the base, when the titan seized it with both his hands, whirled it round about his head, with a roar like a hurricane, and hurled it through the air with deadliest aim toward the fated vessel now abreast the cliff. Erlin was not prepared for this, and as he saw the missile fly, roaring through the air, he uttered a cry of agony. The next moment, ere it had flown one-half the distance between the cliff and vessel, he landed on it. Instantly it was arrested in its onward course, and with the swiftness of a lightning bolt it descended to the earth, and buried itself deep in the sand, just on the water's edge.

"Loud bellowings and wailings filled the air. Hurled back into their cave by some power invisible, the hideous monsters who had met in council, were bound down in chains of adamant and shut up forever in the cliff's dark womb. Their howlings are distinctly heard when the storm against their prison loudly beats. The thunder never fails to stir their fierce wrath, and long and direful are their yells and groans when thus disturbed in the eternal dungeons to which the victories of the fay have doomed their monstrous race."

Having finished this wild legend of diablerie, the narrator rose to his feet, placed his spy-glass beneath his arm, refilled his waning pipe from an antiquated silver tobacco box, which he drew from a deep pouch by his left hip, and seemed about to go from whence he came. I thanked him for his narrative, warmly expressing my gratification, and then courteously asked him to whom I was so greatly indebted. He took his pipe, which he had resumed, from his mouth, and answered me:

"Mortals, after death, hover over these terrestrial scenes, pursue those pleasures or those labors, and mingle in with all those affairs which occupied them while alive. Departed poets have a region of their own, inhabiting romantic solitudes, wandering by the banks of rivulets, and roaming amid sublime scenery, delighting their souls with the essence of that beauty, the grosser parts of which were only enjoyed by them as mortals. Philosophers, statesmen, authors, and all others have each his own spiritual region, which is, in a manner, the soul of the sublunary, for it is to the globe what the soul of man is to his body. It is in this vast soul, which envelopes the earth, that they pass their spiritual existence. Nothing is now dark or obscure to their intellects, nothing beyond the grasp of their comprehension. All things before hid in mystery are now clear as the sun, to their spiritual vision. Navigators, who discover continents, islands, lakes, and rivers, do, in a special manner, haunt the scenes of their earthly fame, and are more immediately their presiding and protecting genii. All these essences or spirits, whatever the variety of their several pursuits, however elevated their rank, are bound to obey the call of mortals, appear before them in their earthly form, and answer to all questions when rightly and sincerely applied to. I am the presiding spirit of this vast river. You wished for me, and I am here."

"You are then—"

"Hendrick Hudson."

A loud clap of thunder at this instant broke above our heads, while the lightning, which accompanied rather than preceded it, blinded me for several seconds. When I recovered the use of my eyes, I looked around and found myself alone.

Twilight was rapidly breaking into night, the clouds began to hang down the sides of the mountain as if heavy with water. Embracing the little daylight that yet remained, I succeeded in regaining the villa of Undercliff, amid tempest of wind and rain, accompanied by wild flashes of lightning, and appalling thunder, which rattled among the hills, awakening, as I now understood the apparent echoes, the howlings of the troubled spirits confined in their cavernous bowels.

The next morning the sky being without a cloud, the atmosphere soft and transparent, the sun bright and cheerful, and all nature smiling and gay, I sought the Kelpie Rock. On the south side I discovered to my entire satisfaction, the deep points of a gigantic hoof six times the size of a horse's and as plainly to be seen as the nose on a man's face, which at once testified to the veracity of the ancient schipper,[31] and the genuineness of his wonderful legend.[32]

---

[31] Modern skipper, an explorer by ship

[32] Author's note: "For the trial of Fay Erlin for loving a mortal—the catastrophe of the council of monsters having led to the detection—the curious dipper and believer in legendary lore, and lover of fairy tales is referred to Drake's inimitable poem, entitled 'The Culprit Fay,' to which, as well as to the history from the pen of that enlightened historian and profound scholar, Mr. Knickerbocker, the writer acknowledges his indebtedness."

Mary Shelley
(1797-1851)

"Mary Shelley, the daughter of William Godwin and Mary Wollstonecraft, was born in London, August, 1797. Her mother dying at her birth, the daughter was tenderly and carefully brought up by her father and stepmother. The little girl soon evinced traits of the hereditary genius which was afterwards so fully developed. In the introduction to one of her novels, she herself says of her youth:

"'It is not singular that, as the daughter of two persons of distinguished literary celebrity, I should very early in life have thought of writing. As a child I scribbled; and my favorite pastime during the hours given me for recreation, was to 'write stories.' Still, I had a dearer pleasure than this, which was the formation of castles in the air; the indulging in waking dreams; the following of trains of thought, which had for their subject the formation of a succession of imaginary incidents. My dreams were at once more fantastic and agreeable than my writings. In the latter I was a close imitator; rather doing as others had done, than putting down the suggestions of my own mind. What I wrote was intended at least for one other eye—my childhood's companion and friend; but my dreams were all my own; I accounted for them to nobody; they were my refuge when annoyed, my dearest pleasure when free. I lived principally in the country as a girl, and passed a considerable time in Scotland. I made occasional visits to the more picturesque parts, but my habitual residence was on the blank and dreary northern shores of the Tay, near Dundee. Blank and dreary on retrospection I call them; they were not so to me then. They were the eyry of freedom, and the pleasant region where unheeded I could commune with the creatures of my fancy. I wrote then, but in a most commonplace style. It was beneath the grounds belonging to our house, or on the bleak sides of the woodless mountains near, that my true compositions, the airy flights of my imagination, were born and fostered. I did not make myself the heroine of my tales. Life appeared to me too commonplace an affair as regarded myself. I could not figure to myself that romantic woes or wonderful events would be my lot; but I was not confined to my own identity, and I could people the hours with creations far more interesting to me at that age than my own sensations.'

"Here is the key of the true womanly character, *disinterestedness*. This young girl did not weave the garland or create the Utopia for herself, but for others. The mind of a boy works differently; he places himself in the center of his creations, and wins the laurel for his own brow.

"In 1815, Miss Wollstonecraft was married to Percy Bysshe Shelley, whose name at once moves the admiration, the pity, and the censure of the world. That Mrs. Shelley loved her husband with a truth mid devotion seldom exceeded, has been proven by her whole career. Their married life was eminently happy, and the fidelity with which she devoted her fine genius to the elucidation of his writings and the defense of his character, is the best eulogium that has been offered to his memory.

"In the summer of 1816, Lord Byron and Mr. and Mrs. Shelley were residing on the banks of the Lake of Geneva. They were in habits of daily intercourse, and when the weather did not allow their boating excursions on the lake, the Shelleys often passed their evenings with Byron at his house at Diodati. "During a week of rain at this time," says Mr. Moore, "having amused themselves with reading German ghost stories, they agreed at last to write something in imitation of them. 'You and I,' said Lord Byron to Mrs. Shelley, 'will publish ours together.' He then began his tale of the 'Vampire;' and having the whole arranged in his head, repeated to them a sketch of the story one evening, but from the narrative being in prose, made but little progress in filling up his outline. The most memorable result, indeed, of their storytelling was Mrs. Shelley's wild and powerful romance of *Frankenstein, or the Modern Prometheus*, one of those original conceptions that take hold of the public mind at once and forever."

"*Frankenstein* was published in 1817, and was instantly recognized as worthy of Godwin's daughter and Shelley's wife, and as, in fact, possessing some of the genius and peculiarities of both. It is formed on the model of St. Leon; but the supernatural power of that romantic visionary produces nothing so striking or awful as the grand conception of *Frankenstein*, the discovery that he can, by his study of natural philosophy, create a living and sentient being.

"In 1817, Shelley and his wife returned to England, and spent several months in Buckinghamshire. In 1818, they returned to Italy; their eldest child died in Rome; the parents then retired to Leghorn for a few months, and after travelling to various places, finally, in 1820, took up their residence at Pisa. In July, 1821, Shelley's death occurred; he was drowned in the Gulf of Lerici.

"Mrs. Shelley had one son who survived his father; with her children she returned to England, and for years supported herself by her writings. In 1844, her son, Henry Florence Shelley, succeeded to the title and estates of his grandfather.

"Mrs. Shelley's second work of fiction, *Walpurga*, was published in 1823. Her other novels are *Lodore*, *Perkin Warbeck*, *Falkner*, and *The Last Man*. She wrote a *Journal of her Travels in Italy and Germany*; also *Lives of Eminent French Poets*. But her last work, *Memoirs of Shelley*, prefixed to the complete edition of his Poems and Letters, displays her character in its loveliest light. She is the guardian angel of her dead husband's fame, as she was of his happiness while he lived. Mrs. Shelley is a woman of original genius; "like her father, she excels in mental analysis," says Mr. Chambers, commenting on *Frankenstein*, "and in the conceptions of the grand and the powerful, but fails in the management of her fable, where probable incidents and familiar life are required or attempted." But in *Lodore* she has shown her power to depict scenes true to nature. Mrs. Shelley died in London, February 1, 1851, in the fifty-third year of her age."[1]

Eighteen thirty was the year that the widowed Mary Shelley, in need of money, sold a new edition of *Frankenstein; or, Prometheus Unbound* for £60. It was the same year Shelley wrote "Transformation," one of the best dwarf stories written in the first half of the nineteen century. The simple, but provocative title, hinted at the transformation that takes place between Doctor Frankenstein and his monster. It also drew on Lord Byron's drama published eight years earlier, "The Deformed Transformed," during the year her husband— Percy Bysshe Shelley—drowned. Lord Byron was quick to point out that his "Transformation" was not entirely his own, rather "founded partly on the story of a novel called 'The Three Brothers,' published many years ago, from which M. G. Lewis's 'Wood Demon' was also taken—and partly on the 'Faust' the great Goethe."[2]

Shelley never used her name in the 1831 annual publication of *The Keepsake*, preferring to be listed simply as the author of *Frankenstein*. The short fantasy story in the magazine was followed by this poem:

> AH! He is gone—and I alone!—
> How dark and dreary seems the time!
> 'Tis this, when the glad sun is flown,
> Night rushes o'er the Indian clime.
>
> Is there no star to cheer this night?
> No soothing twilight for the breast?
> Yes, Memory sheds her fairy light,
> Pleasing as sunset's golden west.
>
> And hope of dawn—oh! Brighter far
> Than clouds that in the orient burn;
> More welcome than the morning star
> Is the dear thought—he will return!

---

[1] *A Cyclopedia of Female Biography Consisting of Sketches of All Women Who Have Been Distinguished by Great Talents, Strength of Character, Piety, Benevolence, or Moral Virtue of Any Kind*, Edited by H. G. Adams, pp. 686-688, 1857

[2] "The Deformed Transformed," Introductory Note, First American Edition and Second English Edition, 1824

TRANSFORMATION
1830

Forthwith this frame of mine was wrench'd
With a woful agony,
Which forced me to begin my tale,
And then it set me free.

Since then, at an uncertain hour,
That agony returns;
And till my ghastly tale is told
This heart within me burns.

Coleridge's "Ancient Mariner."[1]

I HAVE HEARD it said, that, when any strange, supernatural, and necromantic adventure has occurred to a human being, that being, however desirous he may be to conceal the same, feels at certain periods torn up as it were by an intellectual earthquake, and is forced to bare the inner depths of his spirit to another. I am a witness of the truth of this. I have dearly sworn to myself never to reveal to human ears the horrors to which I once, in excess of fiendly pride, delivered myself over. The holy man who heard my confession, and reconciled me to the church, is dead. None knows that once—

Why should it not be thus? Why tell a tale of impious tempting of Providence, and soul-subduing humiliation? Why? answer me, you who are wise in the secrets of human nature! I only know that so it is; and in spite of strong resolve—of a pride that too much masters me—of shame, and even of fear, so to render myself odious to my species—I must speak.

Genoa! my birthplace—proud city! looking on the blue waves of the Mediterranean sea—do you remember me in my boyhood, when your cliffs and promontories, your bright sky and gay vineyards, were my world? Happy time!

---

[1] "The Rime of the Ancyent Marinere," Samuel Taylor Coleridge, 1798

when to the young heart the narrow-bounded universe, which leaves, by its very limitation, free scope to the imagination, enchains our physical energies, and, sole period in our lives, innocence and enjoyment are united. Yet, who can look back to childhood, and not remember its sorrows and its harrowing fears? I was born with the most imperious, haughty, tameless spirit, with which ever mortal was gifted. I quailed before my father only; and he, generous and noble, but capricious and tyrannical, at once fostered and checked the wild impetuosity of my character, making obedience necessary, but inspiring no respect for the motives which guided his commands. To be a man, free, independent; or, in better words, insolent and domineering, was the hope and prayer of my rebel heart.

My father had one friend, a wealthy Genoese noble, who in a political tumult was suddenly sentenced to banishment, and his property confiscated. The Marchese Torella went into exile alone. Like my father, he was a widower. He had one child, the almost infant Juliet, who was left under my father's guardianship. I should certainly have been an unkind master to the lovely girl, but that I was forced by my position to become her protector. A variety of childish incidents all tended to one point,—to make Juliet see in me a rock of refuge; I in her, one, who must perish through the soft sensibility of her nature too rudely visited, but for my guardian care.

We grew up together. The opening rose in May was not more sweet than this dear girl. An irradiation of beauty was spread over her face. Her form, her step, her voice— my heart weeps even now, to think of all of relying, gentle, loving, and pure, that was enshrined in that celestial tenement. When I was eleven and Juliet eight years of age, a cousin of mine, much older than either—he seemed to us a man—took great notice of my playmate; he called her his bride, and asked her to marry him. She refused, and he insisted, drawing her unwillingly towards him. With the countenance and emotions of a maniac I threw myself on him—I strove to draw his sword—I clung to his neck with the ferocious resolve to strangle him. He was obliged to call for assistance to disengage himself from me. On that night I led Juliet to the chapel of our house. I made her touch the sacred relics—I harrowed her child's heart, and profaned her child's lips with an oath, that she would be mine, and mine only.

Well, those days passed away. Torella returned in a few years, and became wealthier and more prosperous than ever. When I was seventeen my father died. He had been magnificent to prodigality. Torella rejoiced that my minority would afford an opportunity for repairing my fortunes. Juliet and I had been affianced beside my father's deathbed—Torella was to be a second parent to me.

I desired to see the world, and I was indulged. I went to Florence, to Rome, to Naples; then I passed to Toulon, and at length reached what had long been the borne of my wishes, Paris. There was wild work in Paris then. The poor king, Charles the Sixth, now sane, now mad, now a monarch, now an abject slave, was the very mockery of humanity. The queen, the dauphin, the Duke of Burgundy, alternately friends and foes now meeting in prodigal feasts, now shedding blood in rivalry-were blind to the miserable state of their country, and the dangers that impended over it, and gave themselves wholly up to dissolute enjoyment or savage strife.

My character still followed me. I was arrogant and self-willed. I loved display, and above all, I threw all control far from me. Who could control me in Paris? My young friends were eager to foster passions which furnished them with pleasures. I was deemed handsome—I was master of every knightly accomplishment. I was disconnected with any political party. I grew a favorite with all. My presumption and arrogance were pardoned in one so young. I became a spoiled child. Who could control me? Not the letters and advice of Torella—only strong necessity visiting me in the abhorred shape of an empty purse. But there were means to refill this void. Acre after acre, estate after estate, I sold. My dress, my jewels, my horses and their caparisons, were almost unrivalled in gorgeous Paris, while the lands of my inheritance passed into possession of others.

The Duke of Orleans was waylaid and murdered by the Duke of Burgundy. Fear and terror possessed all Paris. The dauphin and the queen shut themselves up. Every pleasure was suspended. I grew weary of this state of things, and my heart yearned for my boyhood's haunts. I was nearly a beggar, yet still I would go there, claim my bride, and rebuild my fortunes. A few happy ventures as a merchant would make me rich again. Nevertheless, I would not return in humble guise. My last act was to dispose of my remaining estate near Albaro for half its worth, for ready money. Then I dispatched all kinds of artificers, arras, furniture of regal splendor, to fit up the last relic of my inheritance, my palace in Genoa. I lingered a little longer yet, ashamed at the part of the prodigal returned, which I feared I should play. I sent my horses. One matchless Spanish jennet I dispatched to my promised bride. Its caparisons flamed with jewels and cloth of gold. In every part I caused to be entwined the initials of Juliet and her Guido. My present found favor in hers and in her father's eyes.

Still to return a proclaimed spendthrift, the mark of impertinent wonder, perhaps of scorn, and to encounter singly the reproaches or taunts of my fellow-citizens, was no alluring prospect. As a shield between me and censure, I invited some few of the most reckless of my comrades to accompany me. Thus I went armed against the world, hiding a rankling feeling, half fear and half penitence, by bravado and an insolent display of satisfied vanity.

I arrived in Genoa. I trod the pavement of my ancestral palace. My proud step was no interpreter of my heart, for I deeply felt that, though surrounded by every luxury, I was a beggar. The first step I took in claiming Juliet must widely declare me such. I read contempt or pity in the looks of all. I fancied, so apt is conscience to imagine what it deserves, that rich and poor, young and old, all regarded me with derision. Torella would not come near me. No wonder that my second father should expect a son's deference from me in waiting first on him.

But, galled and stung by a sense of my follies and demerit, I strove to throw the blame on others. We had nightly parties in Palazzo Carega.[2] To sleepless, riotous nights, followed listless, supine mornings. At the "Ave Maria"[3] we showed our dainty persons in the streets, scoffing at the sober citizens, casting insolent glances on the shrinking women. Juliet was not among them—no, no; if she had been there, shame would have driven me away, if love had not brought me to her feet.

---

[2] The Palace Carega Cataldi was built in the center of Genoa, Italy and built between 1558 and 1561

[3] Franz Schubert's composition "Ellen's Third Song" (commonly called "Ave Maria") written in 1825 as one part of a set of songs composed from Sir Walter Scott's poem "The Lady of the Lake"

I grew tired of this. Suddenly I paid the Marchese a visit. He was at his villa, one among the many which deck the suburb of San Pietro d'Arena. It was the month of May—a month of May in that garden of the world the blossoms of the fruit trees were fading among thick, green foliage. The vines were shooting forth. The ground strewed with the fallen olive blooms. The fire-fly was in the myrtle hedge. Heaven and earth wore a mantle of surpassing beauty. Torella welcomed me kindly, though seriously; and even his shade of displeasure soon wore away. Some resemblance to my father-some look and tone of youthful ingenuousness, lurking still in spite of my misdeeds, softened the good old man's heart. He sent for his daughter. He presented me to her as her betrothed.

The chamber became hallowed by a holy light as she entered. Hers was that cherub look, those large, soft eyes, full dimpled cheeks, and mouth of infantine sweetness, that expresses the rare union of happiness and love. Admiration first possessed me. She is mine! was the second proud emotion, and my lips curled with haughty triumph. I had not been the *enfant gate*[4] of the beauties of France not to have learned the art of pleasing the soft heart of woman. If towards men I was overbearing, the deference I paid to them was the more in contrast. I commenced my courtship by the display of a thousand gallantries to Juliet, who, vowed to me from infancy, had never admitted the devotion of others; and who, though accustomed to expressions of admiration, was uninitiated in the language of lovers.

For a few days all went well. Torella never alluded to my extravagance. He treated me as a favorite son. But the time came, as we discussed the preliminaries to my union with his daughter, when this fair face of things should be overcast. A contract had been drawn up in my father's lifetime. I had rendered this, in fact, void, by having squandered the whole of the wealth which was to have been shared by Juliet and myself. Torella, in consequence, chose to consider this bond as cancelled, and proposed another, in which, though the wealth he bestowed was immeasurably increased, there were so many restrictions as to the mode of spending it, that I, who saw independence only in free career being given to my own

---

[4] Spoiled child

imperious will, taunted him as taking advantage of my situation, and refused utterly to subscribe to his conditions. The old man mildly strove to recall me to reason. Roused pride became the tyrant of my thought. I listened with indignation—I repelled him with disdain.

"Juliet, you are mine! Did we not interchange vows in our innocent childhood? Are we not one in the sight of God? and will your cold-hearted, cold-blooded father divide us? Be generous, my love, be just. Take not away a gift, last treasure of your Guido—retract not your vows—let us defy the world, and setting at naught the calculations of age, find in our mutual affection a refuge from every ill."

Fiend I must have been, with such sophistry to endeavor to poison that sanctuary of holy thought and tender love. Juliet shrank from me in fear. Her father was the best and kindest of men, and she strove to show me how, in obeying him, every good would follow. He would receive my tardy submission with warm affection; and generous pardon would follow my repentance. Profitless words for a young and gentle daughter too used to a man accustomed to make his will, law; and to feel in his own heart a despot so terrible and stern, that he could yield obedience to naught save his own imperious desires! My resentment grew with resistance. My wild companions were ready to add fuel to the flame. We laid a plan to carry off Juliet. At first it appeared to be crowned with success. Midway, on our return, we were overtaken by the agonized father and his attendants. A conflict ensued. Before the city guard came to decide the victory in favor of our antagonists, two of Torella's servants were seriously wounded.

This portion of my history weighs most heavily with me. Changed man as I am, I abhor myself in the recollection. May none who hear this tale ever have felt as I. A horse driven to fury by a rider armed with barbed spurs, was not more a slave than I, to the violent tyranny of my temper. A fiend possessed my soul, irritating it to madness. I felt the voice of conscience within me; but if I yielded to it for a brief interval, it was only to be a moment after torn, as by a whirlwind, away—borne along on the stream of desperate rage—the plaything of the storms engendered by pride.

I was imprisoned, and, at the instance of Torella, set free. Again I returned to carry off both him and his child to France; which hapless country, then preyed on by freebooters and gangs of lawless soldiery, offered a grateful refuge to a criminal like me. Our plots were discovered. I was sentenced to banishment; and, as my debts were already enormous, my remaining property was put in the hands of commissioners for their payment. Torella again offered his mediation, requiring only my promise not to renew my abortive attempts on himself and his daughter. I spurned his offers, and fancied that I triumphed when I was thrust out from Genoa, a solitary and penniless exile. My companions were gone. They had been dismissed from the city some weeks before, and were already in France. I was alone—friendless; with neither sword at my side, nor ducat in my purse.

I wandered along the seashore, a whirlwind of passion possessing and tearing my soul. It was as if a live coal had been set burning in my breast. At first I meditated on what I should do. I would join a band of freebooters. Revenge!—the word seemed balm to me:—I hugged it— caressed it—till, like a serpent, it stung me. Then again I would abjure and despise Genoa, that little corner of the world. I would return to Paris, where so many of my friends swarmed; where my services would be eagerly accepted; where I would carve out fortune with my sword, and might, through success, make my paltry birthplace, and the false Torella, rue the day when they drove me, a new Coriolanus, from her walls. I would return to Paris thus, on foot—a beggar—and present myself in my poverty to those I had formerly entertained sumptuously? There was gall in the mere thought of it.

The reality of things began to dawn upon my mind, bringing despair in its train. For several months I had been a prisoner. The evils of my dungeon had whipped my soul to madness, but they had subdued my corporeal frame. I was weak and wan. Torella had used a thousand artifices to administer to my comfort. I had detected and scorned them all and I reaped the harvest of my obduracy. What was to be done? Should I crouch before my foe, and sue for forgiveness?—Die rather ten thousand deaths!— Never would they obtain that victory! Hate—I swore eternal hate! Hate from whom?—to whom?—From a wandering outcast to a mighty noble. I and my feelings were nothing to them. Already had they forgotten one so unworthy. And Juliet!—her angel-face and sylphlike form gleamed among the clouds of my despair with vain beauty; for I had lost her—the glory and flower of the world! Another will call her his!—that smile of paradise will bless another!

Even now my heart fails within me when I recur to this rout of grim-visaged ideas. Now subdued almost to tears, now raving in my agony, still I wandered along the rocky shore, which grew at each step wilder and more desolate. Hanging rocks and hoar precipices overlooked the tideless ocean. Black caverns yawned; and forever, among the seaworn recesses, murmured and dashed the unfruitful waters. Now my way was almost barred by an abrupt promontory, now rendered nearly impracticable by fragments fallen from the cliff. Evening was at hand, when, seaward, arose, as if on the waving of a wizard's wand, a murky web of clouds, blotting the late azure sky, and darkening and disturbing the till now placid deep.

The clouds had strange fantastic shapes; and they changed, and mingled, and seemed to be driven about by a mighty spell. The waves raised their white crests. The thunder first muttered, then roared from across the waste of waters, which took a deep purple dye, flecked with foam. The spot where I stood, looked, on one side, to the wide-spread ocean; on the other, it was barred by a rugged promontory. Round this cape suddenly came, driven by the wind, a vessel. In vain the mariners tried to force a path for her to the open sea—the gale drove her on the rocks. It will perish!—All on board will perish!—Would I were among them! And to my young heart the idea of death came for the first time blended with that of joy. It was an awful sight to behold that vessel struggling with her fate. Hardly could I discern the sailors, but I heard them. It was soon all over!—A rock, just covered by the tossing waves, and so unperceived, lay in wait for its prey. A crash of thunder broke over my head at the moment that, with a frightful shock, the skiff dashed upon her unseen enemy.

In a brief space of time she went to pieces. There I stood in safety; and there were my fellow-creatures, battling, how hopelessly, with annihilation. I thought I saw them struggling—too truly did I hear their shrieks, conquering the barking surges in their shrill agony. The dark breakers threw hither and thither the fragments of the wreck. Soon it disappeared. I had been fascinated to gaze till the end. At last I sank on my knees—I covered my face with my hands. I again looked up. Something was floating on the billows towards the shore. It neared and neared. Was that a human form?—It grew more distinct; and at last a mighty wave, lifting the whole freight, lodged it on a rock. A human being bestriding a sea-chest!—A human being!—Yet was it one? Surely never such had existed before a misshapen dwarf, with squinting eyes, distorted features, and body deformed, till it became a horror to behold. My blood, lately warming towards a fellow-being so snatched from a watery tomb, froze in my heart. The dwarf got off his chest. He tossed his straight, straggling hair from his odious visage.

"By St. Beelzebub!" he exclaimed, "I have been well bested." He looked round and saw me. "Oh, by the fiend! here is another ally of the mighty one. To what saint did you offer prayers, friend—if not to mine? Yet I remember you not on board."

I shrank from the monster and his blasphemy. Again he questioned me, and I muttered some inaudible reply. He continued:—

"Your voice is drowned by this dissonant roar. What a noise the big ocean makes! Schoolboys bursting from their prison are not louder than these waves set free to play. They disturb me. I will have no more of their ill-timed brawling.—Silence, hoary One!—Winds, avaunt!—to your homes! Clouds, fly to the antipodes, and leave our heaven clear!"

As he spoke, he stretched out his two long lank arms, that looked like spider's claws, and seemed to embrace with them the expanse before him. Was it a miracle? The clouds became broken, and fled. The azure sky first peeped out, and then was spread a calm field of blue above us. The stormy gale was exchanged to the softly breathing west. The sea grew calm. The waves dwindled to riplets.

"I like obedience even in these stupid elements," said the dwarf. "How much more in the tameless mind of man! It was a well got up storm, you must allow—and all of my own making."

It was tempting Providence to interchange talk with this magician. But *Power*, in all its shapes, is venerable to man. Awe, curiosity, a clinging fascination, drew me towards him.

"Come, don't be frightened, friend," said the wretch. "I am good humored when pleased; and something does please me in your well-proportioned body and handsome face, though you look a little woebegone. You have suffered a land, a sea wreck. Perhaps I can allay the tempest of your fortunes as I did my own. Shall we be friends?"—And he held out his hand. I could not touch it. "Well, then, companions—that will do as well. And now, while I rest after the buffeting I underwent just now, tell me why, young and gallant as you seem, you wander alone and downcast on this wild seashore."

The voice of the wretch was screeching and horrid, and his contortions as he spoke were frightful to behold. Yet he did gain a kind of influence over me, which I could not master, and I told him my tale. When it was ended, he laughed long and loud. The rocks echoed back the sound. Hell seemed yelling around me.

"Oh, you cousin of Lucifer!" he said. "So you too have fallen through your pride; and, though bright as the son of Morning, you are ready to give up your good looks, your bride, and your well-being, rather than submit to the tyranny of good. I honor your choice, by my soul!—So you have fled, and yield the day; and mean to starve on these rocks, and to let the birds peck out your dead eyes, while your enemy and your betrothed rejoice in your ruin. Your pride is strangely akin to humility, I think."

As he spoke, a thousand fanged thoughts stung me to the heart.

"What would you that I should do?" I cried.

"I!—Oh, nothing, but lie down and say your prayers before you die. But, were I you, I know the deed that should be done."

I drew near him. His supernatural powers made him an oracle in my eyes; yet a strange unearthly thrill quivered through my frame as I said, "Speak!—teach me—what act you advise?"

"Revenge yourself, man!—humble your enemies!—set your foot on the old man's neck, and possess yourself of his daughter!"

"To the east and west I turn," I cried, "and see no means! Had I gold, much could I achieve; but, poor and single, I am powerless."

The dwarf had been seated on his chest as he listened to my story. Now he got off. He touched a spring. It flew open!—What a mine of wealth—of blazing jewels, beaming gold, and pale silver—was displayed therein. A mad desire to possess this treasure was born within me.

"Doubtless," I said, "one so powerful as you could do all things."

"Nay," said the monster, humbly, "I am less omnipotent than I seem. Some things I possess which you may covet; but I would give them all for a small share, or even for a loan of what is yours."

"My possessions are at your service," I replied, bitterly—"my poverty, my exile, my disgrace—I make a free gift of them all."

"Good! I thank you. Add one other thing to your gift, and my treasure is yours."

"As nothing is my sole inheritance, what besides nothing would you have?"

"Your comely face and well-made limbs."

I shivered. Would this all-powerful monster murder me? I had no dagger. I forgot to pray—but I grew pale.

"I ask for a loan, not a gift," said the frightful thing. "Lend me your body for three days—you will have mine to cage your soul the while, and, in payment, my chest. What say you to the bargain?—Three short days."

We are told that it is dangerous to hold unlawful talk; and well do I prove the same. Tamely written down, it may seem incredible that I should lend any ear to this proposition; but, in spite of his unnatural ugliness, there was something fascinating in a being whose voice could govern earth, air, and sea. I felt a keen desire to comply; for with that chest I could command the world. My only hesitation resulted from a fear that he would not be true to his bargain. *Then*, I thought, *I will soon die here on these lonely sands, and the limbs he covets will be mine no more. It is worth the chance.* And, besides, I knew that, by all the rules of art-magic, there were formula and oaths which none of its practisers dared break. I hesitated to reply; and he went on, now displaying his wealth, now speaking of the petty price he demanded, till it seemed madness to refuse. Thus is it. Place our bark in the current of the stream, and down, over fall and cataract it is hurried. Give up our conduct to the wild torrent of passion, and we are away, we know not whither.

He swore many an oath, and I adjured him by many a sacred name; till I saw this wonder of power, this ruler of the elements, shiver like an autumn leaf before my words; and as if the spirit spake unwillingly and per force within him, at last, he, with broken voice, revealed the spell whereby he might be obliged, did he wish to play me false, to render up the unlawful spoil. Our warm life-blood must mingle to make and to mar the charm.

Enough of this unholy theme. I was persuaded—the thing was done. The morrow dawned upon me as I lay on the shingles, and I knew not my own shadow as it fell from me. I felt myself changed to a shape of horror, and cursed my easy faith and blind credulity. The chest was there—there the gold and precious stones for which I had sold the frame of flesh which nature had given me. The sight a little stilled my emotions. Three days would soon be gone.

They did pass. The dwarf had supplied me with a plenteous store of food. At first I could hardly walk, so strange and out of joint were all my limbs; and my voice—it was that of the fiend. But I kept silent, and turned my face to the sun, that I might not see my shadow, and counted the hours, and ruminated on my future conduct. To bring Torella to my feet—to possess my Juliet in spite of him—all this my wealth could easily achieve. During dark night I slept, and dreamt of the accomplishment of my desires. Two suns had set. The third dawned. I was agitated, fearful. Oh expectation, what a frightful thing are you, when kindled more by fear than hope! How do you twist yourself round the heart, torturing its pulsations!

How do you dart unknown pangs all through our feeble mechanism, now seeming to shiver us like broken glass, to nothingness now giving us a fresh strength, which can do nothing, and so torments us by a sensation, such as the strong man must feel who cannot break his fetters, though they bend in his grasp. Slowly paced the bright, bright orb up the eastern sky. Long it lingered in the zenith,[5] and still more slowly wandered down the west. It touched the horizon's verge—it was lost! Its glories were on the summits of the cliff—they grew dun and gray. The evening star shone bright. He will soon be here.

He came not!—By the living heavens, he came not!— and night dragged out its weary length, and, in its

---

[5] Peak position

decaying age, "day began to grizzle its dark hair;"[6] and the sun rose again on the most miserable wretch that ever upbraided its light. Three days thus I passed. The jewels and the gold—oh, how I abhorred them!

Well, well—I will not blacken these pages with demoniac ravings. All too terrible were the thoughts, the raging tumult of ideas that filled my soul. At the end of that time I slept. I had not before since the third sunset; and I dreamt that I was at Juliet's feet, and she smiled, and then she shrieked—for she saw my transformation— and again she smiled, for still her beautiful lover knelt before her. But it was not I—it was he, the fiend, arrayed in my limbs, speaking with my voice, winning her with my looks of love. I strove to warn her, but my tongue refused its office. I strove to tear him from her, but I was rooted to the ground—I awoke with the agony. There were the solitary hoar precipices—there the plashing sea, the quiet strand, and the blue sky over all. What did it mean? was my dream but a mirror of the truth? was he wooing and winning my betrothed? I would on the instant go back to Genoa—but I was banished. I laughed—the dwarf's yell burst from my lips—*I* banished! 0, no! they had not exiled the foul limbs I wore. I might with these enter, without fear of incurring the threatened penalty of death, my own, my native city.

I began to walk towards Genoa. I was somewhat accustomed to my distorted limbs. None were ever so ill adapted for a straight-forward movement. It was with infinite difficulty that I proceeded. Then, too, I desired to avoid all the hamlets strewed here and there on the sea-beach, for I was unwilling to make a display of my hideousness. I was not quite sure that, if seen, the mere boys would not stone me to death as I passed, for a monster. Some ungentle salutations I did receive from the few peasants or fishermen I chanced to meet. But it was dark night before I approached Genoa. The weather was so balmy and sweet that it struck me that the Marchese and his daughter would very probably have left the city for their country retreat. It was from Villa Torella that I had attempted to carry off Juliet. I had spent many an hour reconnoitering the spot, and knew each inch of ground in its vicinity. It was beautifully situated, embosomed in

---

[6] Quote from Lord Byron's poem "Werner," 1822

trees, on the margin of a stream. As I drew near, it became evident that my conjecture was right; nay, moreover, that the hours were being then devoted to feasting and merriment. For the house was lighted up. Strains of soft and gay music were wafted towards me by the breeze. My heart sank within me. Such was the generous kindness of Torella's heart that I felt sure that he would not have indulged in public manifestations of rejoicing just after my unfortunate banishment, but for a cause I dared not dwell upon.

The country people were all alive and flocking about. It became necessary that I should try to conceal myself; and yet I longed to address someone, or to hear others discourse, or in any way to gain intelligence of what was really going on. At length, entering the walks that were in immediate vicinity to the mansion, I found one dark enough to veil my excessive frightfulness; and yet others as well as I were loitering in its shade. I soon gathered all I wanted to know—all that first made my very heart die with horror, and then boil with indignation. Tomorrow Juliet was to be given to the penitent, reformed, beloved Guido—tomorrow my bride was to pledge her vows to a fiend from hell!

And I did this!—my accursed pride—my demoniac violence and wicked self-idolatry had caused this act. For if I had acted as the wretch who had stolen my form had acted if, with a personality at once yielding and dignified, I would have presented myself to Torella, saying, "I have done wrong, forgive me. I am unworthy of your angel-child, but permit me to claim her hereafter, when my altered conduct will manifest that I stop my vices, and endeavor to become in some sort worthy of her. I go to serve against the infidels; and when my zeal for religion and my true penitence for the past will appear to you to cancel my crimes, permit me again to call myself your son." Thus had he spoken; and the penitent was welcomed even as the prodigal son of scripture. The fatted calf was killed for him; and he, still pursuing the same path, displayed such open-hearted regret for his follies, so humble a concession of all his rights, and so ardent a resolve to reacquire them by a life of contrition and virtue, that he quickly conquered the kind, old man; and full pardon, and the gift of his lovely child, followed in swift succession.

O! had an angel from Paradise whispered to me to act this way! But now, what would be the innocent Juliet's fate? Would God permit the foul union—or, some prodigy destroying it, link the dishonored name of Carega with the worst of crimes? Tomorrow at dawn they were to be married. There was but one way to prevent this—to meet mine enemy, and to enforce the ratification of our agreement. I felt that this could only be done by a mortal struggle. I had no sword—if indeed my distorted arms could wield a soldier's weapon—but I had a dagger, and in that lay my every hope. There was no time for pondering or balancing nicely the question. I might die in the attempt; but besides the burning jealousy and despair of my own heart, honor, mere humanity, demanded that I should fall rather than not destroy the machinations of the fiend.

The guests departed. The lights began to disappear. It was evident that the inhabitants of the villa were seeking repose. I hid myself among the trees—the garden grew desert—the gates were closed—I wandered round and came under a window. Ah! well did I know the same!—a soft twilight glimmered in the room—the curtains were half withdrawn. It was the temple of innocence and beauty. Its magnificence was tempered, as it were, by the slight disarrangements occasioned by its being dwelt in, and all the objects scattered around displayed the taste of her who hallowed it by her presence. I saw her enter with a quick light step.

I saw her approach the window. She drew back the curtain yet further, and looked out into the night. Its breezy freshness played among her ringlets, and wafted them from the transparent marble of her brow. She clasped her hands, she raised her eyes to Heaven. I heard her voice.

"Guido!" she softly murmured, "Mine own Guido!" and then, as if overcome by the fullness of her own heart, she sank on her knees—her upraised eyes—her negligent but graceful attitude—the beaming thankfulness that lighted up her face—oh, these are tame words! Heart of mine, you imaginest ever, though you cannot portray, the celestial beauty of that child of light and love.

I heard a step; a quick firm step along the shady avenue. Soon I saw a cavalier, richly dressed, young and, I thought, graceful to look on, advance. I hid myself yet closer. The youth approached. He paused beneath the window. She arose, and again looking out she saw him, and said—I cannot, no, at this distant time I cannot record her terms of soft silver tenderness. To me they were spoken, but they were replied to by him.

"I will not go," he cried. "Here where you have been, where your memory glides like some Heaven-visiting ghost, I will pass the long hours till we meet, never, my Juliet, again, day or night, to part. But do you, my love, retire? The cold morn and fitful breeze will make your cheek pale, and fill with languor your love-lighted eyes. Ah, sweetest! could I press one kiss upon them, I could, I think, repose."

And then he approached still nearer, and I thought he was about to clamber into her chamber. I had hesitated, not to terrify her. Now I was no longer master of myself. I rushed forward—I threw myself on him—I tore him away—I cried, "O loathsome and foul-shaped wretch!"

I need not repeat epithets, all tending, as it appeared, to rail at a person I at present feel some partiality for. A shriek rose from Juliet's lips. I neither heard nor saw—I *felt* only mine enemy, whose throat I grasped, and my dagger's hilt. He struggled, but could not escape. At length hoarsely he breathed these words: "Do!—strike home! destroy this body—you will still live. May your life be long and merry!"

The descending dagger was arrested at the word, and he, feeling my hold relax, extricated himself and drew his sword, while the uproar in the house, and flying of torches from one room to the other, showed that soon we should be separated—and I—oh! far better die, so that he did not survive, I cared not. In the midst of my frenzy there was much calculation—fall I might, and so that he did not survive, I cared not for the death-blow I might deal against myself. While still, therefore, he thought I paused, and while I saw the villainous resolve to take advantage of my hesitation, in the sudden thrust he made at me, I threw myself on his sword, and at the same moment plunged my dagger, with a true desperate aim, in his side. We fell together, rolling over each other, and the tide of blood that flowed from the gaping wound of each mingled on the grass. More I know not—I fainted.

Again I returned to life. Weak almost to death, I found myself stretched on a bed—Juliet was kneeling beside it.

Strange! my first broken request was for a mirror. I was so wan and ghastly, that my poor girl hesitated, as she told me afterwards; but, by the mass! I thought myself a right proper youth when I saw the dear reflection of my own well-known features. I confess it is a weakness, but I avow it, I do entertain a considerable affection for the countenance and limbs I behold, whenever I look at a glass; and have more mirrors in my house, and consult them oftener than any beauty in Venice. Before you too much condemn me, permit me to say that no one better knows than I the value of his own body. No one, probably, except myself, ever having had it stolen from him.

Incoherently I at first talked of the dwarf and his crimes, and reproached Juliet for her too easy admission of his love. She thought me raving, as well she might, and yet it was some time before I could prevail on myself to admit that the Guido whose penitence had won her back for me was myself; and while I cursed bitterly the monstrous dwarf, and blest the well-directed blow that had deprived him of life, I suddenly checked myself when I heard her say, "Amen!" knowing that him whom she reviled was my very self. A little reflection taught me silence. A little practice enabled me to speak of that frightful night without any very excessive blunder.

The wound I had given myself was no mockery of one—it was long before I recovered—and as the benevolent and generous Torella sat beside me, talking such wisdom as might win friends to repentance, and mine own dear Juliet hovered near me, administering to my wants, and cheering me by her smiles, the work of my bodily cure and mental reform went on together. I have never, indeed, wholly recovered my strength. My cheek is paler since— my person a little bent over. Juliet sometimes ventures to allude bitterly to the malice that caused this change, but I kiss her on the moment, and tell her all is for the best. I am a fonder and more faithful husband—and true is this—but for that wound, never had I called her mine.

I did not revisit the seashore, nor seek for the fiend's treasure; yet, while I ponder on the past, I often think, and my confessor was not backward in favoring the idea, that it might be a good rather than an evil spirit, sent by my guardian angel, to show me the folly and misery of pride.

So well at least did I learn this lesson, roughly taught as I was, that I am known now by all my friends and fellow-citizens by the name of Guido il Cortese.

Washington Irving
(1783-1859)

Washington Irving was born April 3, 1783 in New York. He was the youngest of eleven children and his parents were both from Great Britain. Irving studied law, but found little use for it given his aptitude for fiction writing. In 1807 he published the satiric magazine "Salmagundi," along with his brother and a friend. In 1809 he published Diedrich Knickerbocker's "History of New York," that lampooned a number of early Dutch settlers in America. Irving travelled extensively in Europe and became friends with Sir Walter Scott and Charles Dickens. The year 1820 saw Irving's publication of his short story collection *The Sketchbook of Geoffrey Crayon, Gent.*, which contained the wildly popular "Rip Van Winkle" and "The Legend of Sleepy Hollow," which are both read to this day. Two years later he published *Bracebridge Hall; or, The Humorist, A Medley*, which cemented his popularity in Great Britain and America. In 1824, he published *Tales of a Traveller*, which was not as well accepted as some of his earlier fiction. Later in life he would go on to write biographies on such prominent figures as Mahomet and George Washington. Irving died on November 28, 1859 at the age of 76.

A number of towns have claimed to be the one Washington Irving used in "Rip Van Winkle." None appear as on point as Glens Falls, New York for the basis of the village setting in "Rip Van Winkle." The village of Glens

Falls is situated on the Hudson River and in the early nineteenth century claimed a number of prominent Dutchmen, just as in the short fantasy story. Abraham L. Vandenburgh was an attorney who "attended to the legal business of the place" and a general store was owned by L. I. Van Kleeck.[1] A George Vanderheyden also lived in Glens Falls.[2] "In 1812 the old Union Hotel was built by Dr. D. McNeill" and a Union Hotel is featured in Irving's story "by Jonathan Doolittle."[3] The hotel in the story has a sign with painted letters, just as the real Union Hotel did in Glens Falls.[4]

In "Rip Van Winkle" Washington Irving has given the world an enduring fantasy tale with vibrant characters and an excellent storyline; though, as Irving admits in the endnote, the basic concept is not entirely original to him.

---

[1] History of Warren County, H. P. Smith, Chapter XV, p. 422
[2] Ibid, Chapter XX, p. 278
[3] Ibid. at 423
[4] Ibid

Introduction to "Rip Van Winkle"
by
Washington Irving

The following tale was found among the papers of the late Diedrich Knickerbocker, an old gentleman of New York, who was very curious in the Dutch history of the province, and the manners of the descendants, from its primitive settlers. His historical researches, however, did not lie so much among books as among men; for the former are lamentably scanty on his favorite topics; whereas he found the old burghers,[1] and still more their wives, rich in that legendary lore, so invaluable to true history. Whenever, therefore, he happened upon a genuine Dutch family, snugly shut up in its low-roofed farmhouse, under a spreading sycamore, he looked upon it as a little clasped volume of black-letter, and studied it with the zeal of a bookworm.

The result of all these researches was a history of the province during the reign of the Dutch governors, which he published some years since. There have been various opinions as to the literary character of his work, and, to tell the truth, it is not a whit better than it should be. Its chief merit is its scrupulous accuracy, which indeed was a little questioned, on its first appearance, but has since been completely established; and it is now admitted into all historical collections, as a book of unquestionable authority.

The old gentleman died shortly after the publication of his work, and now that he is dead and gone, it cannot do much harm to his memory to say, that his time might have been much better employed in weightier labors. He, however, was apt to ride his hobby his own way; and though it did now and then kick up the dust a little in the eyes of his neighbors, and grieve the spirit of some friends, for whom he felt the truest deference and affection; yet his errors and follies are remembered "more in sorrow than in anger," and it begins to be suspected, that he never

---

[1] Wealthy town citizen who typically controlled various government functions

intended to injure or offend. But however his memory may be appreciated by critics, it is still held dear among many folk, whose good opinion is well worth having; particularly certain biscuit bakers, who have gone so far as to imprint his likeness on their new year cakes, and have thus given him a chance for immortality, almost equal to the being stamped on a Waterloo Medal,[2] or a Queen Anne's farthing.[3]

---

[2] British military medal awarded to soldiers who fought in any of three battles during June of 1815: Battle of Ligny, Quatre Bas, or Waterloo

[3] Expensive, pure metal coin minted in 1714

RIP VAN WINKLE
A POSTHUMOUS WRITING OF
DIEDRICH KNICKERBOCKER
1819

By Woden, God of Saxons,
From whence comes Wensday, that is Wodensday,
Truth is a thing that ever I will keep
Unto thy thylke day in which I creep into
My sepulcher

Cartwright.[1]

WHOEVER HAS MADE a voyage up the Hudson must remember the Kaatskill mountains. They are a dismembered branch of the great Appalachian family, and are seen away to the west of the river, swelling up to a noble height and lording it over the surrounding country. Every change of season, every change of weather, indeed every hour of the day, produces some change in the magical hues and shapes of these mountains, and they are regarded by all the good wives, far and near, as perfect barometers. When the weather is fair and settled, they are clothed in blue and purple, and print their bold outlines on the clear evening sky; but sometimes, when the rest of the landscape is cloudless, they will gather a hood of grey vapors about their summits, which, in the last rays of the setting sun, will glow and light up like a crown of glory.

At the foot of these fairy mountains, the voyager may have descried the light smoke curling up from a village, whose shingle roofs gleam among the trees, just where the blue tints of the upland melt away into the fresh green of

---

[1] William Cartwright (1611-1643) was an English poet and playwright. The epigraph is from Cartwright's 1635 comedic play "The Ordinary" Act. III, Sc. 1, where the speaker (Moth) includes a missing line, "I'll be as faithful to thee as Chanticleer to Madam Partelot," which are the names of Geoffrey Chaucer's (1343-1400) rooster and hen.

the nearer landscape. It is a little village of great antiquity, having been founded by some of the Dutch colonists, in the early times of the province, just about the beginning of the government of the good Peter Stuyvesant, (may he rest in peace!)[2] and there were some of the houses of the original settlers standing within a few years, built of small yellow bricks brought from Holland, having latticed windows and gable fronts, surmounted with weathercocks.

In that same village, and in one of these very houses, (which, to tell the precise truth, was sadly time worn and weather beaten,) there lived many years since, while the country was yet a province of Great Britain, a simple good-natured fellow, of the name of Rip Van Winkle.

He was a descendant of the Van Winkles who figured so gallantly in the chivalrous days of Peter Stuyvesant, and accompanied him to the siege of Fort Christina.[3] He inherited, however, but little of the martial character of his ancestors. I have observed that he was a simple, good natured man; he was, moreover, a kind neighbor, and an obedient henpecked husband.

Indeed, to the latter circumstance might be owing that meekness of spirit which gained him such universal popularity; for those men are most apt to be obsequious and conciliating abroad, who are under the discipline of shrews at home. Their tempers, doubtless, are rendered pliant and malleable in the fiery furnace of domestic tribulation, and a curtain lecture is worth all the sermons in the world for teaching the virtues of patience and long suffering. A termagant wife may therefore, in some respects, be considered a tolerable blessing; and if so, Rip Van Winkle was thrice blessed.

Certain it is, that he was a great favorite among all the good wives of the village, who, as usual with the amiable sex, took his part in all family squabbles; and never failed,

---

[2] A history of Peter the Headstrong is contained in Book VI of *A History of New York from the Beginning of the World to the End of the Dutch Dynasty*, Washington Irving, 1809, and is a caricature of Peter Stuyvesant (1612-1672), the last Dutch General of the colony of New Netherland in America, later ceded to Great Britain and subsequently called New York.

[3] The fort was the first Swedish settlement in America and attacked by Stuyvesant's Dutch military in 1655

whenever they talked those matters over in their evening gossippings, to lay all the blame on Dame Van Winkle. The children of the village, too, would shout with joy whenever he approached. He assisted at their sports, made their playthings, taught them to fly kites and shoot marbles, and told them long stories of ghosts, witches, and Indians. Whenever he went dodging about the village, he was surrounded by a troop of them, hanging on his skirts, clambering on his back, and playing a thousand tricks on him with impunity; and not a dog would bark at him throughout the neighborhood.

The great error in Rip's composition was an insuperable aversion to all kinds of profitable labor. It could not be from the want of assiduity or perseverance; for he would sit on a wet rock, with a rod as long and heavy as a Tartar's lance,[4] and fish all day without a murmur, even though he should not be encouraged by a single nibble. He would carry a fowling piece[5] on his shoulder for hours together, trudging through woods and swamps, and up hill and down dale, to shoot a few squirrels or wild pigeons. He would never refuse to assist a neighbor even in the roughest toil, and was a foremost man at all country frolics for husking Indian corn, or building stone fences. The women of the village, too, used to employ him to run their errands, and to do such little odd jobs as their less obliging husbands would not do for them.—In a word, Rip was ready to attend to any body's business but his own; but as to doing family duty, and keeping his farm in order, he found it impossible.

In fact, he declared it was of no use to work on his farm. It was the most pestilent little piece of ground in the whole country. Everything about it went wrong, and would go wrong, in spite of him. His fences were continually falling to pieces. His cow would either go astray or get among the cabbages. Weeds were sure to grow quicker in his fields than anywhere else. The rain always made a point of setting in just as he had some outdoor work to do; so that though his patrimonial estate had dwindled away under his management, acre by acre, until there was little

---

[4] Russian ethnic group who fought with long spears or lances in the 17th century

[5] Early form of shotgun for shooting birds

more left than a mere patch of Indian corn and potatoes, yet it was the worst conditioned farm in the neighborhood.

His children, too, were as ragged and wild as if they belonged to nobody. His son Rip, an urchin begotten in his own likeness, promised to inherit the habits, with the old clothes of his father. He was generally seen trooping like a colt at his mother's heels, equipped in a pair of his father's cast-off galligaskins,[6] which he had much ado to hold up with one hand, as a fine lady does her train in bad weather.

Rip Van Winkle, however, was one of those happy mortals, of foolish, well-oiled dispositions, who take the world easy, eat white bread or brown, whichever can be got with least thought or trouble, and would rather starve on a penny than work for a pound. If left to himself, he would have whistled life away in perfect contentment; but his wife kept continually dinning in his ears about his idleness, his carelessness, and the ruin he was bringing on his family. Morning, noon, and night, her tongue was incessantly going, and everything he said or did was sure to produce a torrent of household eloquence. Rip had but one way of replying to all lectures of the kind, and that, by frequent use, had grown into a habit. He shrugged his shoulders, shook his head, cast up his eyes, but said nothing. This, however, always provoked a fresh volley from his wife; so that he was fain to draw off his forces, and take to the outside of the house—the only side which, in truth, belongs to a henpecked husband.

Rip's sole domestic adherent was his dog Wolf, who was as much henpecked as his master; for Dame Van Winkle regarded them as companions in idleness, and even looked upon Wolf with an evil eye, as the cause of his master's going so often astray. True it is, in all points of spirit befitting an honorable dog, he was as courageous an animal as ever scoured the woods—but what courage can withstand the ever-during and all-besetting terrors of a woman's tongue? The moment Wolf entered the house his crest fell, his tail drooped to the ground or curled between his legs, he sneaked about with a gallows air, casting many a sidelong glance at Dame Van Winkle, and at the least flourish of a broomstick or ladle, he would fly to the door with yelping precipitation.

---

[6] Extremely baggy pants worn in the 16th and 17th centuries

Times grew worse and worse with Rip Van Winkle as years of matrimony rolled on. A tart temper never mellows with age, and a sharp tongue is the only edge tool that grows keener with constant use. For a long while he used to console himself, when driven from home, by frequenting a kind of perpetual club of the sages, philosophers, and other idle personages of the village, which held its sessions on a bench before a small inn, designated by a rubicund portrait of His Majesty George the Third.[7]

Here they used to sit in the shade, of a long lazy summer's day, talk listlessly over village gossip, or tell endless sleepy stories about nothing. But it would have been worth any statesman's money to have heard the profound discussions that sometimes took place, when by chance an old newspaper fell into their hands from some passing traveler. How solemnly they would listen to the contents, as drawled out by Derrick Van Bummel, the schoolmaster, a dapper learned little man, who was not to be daunted by the most gigantic word in the dictionary; and how sagely they would deliberate upon public events some months after they had taken place.

The opinions of this junto were completely controlled by Nicholas Vedder, a patriarch of the village, and landlord of the inn, at the door of which he took his seat from morning till night, just moving sufficiently to avoid the sun and keep in the shade of a large tree; so that the neighbors could tell the hour by his movements as accurately as by a sun dial. It is true, he was rarely heard to speak, but smoked his pipe incessantly. His adherents, however, (for every great man has his adherents,) perfectly understood him, and knew how to gather his opinions. When anything that was read or related displeased him, he was observed to smoke his pipe vehemently, and send forth short, frequent, and angry puffs; but when pleased, he would inhale the smoke slowly and tranquilly, and emit it in light and placid clouds, and sometimes taking the pipe from his mouth, and letting the fragrant vapor curl about his nose, would gravely nod his head in token of perfect approbation.

From even this strong hold the unlucky Rip was at length routed by his termagant wife, who would suddenly

---

[7] George William Frederick (1738-1820), king of Great Britain and Ireland from 1760-1801

break in upon the tranquility of the assemblage and call the members all to naught; nor was that august personage, Nicholas Vedder himself, sacred from the daring tongue of this terrible virago, who charged him outright with encouraging her husband in habits of idleness,

Poor Rip was at last reduced almost to despair and his only alternative, to escape from the labor of the farm and the clamor of his wife, was to take gun in hand, and stroll away into the woods. Here he would sometimes seat himself at the foot of a tree and share the contents of his wallet with Wolf, with whom he sympathized as a fellow sufferer in persecution.

"Poor Wolf," he would say, "your mistress leads you a dog's life of it; but never mind, my lad, while I live you will never want for a friend to stand by you!"

Wolf would wag his tail, look wistfully in his master's face, and if dogs can feel pity, I verily believe he reciprocated the sentiment with all his heart.

In a long ramble of the kind on a fine autumnal day, Rip had unconsciously scrambled to one of the highest parts of the Kaatskill mountains. He was after his favorite sport of squirrel shooting, and the still solitudes had echoed and re-echoed with the reports of his gun. Panting and fatigued, he threw himself, late in the afternoon, on a green knoll, covered with mountain herbage, that crowned the brow of a precipice. From an opening between the trees he could overlook all the lower country for many a mile of rich woodland. He saw at a distance the lordly Hudson, far, far below him, moving on its silent but majestic course, with the reflection of a purple cloud, or the sail of a lagging bark, here and there sleeping on its glassy bosom, and at last losing itself in the blue highlands.

On the other side he looked down into a deep mountain glen, wild, lonely, and shagged, the bottom filled with fragments from the impending cliffs, and scarcely lighted by the reflected rays of the setting sun. For some time Rip lay musing on this scene. Evening was gradually advancing. The mountains began to throw their long blue shadows over the valleys. He saw that it would be dark long before he could reach the village, and he heaved a heavy sigh when he thought of encountering the terrors of Dame Van Winkle.

As he was about to descend, he heard a voice from a distance, hallooing, "Rip Van Winkle! Rip Van Winkle!"

He looked around, but could see nothing but a crow winging its solitary flight across the mountain. He thought his fancy must have deceived him and turned again to descend, when he heard the same cry ring through the still evening air.

"Rip Van Winkle! Rip Van Winkle!"—at the same time Wolf bristled up his back, and giving a low growl, skulked to his master's side, looking fearfully down into the glen. Rip now felt a vague apprehension stealing over him; he looked anxiously in the same direction, and perceived a strange figure slowly toiling up the rocks, and bending under the weight of something he carried on his back. He was surprised to see any human being in this lonely and unfrequented place, but supposing it to be some one of the neighborhood in need of his assistance, he hastened down to yield it.

On nearer approach he was still more surprised at the singularity of the stranger's appearance. He was a short square built old fellow, with thick bushy hair, and a grizzled beard. His dress was of the antique Dutch fashion—a cloth jerkin[8] strapped round the waist—several pair of breeches,[9] the outer one of ample volume, decorated with rows of buttons down the sides, and bunches at the knees. He bore on his shoulder a stout keg, that seemed full of liquor, and made signs for Rip to approach and assist him with the load.

Though rather shy and distrustful of this new acquaintance, Rip complied with his usual alacrity, and mutually relieving each other, they clambered up a narrow gully, apparently the dry bed of a mountain torrent. As they ascended, Rip every now and then heard long rolling peals, like distant thunder, that seemed to issue out of a deep ravine, or rather cleft between lofty rocks, toward which their rugged path conducted. He paused for an instant, but supposing it to be the muttering of one of those transient thundershowers which often take place in mountain heights, he proceeded. Passing through the ravine, they came to a hollow, like a small amphitheater, surrounded by perpendicular precipices over the brinks of

---

[8] Sleeveless coat with a belt at waist level
[9] Pants

which impending trees shot their branches, so that you only caught glimpses of the azure sky and the bright evening cloud. During the whole time Rip and his companion had labored on in silence; for though the former marveled greatly on what could be the object of carrying a keg of liquor up this wild mountain, yet there was something strange and incomprehensible about the unknown, that inspired awe and checked familiarity.

On entering the amphitheater, new objects of wonder presented themselves. On a level spot in the center was a company of odd looking personages playing at nine-pins.[10] They were dressed in a quaint outlandish fashion: some wore short doublets,[11] others jerkins, with long knives in their belts, and most of them had enormous breeches, of similar style with that of the guide's.

Their visages, too, were peculiar: one had a large head, broad face, and small piggish eyes. The face of another seemed to consist entirely of nose, and was surmounted by a white sugarloaf hat,[12] set off with a little red cockstail. They all had beards, of various shapes and colors. There was one who seemed to be the commander. He was a stout old gentleman, with a weather-beaten countenance. He wore a laced doublet, broad belt and hanger, high crowned hat and feather, red stockings, and high heeled shoes, with roses in them. The whole group reminded Rip of the figures in an old Flemish painting, in the parlor of Dominie Van Schaick, the village parson, and which had been brought over from Holland at the time of the settlement.

What seemed particularly odd to Rip, was, that though these folks were evidently amusing themselves, yet they maintained the gravest faces, the most mysterious silence, and were, withal, the most melancholy party of pleasure he had ever witnessed. Nothing interrupted the stillness of the scene, but the noise of the balls, which, whenever they were rolled, echoed along the mountains like rumbling peals of thunder.

As Rip and his companion approached them, they suddenly desisted from their play, and stared at him with

---

[10] Bowling game played with nine wooden pins and a wooden ball

[11] Short jackets

[12] Tall, conical hat; there is also a Sugar Loaf Mountain on the Hudson River

such fixed statue-like gaze, and such strange, uncouth, lack-lustre countenances, that his heart turned within him, and his knees smote together. His companion now emptied the contents of the keg into large flagons,[13] and made signs to him to wait upon the company. He obeyed with fear and trembling. They quaffed the liquor in profound silence, and then returned to their game.

By degrees, Rip's awe and apprehension subsided. He even ventured, when no eye was fixed upon him, to taste the beverage, which he found had much of the flavor of excellent Hollands.[14] He was naturally a thirsty soul, and was soon tempted to repeat the draught. One taste provoked another, and he reiterated his visits to the flagon so often, that at length his senses were overpowered, his eyes swam in his head, his head gradually declined, and he fell into a deep sleep.

On waking, he found himself on the green knoll from whence he had first seen the old man of the glen. He rubbed his eyes—it was a bright sunny morning. The birds were hopping and twittering among the bushes, and the eagle was wheeling aloft, and breasting the pure mountain breeze. *Surely,* thought Rip, *I have not slept here all night.* He recalled the occurrences before he fell asleep. The strange man with a keg of liquor—the mountain ravine—the wild retreat among the rocks —the woebegone party at nine-pins—the flagon—*Oh! that flagon! that wicked flagon!* Thought Rip—*what excuse shall I make to Dame Van Winkle?*

He looked round for his gun, but in place of the clean well-oiled fowling-piece, he found an old firelock lying by him, the barrel encrusted with rust, the lock falling off, and the stock worm-eaten. He now suspected that the grave roisters[15] of the mountain had put a trick upon him, and having dosed him with liquor, had robbed him of his gun. Wolf, too, had disappeared, but he might have strayed away after a squirrel or partridge. He whistled after him and shouted his name, but all in vain. The echoes repeated his whistle and shout, but no dog was to be seen.

---

[13] Large drinking mug with a handle
[14] Dutch gin
[15] Revelers or tricksters

He determined to revisit the scene of the last evening's gambol, and if he met with any of the party, to demand his dog and gun. As he rose to walk he found himself stiff in the joints, and wanting in his usual activity. *These mountain beds do not agree with me,* thought Rip, *and if this frolic should lay me up with a fit of the rheumatism, I shall have a blessed time with Dame Van Winkle.*

With some difficulty he got down into the glen. He found the gully up which he and his companion had ascended the preceding evening; but to his astonishment a mountain stream was now foaming down it, leaping from rock to rock, and filling the glen with babbling murmurs. He, however, made shift to scramble up its sides, working his toilsome way through thickets of birch, sassafras, and witch hazel, and sometimes tripped up or entangled by the wild grape vines that twisted their coils and tendrils from tree to tree, and spread a kind of network in his path.

At length he reached to where the ravine had opened through the cliffs to the amphitheater; but no traces of such opening remained. The rocks presented a high impenetrable wall over which the torrent came tumbling in a sheet of feathery foam, and fell into a broad deep basin, black from the shadows of the surrounding forest. Here, then, poor Rip was brought to a stand. He again called and whistled after his dog. He was only answered by the cawing of a flock of idle crows, sporting high in the air about a dry tree that overhung a sunny precipice; and who, secure in their elevation, seemed to look down and scoff at the poor man's perplexities.

What was to be done? The morning was passing away, and Rip felt famished for want of his breakfast. He grieved to give up his dog and gun. He dreaded to meet his wife; but it would not do to starve among the mountains. He shook his head, shouldered the rusty firelock, and, with a heart full of trouble and anxiety, turned his steps homeward.

As he approached the village he met a number of people, but none whom he knew, which somewhat surprised him, for he had thought himself acquainted with everyone in the country round. Their dress, too, was of a different fashion from that to which he was accustomed. They all stared at him with equal marks of surprise, and whenever they cast eyes on him, invariably stroked their chins. The constant recurrence of this gesture induced

Rip, involuntarily, to do the same, when, to his astonishment, he found his beard had grown a foot long!

He had now entered the skirts of the village. A troop of strange children ran at his heels, hooting after him, and pointing at his gray beard. The dogs too, not one of which he recognized for an old acquaintance, barked at him as he passed. The very village was altered. It was larger and more populous. There were rows of houses which he had never seen before, and those which had been his familiar haunts had disappeared. Strange names were over the doors—strange faces at the windows—everything was strange. His mind now misgave him. He began to doubt whether both he and the world around him were not bewitched. Surely this was his native village, which he had left but the day before. There stood the Kaatskill mountains—there ran the silver Hudson at a distance— there was every hill and dale precisely as it had always been—Rip was sorely perplexed—*That flagon last night,* he thought, *has addled my poor head sadly!*

It was with some difficulty that he found the way to his own house, which he approached with silent awe, expecting every moment to hear the shrill voice of Dame Van Winkle. He found the house gone to decay—the roof fallen in, the windows shattered, and the doors off the hinges. A half-starved dog that looked like Wolf was skulking about it. Rip called him by name, but the cur snarled, showed his teeth, and passed on. This was an unkind cut indeed—"My very dog," sighed poor Rip, "has forgotten me!"

He entered the house, which, to tell the truth, Dame Van Winkle had always kept in neat order. It was empty, forlorn, and apparently abandoned. This desolateness overcame all his connubial fears—he called loudly for his wife and children—the lonely chambers rung for a moment with his voice, and then all again was silence.

He now hurried forth, and hastened to his old resort, the village inn—but it too was gone. A large rickety wooden building stood in its place, with great gaping windows, some of them broken and mended with old hats and petticoats, and over the door was painted, "The Union

Hotel,[16] by Jonathan Doolittle."[17] Instead of the great tree that used to shelter the quiet little Dutch inn of yore, there now was reared a tall naked pole, with something on top that looked like a red night cap, and from it was fluttering a flag, on which was a singular assemblage of stars and stripes—all this was strange and incomprehensible.[18] He recognized on the sign, however, the ruby face of King George, under which he had smoked so many a peaceful pipe; but even this was singularly metamorphosed. The red coat was changed for one of blue and buff, a sword was held in the hand instead of a scepter, the head was decorated with a cocked hat, and underneath was painted in large characters, General Washington.[19]

There was, as usual, a crowd of folk about the door, but none that Rip recollected. The very character of the people seemed changed. There was a busy, bustling, disputatious tone about it, instead of the accustomed phlegm and drowsy tranquility. He looked in vain for the sage Nicholas Vedder, with his broad face, double chin, and fair long pipe, uttering clouds of tobacco smoke instead of idle speeches; or Van Bummel, the schoolmaster, doling forth the contents of an ancient newspaper. In place of these, a lean bilious-looking fellow,[20] with his pockets full of handbills,[21] was haranguing vehemently about rights of citizens—election—

---

[16] The Union Hotel is a metaphor for the American Union and the damage suffered in the American Revolutionary War with Great Britain.

[17] Perhaps a reference to Jonathan Trumbull (1710-1785), which rhymes with Doolittle. Trumbull was a governor of Connecticut who declined the request of British General Thomas Gage for help. Trumbull assisted George Washington and would be called "Brother Jonathan" for his help.

[18] The American flag during the American Revolutionary War consisted of six white stripes, seven red stripes and thirteen white stars composed in a circle on a blue background

[19] George Washington (1732-1799) who led America against the British in the American Revolutionary War

[20] Brother Jonathan or a symbol of America during the American Revolutionary War

[21] Propaganda used by American soldiers to get British soldiers to defect during the American Revolutionary War

members of congress—liberty—Bunker's hill[22]—heroes of seventy-six—and other words, that were a perfect Babylonish jargon to the bewildered Van Winkle.

The appearance of Rip, with his long grizzled beard, his rusty fowling piece, his uncouth dress, and the army of women and children that had gathered at his heels, soon attracted the attention of the tavern politicians. They crowded round him, eyeing him from head to foot, with great curiosity. The orator bustled up to him, and drawing him partly aside, inquired "on which side he voted?"

Rip stared in vacant stupidity.

Another short but busy little fellow pulled him by the arm, and rising on tiptoe, inquired in his ear, "whether he was Federal or Democrat."

Rip was equally at a loss to comprehend the question; when a knowing, self-important old gentleman, in a sharp cocked hat, made his way through the crowd, putting them to the right and left with his elbows as he passed, and planting himself before Van Winkle, with one arm akimbo, the other resting on his cane,[23] his keen eyes and sharp hat penetrating, as it were, into his very soul, demanded, in an austere tone, "what brought him to the election with a gun on his shoulder, and a mob at his heels, and whether he meant to breed a riot in the village?"

"Alas! gentlemen," cried Rip, somewhat dismayed, "I am a poor quiet man, a native of the place, and a loyal subject of the King, God bless him!"

Here a general shout burst from the bystanders—"A tory! A tory! A spy! A refugee! Hustle him! Away with him!"

It was with great difficulty that the self-important man in the cocked hat restored order; and having assumed a tenfold austerity of brow, demanded again of the unknown culprit, what he came there for, and whom he was seeking. The poor man humbly assured him that he

---

[22] Battle of Bunker Hill in 1775, which the British won over the Americans

[23] Perhaps a caricature of Benjamin Franklin (1706-1790) who wore a pointed hat and brokered peace toward the end of the American Revolutionary War. He did not, however, receive his walking cane from the French until 1780, which means it was a mistake by Washington Irving to portray him with a cane around the time of the American Revolutionary War.

meant no harm, but merely came there in search of some of his neighbors, who used to keep about the tavern.

"Well—who are they?—Name them."

Rip thought for a moment, and inquired, "Where's Nicholas Vedder?"

There was a silence for a little while, when an old man replied, in a thin piping voice, "Nicholas Vedder? Why he is dead and gone these eighteen years! There was a wooden tombstone in the churchyard that used to tell all about him, but that's rotted and gone too."

"Where's Brom Butcher?"

"Oh, he went off to the army in the beginning of the war. Some say he was killed at the storming of Stoney-Point[24]—others say he was drowned in a squall at the foot of Antony's Nose.[25] I don't know—he never came back again."

"Where's Van Bummel, the schoolmaster?"

"He went off to the wars too, was a great militia general, and is now in Congress."

Rip's heart died away at hearing of these sad changes in his home and friends and finding himself thus alone in the world. Every answer puzzled him, too, by treating of such enormous lapses of time, and of matters which he could not understand: war—congress—Stoney-Point;—he had no courage to ask after any more friends, but cried out in despair, "does nobody here know Rip Van Winkle?"

"Oh, Rip Van Winkle!" exclaimed two or three, "Oh, to be sure! That's Rip Van Winkle yonder, leaning against the tree."

Rip looked and beheld a precise counterpart of himself as he went up the mountain: apparently as lazy, and certainly as ragged. The poor fellow was now completely confounded. He doubted his own identity, and whether he was himself or another man. In the midst of his bewilderment, the man in the cocked hat demanded who he was, and "What, was his name?"

"God knows," he exclaimed, at his wit's end. "I'm not myself—I'm somebody else—that's me yonder—no—that's somebody else, got into my shoes—I was myself last night, but I fell asleep on the mountain, and they've changed my

---

[24] Fortified peninsula a dozen miles south of West Point that jutted into the Hudson River that was stormed by British soldiers in 1779
[25] Hill that meets the Hudson River

gun, and everything's changed, and I'm changed, and I can't tell what's my name, or who I am!"

The bystanders began now to look at each other, nod, wink significantly, and tap their fingers against their foreheads. There was a whisper, also, about securing the gun, and keeping the old fellow from doing mischief, at the very suggestion of which the self-important man in the cocked hat retired with some precipitation. At this critical moment a fresh comely woman pressed through the throng to get a peep at the grey bearded man. She had a chubby child in her arms, which, frightened at his looks, began to cry. "Hush, Rip," she cried, "hush, you little fool. The old man won't hurt you."

The name of the child, the air of the mother, the tone of her voice, all awakened a train of recollections in his mind. "What is your name, my good woman?" he asked.

"Judith Gardenier."

"And your father's name?"

"Ah, poor man, his name was Rip Van Winkle. It's twenty years since he went away from home with his gun, and never has been heard of since—his dog came home without him; but whether he shot himself, or was carried away by the Indians, nobody can tell. I was then but a little girl."

Rip had but one question more to ask; but he put it with a faltering voice:

"Where's your mother?"

Oh, she too had died but a short time since. She broke a blood vessel in a fit of passion at a New-England peddler.

There was a drop of comfort, at least, in this intelligence. The honest man could contain himself no longer.—He caught his daughter and her child in his arms.—"I am your father!" he cried—"Young Rip Van Winkle once—old Rip Van Winkle now!—Does nobody know poor Rip Van Winkle?"

All stood amazed, until an old woman, tottering out from among the crowd, put her hand to her brow, and peering under it in his face for a moment, exclaimed, "Sure enough! It is Rip Van Winkle—It is himself! Welcome home again, old neighbor—Why, where have you been these twenty long years?"

Rip's story was soon told, for the whole twenty years had been to him but as one night. The neighbors stared when they heard it; some were seen to wink at each other, and put their tongues in their cheeks: and the self-important man in the cocked hat, who, when the alarm was over, had returned to the field, screwed down the corners of his mouth and shook his head—upon which there was a general shaking of the head throughout the assemblage.

It was determined, however, to take the opinion of old Peter Vanderdonk, who was seen slowly advancing up the road. He was a descendant of the historian of that name,[26] who wrote one of the earliest accounts of the province.[27] Peter was the most ancient inhabitant of the village, and well versed in all the wonderful events and traditions of the neighborhood. He recollected Rip at once, and corroborated his story in the most satisfactory manner. He assured the company that it was a fact, handed down from his ancestor the historian, that the Kaatskill mountains had always been haunted by strange beings. That it was affirmed that the great Hendrick Hudson,[28] the first discoverer of the river and country, kept a kind of vigil there every twenty years, with his crew of the Half-moon, being permitted in this way to revisit the scenes of his enterprise and keep a guardian eye upon the river, and the great city called by his name. That his father had once seen them in their old Dutch dresses playing at nine pins in a hollow of the mountain; and that he himself had heard, one summer afternoon, the sound of their balls, like distant peals of thunder.

To make a long story short, the company broke up, and returned to the more important concerns of the election.[29]

Rip's daughter took him home to live with her. She had a snug, well-furnished house, and a stout cheery

---

[26] Adriaen van der Donck (1618-1655) was an attorney and historian who chronicled life in New Netherlands before it became part of America.

[27] In 1665 Adriaen van der Donck published *A Description of New Netherland. Iroquoians and their World.*

[28] Henry Hudson (1560/70s-1611) was an Englishman who explored the Hudson River area in the seventeenth century.

[29] America's first election was held in 1796, which means that Rip fell asleep twenty years before the year America declared independence from the British in July of 1776.

farmer for a husband, whom Rip recollected for one of the urchins that used to climb upon his back. As to Rip's son and heir, who was the ditto of himself, seen leaning against the tree, he was employed to work on the farm; but evinced an hereditary disposition to attend to anything else but his business.

Rip now resumed his old walks and habits. He soon found many of his former cronies, though all rather the worse for the wear and tear of time; and preferred making friends among the rising generation, with whom he soon grew into great favor.

Having nothing to do at home, and being arrived at that happy age when a man can do nothing with impunity, he took his place once more on the bench at the inn door, and was reverenced as one of the patriarchs of the village, and a chronicle of the old times "before the war." It was some time before he could get into the regular track of gossip, or could be made to comprehend the strange events that had taken place during his torpor. How that there had been a revolutionary war—that the country had thrown off the yoke of old England—and that, instead of being a subject of his Majesty George the Third, he was now a free citizen of the United States.

Rip, in fact, was no politician. The changes of states and empires made but little impression on him; but there was one species of despotism under which he had long groaned, and that was—petticoat government.[30] Happily, that was at an end. He had got his neck out of the yoke of matrimony, and could go in and out whenever he pleased, without dreading the tyranny of Dame Van Winkle. Whenever her name was mentioned, however, he shook his head, shrugged his shoulders, and cast up his eyes; which might pass either for an expression of resignation to his fate, or joy at his deliverance.

He used to tell his story to every stranger that arrived at Mr. Doolittle's hotel. He was observed, at first, to vary on some points every time he told it, which was, doubtless, owing to his having so recently awaked. It at last settled down precisely to the tale I have related, and

---

[30] In this instance, reference to women running the home in a domineering, almost military fashion as Rip was subjected to by his wife

not a man, woman, or child in the neighborhood, but knew it by heart.

Some always pretended to doubt the reality of it, and insisted that Rip had been out of his head, and that this was one point on which he always remained flighty. The old Dutch inhabitants, however, almost universally gave it full credit. Even to this day they never hear a thunder storm of a summer afternoon about the Kaatskill, but they say Hendrick Hudson and his crew are at their game of nine pins; and it is a common wish of all henpecked husbands in the neighborhood, when life hangs heavy on their hands, that they might have a quieting draught out of Rip Van Winkle's flagon.[31]

ENDNOTE

The foregoing Tale, one would suspect, had been suggested to Mr. Knickerbocker by a little German superstition about the Emperor Frederick *der Rothbart,*[32] and the Kypphaliser mountain: the subjoined note, however, which he had appended to the tale, shows that it is an absolute fact, narrated with his usual fidelity:

"The story of Rip Van Winkle may seem incredible to many, but nevertheless I give it my full belief, for I know the vicinity of our old Dutch settlements to have been very subject to marvelous events and appearances. Indeed, I have heard many stranger stories than this, in the villages along the Hudson; all of which were too well authenticated to admit of a doubt. I have even talked with Rip Van Winkle myself, who, when last I saw him, was a very venerable old man, and so perfectly rational and consistent on every other point, that I think no conscientious person could refuse to take this into the bargain; nay, I have seen a certificate on the subject taken before a country justice, and signed with a cross, in the justice's own hand writing. The story, therefore, is beyond the possibility of doubt."

"D.K."

---

[31] Drinking flask

[32] In German folklore, Frederick I (1121-1190)—referred to as Barbarossa, *der Rothbart* (Redbeard)—fell into deep sleep instead of dying, from which he would awake when his country was in need of him.

POSTSCRIPT

The following are travelling notes from a memorandum-book of Mr. Knickerbocker: —

The Kaatsberg, or Catskill Mountains, have always been a region full of fable. The Indians considered them the abode of spirits, who influenced the weather, spreading sunshine or clouds over the landscape, and sending good or bad hunting seasons. They were ruled by an old squaw spirit, said to be their mother. She dwelt on the highest peak of the Catskills, and had charge of the doors of day and night to open and shut them at the proper hour. She hung up the new moons in the skies, and cut up the old ones into stars. In times of drought, if properly propitiated, she would spin light summer clouds out of cobwebs and morning dew, and send them off from the crest of the mountain, flake after flake, like flakes of carded cotton, to float in the air; until, dissolved by the heat of the sun, they would fall in gentle showers, causing the grass to spring, the fruits to ripen, and the corn to grow an inch an hour. If displeased, however, she would brew up clouds black as ink, sitting in the midst of them like a bottle-bellied spider in the midst of its web; and when these clouds broke, woe betide the valleys!

In old times, say the Indian traditions, there was a kind of Manitou or Spirit, who kept about the wildest recesses of the Catskill Mountains, and took a mischievous pleasure in wreaking all kinds of evils and vexations upon the red men. Sometimes he would assume the form of a bear, a panther, or a deer, lead the bewildered hunter a weary chase through tangled forest and among ragged rocks; and then spring off with a loud ho! ho! leaving him aghast on the brink of a beetling precipice or raging torrent.

The favorite abode of this Manitou is still shown. It is a great rock or cliff on the loneliest part of the mountains, and from the flowering vines which clamber about it, and the wild flowers which abound in its neighborhood, is known by the name of the Garden Rock. Near the foot of it is a small lake, the haunt of the solitary bittern, with water-snakes basking in the sun on the leaves of the pond-lilies which lie on the surface. This place was held in great awe by the Indians, insomuch that the boldest hunter would not pursue his game within its precincts.

Once upon a time, however, a hunter, who had lost his way, penetrated to the Garden Rock, where he beheld a number of gourds placed in the crotches of trees. One of these he seized and made off with it, but in the hurry of his retreat he let it fall among the rocks, when a great stream gushed forth, which washed him away and swept him down precipices, where he was dashed to pieces, and the stream made its way to the Hudson, and continues to flow to the present day; being the identical stream known by the name of the Kaaters-kill.

Who is the mysterious George Darley, born in Dublin, Ireland during 1795 and who lived until 1846? How did this relatively unknown mathematician and poet manage to pen not only one of the best fantasy short stories for the first half of the nineteenth century, but also the cornerstone of modern fairy tales?

After much research there are no easy answers and what makes Darley even more mysterious was his plentiful use of pseudonyms such as "G. Crayon, jun" and "Guy Penseval" and "John Lacy." No picture of him is available, either.

The stuttering, introverted Darley was, foremost, an Irish poet and little attention was paid to his "Lillian of the Vale" subsequent to its initial publication in 1824. Fifty years after his death, the September 18, 1897 issue of the *Athenæum* magazine echoes this sad truth, though it does reference his sonnet "I've Been Roaming" that first appeared in "Lillian of the Vale":

"Fate has treated Darley somewhat harshly, as the verdicts of his own day suggest. Tennyson offered at his own expense to print his poetry; Carlyle—never over generous of good words for his contemporaries—thought him a considerable mathematician; and his critical power, well known to his brilliant circle of friends, contributed much to the *London Magazine*—then at its zenith, with "Elia" and other stars as contributors—and more to the *Athenæum*, for which he did good work till the day of his death, though this side of his literary activity seems to have escaped Mr. Streatfeild. And today, except as the author of the words "I've been roaming," associated with a fine old English tune, he is probably almost unknown. The reason is not far to seek.

"An impediment in his speech, an exquisite and fantastic taste, an outspoken temper at war with the pretentious, and intolerant of sham, all led Darley to shrink from a world which he feared would not understand him. Writing often under varying pseudonyms, he courted retirement as eagerly as some writers have sought advertisement. Hence to the world of today Darley, dead more than fifty years since, is almost a new poet, and the critic may hesitate between two ways of reviewing."

At first glance, Darley appears to be a one-hit wonder in the fantasy genre; and this is certainly true if viewed from a short story perspective. He was, however, active in writing fantasy poems and sonnets and dramas such as "Syliva; or, The May Queen," "The Mermaiden's Vesper-Hymn," "The Sea-Bride," and "Nepenthe."

The venerable Edgar Allan Poe thought that Darley's treatment of fairies in the short story had "wonderfully succeeded."[1] This is no surprise since Darley's philosophy of art aligned with Poe's. Darley stated in the *Athenæum* magazine of October 8, 1836, "the primary law of the Fine Arts consists in Beauty" as opposed to the teaching of *morals* that was so widely popular in the Romantic Age. In "Lilian of the Vale" Darley truly did produce a work of beautiful art that wonderfully succeeded.

---

[1] "Fancy and Imagination," Edgar Allan Poe, *The Works of the Late Edgar Allan Poe*, 1850, p. 377

LILIAN OF THE VALE
1824

HAVING PARTIALLY RECOVERED from a nervous distemper, brought on by a severe course of academical studies, I determined to withdraw for the summer months into the country, where my constitution, naturally weak, might be invigorated, and my mind be diverted from preying on my body, by the novelty and variety of such amusements as woods, and rivers, and mountains, and valleys, afford. Both inclination and necessity (for I was not affluent) induced me to seek a place of retirement at once humble and private, where my expenditure would be inconsiderable, and my actions might escape from that ceremonious restraint, which the forms of society impose upon its members.

I had travelled for some time in search of such an abode, but with little success, when one evening as I was returning, quite chagrined, to the village where I had lain the night before, my eyes were attracted to a narrow sheepwalk—which deviated nearly at right angles from the high road—by something which I thought resembled an ornament of dress lying in the middle of the path. On taking it up, I found it to be a pale blue ribband,[1] simply folded in the form of a star-knot, and held together by a silken thread of the same color.

This was some proof at least, that a habitation was not far distant, and I immediately determined to attempt discovering it; for, beside the desire of returning the trifle to its owner, I was strongly tinctured with that theory which appropriates much of our future destiny to such accidental occurrences, and I firmly believed that this pathway and no other would lead me to the object in search of which I had set out; especially as the aforesaid ribband did not lie near the road I was pursuing, but a considerable distance from it on the bypath, thereby obviously pointing out to me the way I should choose.

The path I speak of sunk down between two hills, descending much below the level of the high road, and at

---

[1] Ribbon

length opening into a green platform which overlooked a still deeper declivity. I will never forget the enchanting prospect which offered itself to my view, as I stood in the green recess, formed by the two banks, which rose from the platform, and concealed both it and the steepdown valley it overhung, from the passengers on the high road. I seemed as if suspended in middle air, for the purpose of surveying the hollow woodland beneath me to the greatest advantage; for the precipitous descent of the mountain, on whose side I was placed, prevented me from seeing that there was anything under my feet but the surface of the platform itself.

The valley was of considerable extent, and terminated either way in a dark glen. It was perfectly verdant, except where its green mantle was relieved by the deeper tints of several masses of foliage with which the lawns were interspersed, by a few glistening rocks, or by the bright surface of a stream which ran at the bottom, forming innumerable cascades and waterfalls, which gave an uncommon sweetness and purity to the air. At one end of the valley appeared a small cottage scarcely indeed apparent, from the number of trees which surrounded it, and open only in front towards the river, on whose opposite side it lay. A few wreaths of thin blue smoke curling above it, showed it to be inhabited.

Here then (I thought), *will my labors at length cease, if all the wealth I am master of can purchase a corner in such a paradise.*

Looking about to see how I should descend from my present altitude to this Eden, a little goat made its appearance on the edge of the precipice, just where it was met by the bank forming the side of the recess where I stood, and gazing full at me for some time, disappeared. I approached the place where it had vanished, and found that the former pathway still wound by the foot of the bank wall, and continued in a slanting direction down the side of the precipice, till it ended at the ford which lay across the river, and led up to the cottage door. With some difficulty and considerable danger I doubled this promontory, and descended cautiously, my four-footed guide running on before me, and stopping at intervals to see if I followed.

Surely (I thought), still theorizing as I followed my active conductor to the bottom, *my fate lies this way; here*

*have I a second regulator of my path; there must be
something in these governing accidents.*

I found the river much wider and more rapid than I
expected. A large tree, supported at each end on massive
stones, lay across the deepest part of the stream, where
there were no rocks to serve as steps. Over this my nimble
vaunt-courier trotted, and in a few moments led me to the
threshold of the cottage, which it entered
unceremoniously.

As my figure darkened the door, a matron, who sat
within, raised her eyes from the book which lay upon her
knee, and somewhat astonished, I suppose, at the
suddenness of my appearance, waited without speaking
till I had explained myself. Having apologized for my
intrusion, and related the circumstances which
occasioned it, I briefly mentioned the object in search of
which I was travelling. The matron civilly replied, that her
cottage, from its smallness, was ill adapted to my
purposes, but that if I was satisfied with such an humble
residence, if I thought my health would be improved by
the situation, I was welcome to a part of her house; that
she only regretted her inability to provide me with a
suitable apartment.

I agreed with the good woman on her own terms, and
finding myself fatigued by my journey, I soon retired to my
chamber. It was a small room, neatly but simply
furnished. A little bed lay in one corner. A woman's
dressing-stand, and a couple of old-fashioned chairs, with
an oaken table, nearly completed the inventory. A few
books, chiefly moral and religious, stood on a shelf near
the window. One of these I opened and found the word
Lilian,[2] written in a delicate way, on the title page. Without
waiting to make any further observations, I went to bed
and fell asleep immediately.

When the soul is entranced in slumber, and we are as
if divided between life and death, there are sounds often
heard in such moments, which seem to partake of another
and a superior world; sounds of that wild and visionary
description to which, waking, we can find no parallel. With
such celestial music in my ears I awoke in the morning,
but the sounds seemed to die away as I returned to the

---

[2] Lilian is the formal name of Lily, which is derived from the flower of
the same name.

consciousness of earthly existence. While I was regretting that my dream was not reality, and before the echoes of its ideal symphony had ceased to vibrate in my brain, I thought I heard the same notes distinctly repeated by a voice; human indeed, but more exquisitely sweet than ever I had heard on earth before. The imperfect sensations of sleep had given it its spirituality, but waking perception left it all its wildness and melody. The words, struck apparently by a silver tongue, penetrated to my brain, while lost in breathless transport my vision seemed to return. Again it sung:—

> Vale of the Waterfalls!
> Glen of the River!
> Where the white torrents roll
> Fast and for ever!
>
> Wild sings the mountain-lark,
> Bird of the air!
> And down in the valley
> There's music as rare.
>
> Sweet blow the mountain-bells,
> High o'er the dale,
> Waking the little bells
> Down in the vale.
>
> Fresh breathes the morning-wind,
> Bright looks the day,—
> Up to the heather-hills!
> Lilian, away!

Raising myself on one elbow to catch these delicious sounds, and looking through the lattice which commanded a view of the ford, and the opposite side of the valley, I saw a light female figure glide swiftly over the sylvan bridge, and with the speed of wind fly up the pathway which I had descended yester-evening.

I arose instantly, and going to the window beheld her, accompanied by the little goat, rapidly ascending the precipice. When she had gained the platform, she turned towards the sun, which rose on the other side of the vale, and after a few moments, apparently given to contemplation of its splendor, disappeared between the banks which formed the verdant recess. Though the morning was not far advanced, I felt too much interested, by the song I had heard, and the form I had seen, to think of returning to bed.

I hastily dressed myself, and taking up one of the books which lay near me, fixed my eyes on the written characters which I had observed the night before. I know not how long I remained in this state of abstraction, when the shadow of the good woman of the house, passing over the book, awakened me from my reverie. In a few minutes she repassed my window, and proceeded to the other end of the cottage, where a thick copsewood reaching from it to the river, shut out the view of the mountains behind.

A green plat, fresh and dewy, lay in front of the cottage, and sloping down to the river, mingled its short herbage with the sedgy borders of the channel. A rustic bench, shadowed by the overhanging copse, formed a kind of bower in which the matron now sat, looking anxiously towards the path which led down from the hills.

As she sat there, I had a good opportunity of observing her appearance. It was that of one who had seen better days, who had felt misfortunes keenly but not impatiently; melancholy predominated in her countenance, but resignation strove hard for superiority.

Sickness more than age had robbed her of youth's graces; but though the rose had faded on her cheek, the lily still remained in all its former delicacy. Turning towards my window, her eye caught mine, and I instantly went forth to salute her. She inquired kindly for my health, hoped a few days would restore it, and told me that her daughter had gone to pull some herbs which she thought would be of use to me, and would soon return. I asked if it was her daughter whom I had heard that morning singing so exquisitely.

"Yes (she said), my Lilian is more like a bird of the air, than a thing of the earth. In joy she sings of her happiness. In woe she sings away her sadness. When in neither, like the birds she sings for very thoughtlessness."

"And if I may judge (I said) by the rapidity with which she ascended the precipice,—she must have their wings too, as well as their song."

The matron smiled. "Lilian has lived here for fourteen years, from infancy to girlhood; and these mountains are grown so familiar to her, that she might tread them blindfolded. In truth, sir, she is a wild one. When her duty to me does not require her presence, she spends her time wandering through the recesses of this valley and the surrounding hills. She goes singing her little roundelays over the whole wilderness, and there is scarcely a rock, a cave, or a precipice, which has not echoed to her song."

"Forgive me if I ask whether you are a native of this valley. Your conversation would lead me to think not."

"Alas, sir! I saw many years of sorrow before I came to this solitude. My husband was an officer of distinction in the army—but, hush! (she said, putting her finger to her lips,) Lilian is coming;—and I think it but fair to keep the canker from the bud, let the old tree decay as it will," she added, forcing a smile as her daughter approached.

At the end of the arbor where I sat, the foliage was sufficiently thick to conceal me, yet not so dense as to prevent my seeing what might pass without. Receiving a significant smile from the widow, I withdrew myself farther into the shade, just as the girl reached the foot of the bridge. When she came to the middle where the water was deepest, she stopped, and clasping her hands, while she drew them to her neck with that natural grace which belongs to the period of extreme youthfulness, at the same time bending her aerial form into the attitude of one supplicating inwardly, she looked at her mother with an intensity of expression, which denoted more heartfelt feelings than words could possibly convey.

This beautiful apparition seemed to have but just escaped the age of childhood; or rather, extreme innocence had prolonged that portion of her life beyond its due period. Her figure was small, but exquisitely proportioned, as was evident from her delicate arms bare almost to the shoulder, and her tiny feet and ankles which the mountain dress she wore was not calculated to conceal. Her hair was of a glossy fairness, and her complexion of that fine bloom which arises from health and purity of blood. Considerably heightened by exercise, the glow of her cheek was only surpassed by the bright redness of her mouth, which seemed indeed the very bed of sweetness. Eyes, with which we are inclined to imagine angels, were heavenly blue and liquid from the overflowing of a tender and sensitive heart. A simple white wrapper of very thin muslin,[3] showing off the harmony and gracefulness of her figure to the greatest advantage, and more like a mist than a garment, shrouded this little goddess; and as the foam of the cataract[4] curled to her foot, or burst in a thousand frothy shapes around her, she stood like the Naiad of the River,[5] which thundered in unruly joy at receiving her among its billows.

In this attitude she advanced, brightening as she approached her mother, and mincing her steps with girlish sportiveness, till she came within a few paces of the bower. Then unclasping her hands and spreading her arms, as if to embrace her anxious parent, like a spirit at play, she began a kind of fantastic dance; and as her nimble fairy feet twinkled on the green turf, and her thin garb floated on her shoulders like wings, I thought the veritable Ariel[6] swam before my sight. Fondly tantalizing her delighted mother, who sat with outstretched arms to receive her, while tears of joy trickled from her eyes, the playful girl still continued—without actually touching—to hover round her, accompanying her fantastic movements with a little song of the wildest sweetest cadency.

> I've been roaming! I've been roaming!
> Where the meadow dew is sweet,
> And I'm coming! and I'm coming!
> With its pearls upon my feet.
>
> I've been roaming! I've been roaming!
> O'er red rose and lily fair,
> And I'm coming! and I'm coming!
> With their blossoms in my hair.
>
> I've been roaming! I've been roaming!
> Where the honeysuckle creeps,
> And I'm coming! and I'm coming!
> With its kisses on my lips.

Here the fairy threw herself into her mother's breast, and was covered with kisses, as fervently repaid.

---

[3] Thin, white cotton material
[4] Stream issuing from a crevice in a mountain
[5] Daughter of the river god in Greek mythology
[6] Archangel in Christian Apocrypha

The favorite goat, which had been her companion, now presented itself at the entrance of the bower, having a little basket of light osier[7] suspended from one of its horns, and containing a profusion of flowers which its mistress had gathered in her excursions.

In rising from her mother's lap to relieve her companion from its charge, my figure met her view. A blush, at the recollection that she had been seen by a stranger, overspread her whole face, bosom, and even her arms, with the deepest crimson. When the good woman presented her to me as her daughter, with her cheek half averted, she made me a simple curtsey, and retired almost like a child behind her mother. In a little time we went to breakfast in the arbor, and the business of the scene was a relief to her embarrassment, but she remained in total silence, while at every turn of my head the blood mantled involuntarily to her cheek and bosom.

In this secluded valley, where perhaps no one of my sex above the grade of a peasant had ever appeared, and from which society was naturally excluded, neither her bashfulness nor her reserve surprised me, especially when I considered her extreme youth; but that such a beautiful creation could exist upon earth, without drawing the world to adore it as the symbol of heavenly perfection, was to me totally inexplicable.

Sensations which I never had experienced before, sensations under which my entire frame trembled with an agitation at once excessive and pleasurable, now took possession of my soul. I seemed to have plunged into a new world, a world of superior purity, where the softness of the air, and the brightness of the verdure, had exalted my feelings to a height of enthusiasm and intense sensitiveness, which we attribute to the inhabitants of our visionary vales of eternal blessedness. Shut in from the common occurrences of life which might destroy the illusion, placed amid scenery so romantic, so melancholy, so lovely, it was no wonder if to one of my fervid imagination, his nature should seem to be exalted by the place, rather than the beauty of the scene to be exaggerated by his enthusiastic disposition.

I forgot the actual world,—forgot that I was in it, and gave myself wholly up to the dreams of fancy. The sylvan

---

[7] Willow having long and pliable shoots used in basket weaving

Goddess, or spirit of this place, had now become familiar, and as she hovered around my path, pointing out the freshest spots where I might recline while she sung me into slumber, and showed me the various flowery treasures of her enchanted garden, I thought of Eden, of Elysium, of Paradise, fancied I had already by some forgotten means been transported to one of these delightful abodes, and her own angelic airy form confirmed the delusion.

In fact, this singular girl had a character of mind and frame which was quite preternatural. She was a perfect, I had almost said *real*, Wood-nymph.[8] Her form, her actions, her thoughts, were those that belong to such a being. She seemed to have imbibed the very spirit of germination which pervaded the wild productions of her native valley. The tenderness and diminutive symmetry of its herbage, had imparted a like delicacy and grace to her form. The purity and fineness of its elements had infused themselves into her blood. The wildness of its imagery, its sublimity, and its beauty, had assimilated the disposition of her mind to themselves. She was something between earthly and celestial. She had the form of a mortal, but the habits of a spirit.

For the first two or three days which I spent in the Vale of the Waterfalls (as it was called), Lilian was distant and reserved, but when a little habituated to my presence, with the freedom which we see in childhood when fear has subsided, she became affectionate and familiar, nor was there ever in her manners that coyness which generally distinguishes maidenhood. She seemed to be totally unconscious that it was necessary, and gave herself to my society as she would to that of a brother.

I became her inseparable companion. She would lead me through the devious paths of the wilderness, and bring me to the several grottos and fountains, and fresh rolling streams, with which this solitude abounded. She would guide my steps over little hillocks blooming with the loveliest flowers, and glades of the sweetest verdure; then having embosomed me among these inextricable recesses, disappear like a wraith[9] in some dell or hollow, and start up again when I least expected her.

---

[8] A tree spirit in Greek mythology
[9] Spirit

One day as I sat alone under the shade of a rock, I felt something rustle softly in my bosom, and looking round perceived the girl skipping down from the rock, with the ribband which had first seduced me to this valley in her hand, and laughing gaily as she waved it round her head. She had silently mounted the rock behind me, and snatched the ribband from my breast, where I had preserved it. I attempted to recover it, but she escaped me like a shadow before I had run a dozen paces. In a short time she re-appeared, and coming up to me, threw a little knot of blue flowers into my bosom, singing—

> Sweet blue-bells we,
>   Mid flowers of the lea
> The likest in hue to heaven,
> Our bonnets so blue
>   Are tinged with the dew
> That drops from the sky at Even.

> Our bloom more sweet
>   Than dark violet,
> Or tulip's purple stain,
> At every return
>   Of the dew-breathing morn,
> Grows brighter and brighter again!

A very remarkable circumstance attending my acquaintance with this creature was, that, except on the above occasion, I never knew what it was to feel her touch; and even here, the sensation was more that of a breeze rustling in my bosom, than of a mortal hand. Though perfectly familiar and unsuspicious, whenever I approached within the possibility of touching her, she seemed to flit from me by imperceptible degrees, so that I could not at this moment assert, except from the evidence of sight and reasoning, that she was actually corporeal.[10]

Indeed all her habits and actions partook of another nature. She spoke little; expressing herself mostly by gestures or inarticulate modulations of voice. When she did utter words, they were breathed in a kind of recitative or cadence, or, as was most generally the case, her sentiments were conveyed in the form of a song. I have

---

[10] Material or physical

given a few specimens of these and although simplicity is their principal attribute, when aided by her angelic voice and expressive gestures, they were the wildest and sweetest imaginable. In fact she had a natural turn for poetry. Education had nothing to do with it.

Both her poetry and the music with which she accompanied it, were irregular and inartificial, like the song of a bird, the murmur of a brook, or the sigh of a tree—more the involuntary emanations than the premeditated combinations of sounds. Such of her songs as I can recall to memory—for as she sung from momentary impulse it was extremely difficult to find her repeating the same words except on similar occasions—such of these as I could collect on the instant will appear in order, while I endeavor to give some notion of this extraordinary girl, with whom the happiest, if not the most rational moments of my life were spent.

Her mother has often told me that she did not know how Lilian subsisted. She would never sit down to a regular meal, but would sometimes take a morsel of bread with her when she purposed a distant excursion, and even this would be found strewed on some pathway for the birds who might happen to light there. She was impatient of confinement; and often when her mother had seen her to bed, ongoing into her room an hour after, it would be found empty, and Lilian escaped unseen to wander by moonlight in the valley. This happened frequently during my residence there; and once being excited by curiosity, I went out in search of her and found her in the bottom of a dell—drinking dew out of the cups of flowers.

"Lilian," I said, "why have we lost you?"

"My sisters! My sisters!" she answered impatiently.

"What sisters?"

"Look! Look!" she said, pointing to some fantastic shapes into which the spray of the distant cataract were formed by the reflection of the moon.

"I see nothing but the river foam dancing in the moonbeams."

"These," she replied, "these are my sisters,—the only sisters Lilian ever knew. Listen! Do they not speak to each other?"

"Come, you are too romantic, Lilian. The water as it falls murmurs indistinctly, and at this distance misleads you."

"Nearer then!" the girl said. "I must hear what they say."

And before I could interpose, she rushed to the brow of the cataract and disappeared. Uttering a cry of terror I followed, and just as I had reached the spot where she vanished, her mother came to tell me that Lilian had returned to the cottage.

I retired to my chamber, lost in astonishment at this singular occurrence. In the morning, when her mother talked with Lilian about the imprudence of wandering in the night air, she replied in a roundelay.[11]

The wren hath her nest at the root of a tree,
And the tufted moss is the couch of the bee,
Where rain nor cold hath power to harm her;
The bed of the eagle is built in the sky,
And the bittern in rushes doth nightly lie;
Then why should Lilian's bed be warmer?

Her senses were incontestably more acute than belongs to the nature of mortality. She would often stop in the midst of our conversation, to listen, as she said,—to the wind walking over the flowers; and accordingly in a little time I would perceive the breeze to swell into a transient gust as it passed by the place where we stood. Whether in some instances her romantic imagination might not have suggested ideal murmurs I will not decide, but her delicate perceptions of sound were mostly verified by fact. I remember sitting with her one sunny day on the river bank in a sequestered part of the vale, when, after a fit of contemplative silence, on my addressing myself to break it, she raised her head, and motioning me to be still, began in a low tremulous voice, scarcely distinguishable from the mixed murmur which rises from the breast of the woodland in summertime, a kind of irregular chaunt—

Hear! Hear!
How the vale-bells tinkle all around
As the sweet wind shakes them—hear!
What a wild and sylvan sound!

---

[11] Short, uncomplicated song

> Hear! Hear!
> How the soft waves talk beneath the bank,
> And rush sighs to willow—hear!
>   Most reeds sigh to willow dank!
>
> Hear! Hear!
> How the blue fly hizzes in the air
> With his voice in his tiny wings—hear!
>   He sings at his flowery fare!
>
> Hear! Hear!
> How the wood-bird murmurs in the dark,
> And the distant cuckoo chimes—hear!
>   From the sun-cloud trills the lark!

She could discriminate accurately between the scents of flowers of the same species, so as to name them blindfolded. Her sight was so fine that she would detect the minnows lying on the bed of a stream, in the darkest weather, when to me they were indistinguishable from the slimy pebbles on the bottom. On putting down a straw to the place she pointed out, they flitted. Her other senses were equally discriminative.

But in what she chiefly resembled our notions of spirit, was the lightness, grace, and peculiar swiftness of her motion. Something between flying and dancing. Her movements were so rapid that sometimes it required no great stretch of superstition to believe that she actually vanished into the air. The wild and restless life she led, wandering over hill, dell, rock and precipice, had given an elasticity to her foot, which made her seem to tread on air; while the slightness of her limbs, formed on the most delicate model of beauty and grace, appeared by the tremulous instability which they gave to her frame, to indicate a necessity for perpetual and ever-varying motion.

I had often dreamed of Attendant Spirits,[12] Sylphs,[13] Houris,[14] Semi-deities,[15] and imagined beings partaking of a double nature, the spiritual and corporeal, beings of an intermediate class, whose outlines and figures were

---

[12] Spirits who specifically watch over one person
[13] Air-spirit
[14] Pure, female spirits with large eyes
[15] Small gods

human, but whose form was insubstantial; whose actions, habits, and thoughts were not preternatural, nor supernatural wholly, but such as human actions, habits, and thoughts, would be when refined by some celestial alchemy which would clear them of their grossness without divesting them of their specific essence. With such visionary beings had my waking dreams been peopled, but never until now were these conceptions apparently realized. This creature adequately represented my preconceived notion of an intermediate being.

The surface of the Vale of the Waterfalls was not uniform, but was broken into numberless hillocks and dells in miniature, interspersed with the several varieties of rock, cleft, grove, glade, and declivity. Amid these romantic solitudes was Lilian ever straying. Every singular or characteristic point of the Vale, was to her in place of a companion. Hillocks, rocks, shrubs, and flowers, the people of the wilderness, were to her in place of society. I have frequently wandered for the whole day in search of her, and perhaps found her at length in a shady nook singing to the wild flowers, or on a sunny bank dancing round a knot of cowslips, or hovering on the brink of the torrent chanting her mystic verses to its monotonous numbers.

Sometimes I accompanied her from the cottage door, while she rambled like a wild bee from bank to dell, and from shrub to flower, conversing with her by snatches, but never finding it possible to confine her either to one subject or one place. The character of her thoughts was wildness mingled with deep tenderness and melancholy; but she was at times gay and playful. A high strain of sublimity would often convert the sylph into a sybil,[16] when the changes in the face of nature gave a gloomy color to her mind; for her wildness, melancholy, gaiety, and sublimity of imagination, were nothing but the transcripts of those passions which seem to animate the system of natural things. When a wild rock or a solitary cave attracted her notice, she grew romantic or melancholy. When a sunny flower or a darkly-waving pine caught her eye, she became gay or gloomy accordingly.

---

[16] In Greek mythology there were ten female sybils, each with the gift of prophecy sometimes through the use of an oracle; all had booming voices and lived in caves.

But as the predominating features of the solitude even in its most charming dress were melancholy and wildness, so the general characteristics of her thoughts were sadness and romance.

We sat one evening on the side of the river, just at the foot of the principal cataract, where the waves plunging from on high down into a rocky basin, shook the very bank we sat on by their fall, and drowning each other in the pool, raised a continual din and echo by their struggles and tumultuous contentions. The wind had swept in frequent gusts through the vale during the latter part of the day, but as night approached the old trees began to groan with a heavier blast, and the wild birds flew with fearful screams to the groves. The small flowers closed up their breasts rapidly, and committed themselves to the storm, while the river seemed to foam and swell under the chafing wing of the tempest. In a few minutes the rack began. Thunder broke in tremendous peals over our heads, leaves flew in eddies through the air, the shrill reed whistled, and the swinging pine moaned loudly in the night wind, while the caves and narrow passages between rocks swelled the terrific chorus by their hollow voices.

Shuddering, I turned to Lilian. She had risen, and was hanging over the brink of the whirlpool, muttering something which, by its wildness and incoherence, resembled an incantation. Her delicate white arms were crossed on her bosom, her long hair flew over her shoulders on the wind, and her little cheek grew pale as she uttered her mystic numbers to the roar of the torrent.

"Lilian," I said, "come away, the night grows terrific." She answered not, but elevating her voice till it nearly reached a scream, and mingled with the noise of the waves like the cry of one drowning, she chanted a wild rhapsody, her eye almost lighted to frenzy, and her check whitening every moment—

 The woods are sighing!
 And the wild birds crying!
And loud and sorely the wild waters weep!
 Dark pines are groaning!
 And night winds are moaning!
And muttering thunder rumbles hoarse and deep!

Ghastly, frantic, and appalling, she broke into a yet wilder measure:

> Come, Sisters, come, come!
> Bring the storm, and bring the rain,
> Let the raving winds loose upon the swelling billows
> Down, Spirits, down, down!
> Shake the oak, and split the rock,
> Scream amid the dashing waves, and shriek among the willows!

Her voice ended in a wild shriek, and she disappeared. I had no courage to follow up this adventure. Her character seemed to change here; enthusiasm degenerated into frenzy, and gentleness gave way to more than sibylline extravagance of voice and gesture. I returned to the cottage, and as I did not wish to be questioned by the woman concerning her daughter, I retired immediately to my chamber.

There was something of a foreboding nature in this last incident. The morning after, I received a post letter from the neighboring town where the widow had gone for provisions, letting me know that my father was on his deathbed, and requiring my immediate attendance to receive his last blessing. This was imperative. And though I had neither seen nor heard of Lilian since the preceding night, after having taken a hasty leave of her mother, I set off immediately to the village where I might procure some mode of conveyance to my father's residence. The direct path from the Vale of the Waterfalls to the village lay through one of the glens or dingles in which the valley terminated. The sides of the mountains which formed this defile were so precipitous that they almost met overhead, and they were moreover clothed with a dark mantle of hanging fir, which increased the gloom and horror of the place.

At the very bottom lay the path, and as I looked up the sides of this dreary profound, which seemed the very realization of the Valley of the Shadow of Death,[17] my fancy grew bewildered. Though waking, I seemed to walk in a dream, and a thousand dim and terrible phantoms

---

[17] Psalm 23:4 "Yea, though I walk through the Valley of the Shadow of Death . . . ."

appeared to rise from the brambles under my feet, and darken still more the obscurity which encompassed me.

The incidents of last night returned forcibly to my mind. There was something mysterious, unreal, and preternatural in everything connected with that Vale, and this was a fit place for executing the final catastrophe. As I passed on, at intervals some horrid thing would brush by me, and a wet flaccid wing like that of a monstrous bat would flap me in the face. Sometimes a phantom would come and whisper busily in my ear, yet I heard nothing. And I saw many hideous shapes, who by their distortions were apparently in the acts of screaming, laughing, and making other abominable noises, yet the air was as silent as death.

All of a sudden, this subterranean passage of horror and darkness opened into the bright fields of day. I was reinspirited; but the recollection of the dreary glen, the vale, Lilian and her preternatural disappearance, still remained. Pondering on these subjects, and endeavoring to account for them in some probable manner, I proceeded through the open valley into which the sides of the glen had widened, and passing by a tuft of green bushes, I thought I heard from within them someone weeping like a deserted child. I immediately opened them, and to my astonishment found Lilian sitting on the green plat in the midst with her head in her lap, lamenting piteously, and drowned in a flood of tears.

She rose and spread her arms to receive me. I flew to her embrace, but when I thought to have caught her to my bosom, she was still at the same distance from me as before.

"Lilian," I said, "why do you avoid me? I am going."

"I know it," she replied, "and I came to take my last farewell."

"Not the last, not the last, dear girl! (I said, forgetting yesterday's adventure) if heaven will spare us for each other. When I have paid the duties which I owe to my father, I will return to love and Lilian."

"Lilian," she said, faintly smiling, "Lilian will then be no more!"

As I stood, unable from the impressiveness of her manner to make any answer, whether it was imagination, or that the echo in this place was extraordinarily powerful, I heard her last words repeated several times up the mountains, and "No more! No more! No more!" at length died away in hollow sighs among the rocks of the valley. Perceiving me silent, she said, "Come, I will delay you no longer. Depart to your home! On that glade," (pointing to a sloping bank at some distance,) "we separate forever!"

We proceeded in silence. When we had reached the spot, she stopped; and turning to me, her innocent bosom filled with tears, and her blue eyes dropping crystal, she pointed towards the vale which lay behind us, and in a voice scarcely audible with sorrow, "Listen," she said, "to the Rover's Farewell"—

Farewell the groves, and farewell the bowers!
Ye rocks, ye mountains, and ye streams, farewell!
Farewell the bloom and sweet breath of flowers!
Farewell for ever-more! a long farewell!

Farewell, O Vale of fast falling water!
Ye banks, ye bushes, and ye glades, farewell!
Farewell, lone parent of one wayward daughter!
Farewell for ever,—a long, long farewell!

And farewell, Lilian! . . .

Here she was interrupted by a loud laugh uttered over my shoulder. I turned to see from whom it came, but no one appeared. On turning again towards Lilian, she was gone. Immoveable with astonishment, I stood for some time stupefied, but recovering my senses, I called several times, "Lilian, Lilian! Dear Lilian, answer me!"

She appeared a long way off, at the entrance of the valley, with her hands covering her face, and walking slowly towards her home. I now recollected my father, and considering that it would be useless to pursue this adventure any farther at present, summoning up my courage, I proceeded onwards to the village. I had scarcely walked twenty paces, when, to my utter surprise, this apparition stood before me again in the midst of the path, but when I approached, disappeared and appeared on the top of some rock or prominence at a distance, where her small figure whitening in the sun would seem to kiss its hand to me as I passed. In this way, she continued to accompany me, till the signs of population began to appear. She had gradually kept behind me as I approached the high road, and when I at length reached it, on looking round I perceived her standing on a high rock at some distance, the sunbeams glistening in her eyes which were filled with tears, while she kissed her hand repeatedly, till she faded entirely from my view.

When I reached my father's house, I found him partially recovered. I accompanied him to Italy, where he had been ordered by his physicians,—too late however for his preservation. He died within a few miles of Turin. My attention to him on his deathbed was necessarily unremitting; and this, combined with my own previous delicate state of health, occasioned a relapse of my nervous disorder.

With some difficulty I recovered so much of my health as to think of returning to my native country, to which the desire of revisiting the Vale of the Waterfalls and investigating its mysteries completely was no small inducement. The unceasing attendance which my father's illness required on my part, added to the novelty of scene and society, had prevented me from dwelling intensely on the extraordinary incidents which I so lately experienced; but my thoughts now reverted naturally to them, as well from my innate tendency to the romantic, as from the singularity of the facts themselves, and the influence of my late illness and my father's death, in rendering such melancholy recollections attractive. The cottage where my father died was situated on the borders of a lake in the bosom of a deep valley among the Piedmontese hills, and I was sitting about the close of the evening in the room that had been his, ruminating successively on him and on Lilian.

The window where I sat looked out on the lake which lay in calm unruffled stillness before me, and the blue mountains towards the west were just sinking into that mellow haze which characterizes the softness of an Italian evening. The lattice was open, and I leaned forward to catch the summer breeze as it gently moved the tendrils of a jessamine which crept to the roof of the cottage. A rustic bench outside rose nearly to the level of the window;— Lilian came and sat down on it. I started at the sight, but looking steadfastly on the figure, I saw it melt gradually into air.

In a little time it appeared standing on the bright surface of the lake, but disappeared in the same manner as before; then on a rock at some distance, and again vanished. I had no doubt but this was a shadow raised by my own imagination, pursuing the same train of ideas intensely. Indeed the figure I now saw was very different from the original in the Vale of the Waterfalls. The form was evidently insubstantial. The figure, though preserving its characteristic outlines, was emaciated and stiff. The bloom had totally faded from its cheek and lip, and was replaced by the wan sickliness of death. The eyes were glazed and motionless.

"Lilian is dead," I said. While I journeyed home, the figure occasionally appeared, but at each time more faintly than before, till it vanished entirely.

On reaching England, the Vale of the Waterfalls was my first object. I quickly sought out the village near to which it lay, and pursuing my former steps, soon found myself in the midst of the valley. It was beautiful as ever, but to me appeared to wear less the air of enchantment than when I had left it. I turned to the cottage.

It was in ruins.

The bower was overgrown with nettles and tall weeds. The smooth plat had shot up into long rank grass that waved heavily in the breeze, and emitted a close suffocating odor. As I stood ruminating on these changes, my heart swelling with the melancholy conviction that Lilian was indeed no more, a peasant appeared on the hills, carrying a mattock[18] and other instruments. Upon his approach I made inquiries concerning the widow and her daughter. He replied that the person who had lived in the cottage was dead some months, that she never had any daughter to his knowledge, but lived quite alone; that the only person he had ever heard of in the valley, beside her, was a young man who came there for the recovery of his health, but he remained for a short time only; that the cottage now belonged to himself, and he was repairing it for his own family.

This account, to me, appeared very singular. I went to the entrance of the dreary glen where I had experienced such horrors. The mountains seemed to have opened overhead, and the place was comparatively lightsome. I passed through it safely, and came to the circle of green bushes where I had found Lilian weeping. A rude stone

---

[18] Hand tool

cross stood in the midst. It was apparently of very great age, yet I never had observed it before. These things were still more extraordinary. On returning to the village, the inhabitants gave me the same account as the peasant and when I spoke of Lilian they seemed not to understand me. Many of them recognized me, yet I could gain no farther satisfaction. They also called the vale by a different name.

I have frequently revisited this valley, but never could obtain any intelligence concerning the extraordinary being whom it was my fortune alone to have met there. An impenetrable veil seemed to have been drawn over her history, and I am at length compelled to give up all attempts at investigating it. That she was mortal and had actual existence, the evidence of my senses, and my disbelief in the theory of spirits visiting this world, induce me to assert.

Yet it is totally unaccountable how such a being could exist, and the whole world, with but one exception, remain ignorant of it. I have never been able to come to any conclusion on this point. Sometimes, indeed I am inclined to think that this vision of Lilian of the Vale was a mere creation of my own brain, naturally very imaginative, and at the period of this adventure disturbed and overheated by the fever which accompanies a nervous disease such as mine.

John MacKay Wilson
(1804-1835)

"The Doom of Soulis" was published in the year John MacKay Wilson died at the young age of 31. He was a Scottish author, songist and dramatist. He took on the ambitious editing project of publishing a magazine "every Saturday" that he called *Tales of Border*. A number of short stories contained in the magazine were his own, including "The Poor Scholar" that is partially autobiographical.

Wilson would die the following year, literally having worked himself into the grave. His wife, Sara, succeeded him and would go on to republish many of his tales throughout her life, including in 1869 when Walter Scott's publishing company printed all 24 volumes of *Tales of Border*. Of the sixty-six short stories Wilson penned for his magazine, "The Doom of Soulis" was one of them and is his best fantasy story; though the germ of the tale was based on legend. William II de Soulis was a Scottish noble who could not have a more fitting surname.

THE DOOM OF SOULIS
1835

"They rolled him up in a sheet of lead,
  A sheet of lead for a funeral pall;
They plunged him in the caldron red,
  And melted him, lead, and bones and all." –*Leyden.*[1]

A GAZETTER WOULD inform you that Denholm is a village beautifully situated near the banks of the Teviot, about midway between Jedburgh and Hawick, and in the parish of Carers, and perhaps,—if of modern date, it would add that it has the honor of being the birthplace of Dr. Leyden. However, it was somewhat early on a summer morning, a few years ago, that a young man, a stranger, with a fishing rod in hand, and a creel fastened to his shoulders, entered the village. He stood in the midst of it, and turning round—"This then," he said, "is the birthplace of Leyden—the son of genius—the martyr of study—the friend of Scott!"[2]

Few of the villagers were around, and the first person he met,—who carried a spade over his shoulder, and appeared to be a ditcher,[3]—he inquired if he could show him the house in which the bard and scholar was born.

"Ou aye, Sir," said the man, "I wate can I—I'll shew ye that instantly, and proud to shew you it too."

That is good, thought the stranger, *the prophet is dead, but yet he speaks—he has honor in his own country.*

The ditcher conducted him across the green and past the end of a house that was described as being the schoolhouse, and was newly built, and led him towards a humble building, the height of which was but a single story and which was occupied by a millwright as a

---

[1] Scottish poet, John Leyden (1775-1811)
[2] Scottish author, Sir Walter Scott (1771-1832)
[3] Ditch digger

workshop. Yet, again the stranger rejoiced to find that the occupier venerated his premises for the poet's sake, and that he honored the genius of him who was born there.

"Dash it!"[4] said the stranger, quoting the habitual phrase of poor Leyden, "I will not fish today." And I wonder not at his having so said, for it is not every day that we can stand beneath the thatch-clad roof,—or any other roof—where was born one whose name time will bear written in undying characters on its wings, until those wings droop in the darkness of eternity.

The stranger proceeded up the Teviot, oftentimes thinking of Leyden, of all that he had written, and occasionally repeating passages aloud. He almost forgot that he had a rod in his hand—his eyes did anything but follow the fly, and I need hardly say, his success was not great.

About midday he sat down on the green bank by himself to enjoy a sandwich and a small flask of spirits, which almost every angler, who can afford it, carries with him. But he had not sat long, when a venerable-looking old man saluted him with—

"Here's a bonny day, sir." The old man stood as he spoke. There was something prepossessing in his appearance. He had a weather-beaten face, with thin white hair, blue eyes that had lost some of their former lustre. His shoulders were rather bent and he seemed to be a man who was certainly neither rich nor affluent, but who was at ease with the world, and the world was at ease with him.

They entered into conversation and sat down together. The old man seemed like one of those characters that you will occasionally find fraught with the traditions of the Borders,[5] and still tainted with, and half believing in their ancient superstitions. I wish not to infer that superstition was carried to a greater height of absurdity on the Borders than in other parts of England and Scotland, nor even that the inhabitants of the north were as remarkable in the early days for their superstitions as they are now for their intelligence,—for every nation has its superstitions,

---

[4] Wilson note: "A common expression of John Leyden's, and perhaps was in some degree expressive of his headlong and determined character."
[5] Area near the dividing line between Scotland and England

and I am persuaded that most of them might be traced to a common origin.

Yet, though the same in origin, they change their likeness with the character of a nation or district. People unconsciously made their superstitions to suit themselves. though their imaginary effects still terrified them. There was therefore something characteristic in the fables of our forefathers, which fables they believed as facts. The cunning deceived the ignorant, the ignorant were willing to deceive themselves and what we now laugh at as the clever trick of a *hocus-pocus* man, was scarce more than a century-ago received as a miracle,—as a thing performed by the hand of the "prince of the powers of the air."[6]

Religion without knowledge, and still swaddled in darkness, fostered the idle fear: yea, there are few superstitions, though prostituted by wickedness, that did not owe their existence to some glimmering idea of religion. They had not seen the lamp that lightens the soul and leads it to knowledge, but having perceived its far-off reflection, plunged into the quagmire of error, and hence proceeded superstition.

But I digress into a descant on the superstitions of our fathers, nor should I have done so, but that it is impossible to write a Border Tale of the olden time without bringing them forward; and when I do, it is not with the intention of instilling into the mind of my readers the old idea of sorcery, witchcraft, and visible spirits, but of showing what was the belief and conduct of our forefathers. Therefore without further comment, I will cut short these remarks, and simply observe that the thoughts of the younger stranger still running upon Leyden, he turned to the elder after they had sat together for some time, and said—"Did you know Dr. Leyden, sir?"

"Ken him!" said the old man. "Fifty years ago I've wrought a day's—work beside his father for months!"

They continued their conversation for some time, and the younger inquired of the elder, if he were acquainted with Leyden's ballad of Lord Soulis?

"Why I have heard a verse or twa o' the ballant, sir," said the old man, "but I'm sure everybody kens the story. However, if ye're no perfectly acquaint wi' it. I'm sure I'm

---

[6] Quote from King James version of Ephesians 2:3

willing to let ye hear it wi' great pleasure, and a remarkable story it is,—and just as true, sir, ye may take my word on't, as that I'm raising this bottle to my lips."

So saying, the old man raised the flask to his mouth, and after a regular fisher's draught, added—

"Weel Sir, I'll let ye hear the story about Lord Soulis.[7]

You have no doubt heard of Hermitage Castle, which stands upon the river of that name, at no great distance from Hawick. In the days of the great and good king Robert the Bruce,[8] that castle was inhabited by Lord Soulis. He was a man whose very name spread terror far and wide, for he was a tyrant and a sorcerer. He had a giant's strength, an evil eye, and a demon's heart, and he kept his *familiar*[9] locked in a chest. Peer and peasant became pale at the name of Lord Soulis. His hand smote down the strong, his eye blasted the healthy. He oppressed the poor and he robbed the rich. He ruled over his vassals with a rod of iron. From the banks of the Tweed, the Teviot, and the Jed, with their tributaries, to beyond the Lothians, an incessant cry was raised against him to Heaven and to the king. But his life was protected by a charm, and mortal weapons could not prevail against him. (The seriousness with which the narrator said this, showed that he gave full credit to the tradition, and believed in Lord Soulis as a sorcerer.)

He was a man of great stature, and his person was exceedingly powerful. He also had royal blood in his veins, and laid claim to the crown of Scotland in opposition to the Bruce. But two things troubled him, and the one was to place the crown of Scotland on his head—the other to possess the hand of a fair and rich maiden named Marion, who was about to wed Walter, the young heir of Branxholm—the stoutest and the boldest youth on all the wide Borders. Soulis was a man who was not only of a cruel heart, but it was filled with forbidden thoughts; and to accomplish his purposes, he went down into the

---

[7] William II de Soulis (??-1320), a noble of the Scottish border who resided in Hermitage Castle was a proprietor of Eccles in Berwickshire.

[8] Robert I (1274-1329), who served as king of Scots until his death

[9] Wilson note: "Each sorcerer was supposed to have his Familiar spirit that accompanied him, but Soulis was said to keep his locked in a chest."

dungeon of his castle, in the dead of night, that no man might see him perform the "deed without a name."

He carried a small lamp in his hand, which threw around a lurid light, like a glow-worm in a sepulchre; and as he went, he locked the doors behind him. He carried a cat in his arms. Behind him a dog followed timidly, and before him into the dungeon he drove a young bull that had "never nipped the grass." He entered the deep and the gloomy vault, and with a loud voice exclaimed—

"Spirit of darkness!—I come!"

He placed the feeble lamp on the ground in the middle of the vault; and with a pick-axe which he had previously prepared, he dug a pit and buried the cat alive, and as the poor, suffocating creature mewed, he exclaimed the louder—

"Spirit of darkness come!"

He then leaped on the grave of the living animal, and seizing the dog by the neck, he dashed it violently against the wall, towards the left corner where he stood, and unable to rise, it lay howling long and piteously on the floor. Then he plunged his knife into the throat of the young bull, and while its bleatings mingled with the howling of the dying dog, amidst what might be called the blue darkness of the vault, he received the blood in the palms of his hands, and he stalked around the dungeon, sprinkling it in circles, and crying with a loud voice—

"Spirit of darkness hear me!"

Again he digged a pit, and seizing the dying animal, he hurled it into a grave, feet upwards;[10] and again he groaned while the sweat stood on his brow—"Come spirit!—come!"

He took a horseshoe that had lain in the vault for years, and which was called in the family—the spirit's shoe, and he nailed it against the door, so that it hung obliquely,[11] and as he gave the last blow to the nail, again he cried—

---

[10] These are the recorded practices which sorcerers resorted to, when they wished to have a *glimpse* of invisible spirits.

[11] Wilson note: "In the account of the trial of Elizabeth Bathgate, wife of Alexander Pae, in Eyeinonth, one of the accusations in the indictment against her was that she had 'ane horseshoe in one darnet and secret pairt of your dur, keepit by yon thairopoun as ane devilish meanis and instructioun from the devill.'"

"Spirit I obey thee!—come!"

Afterwards he took his place in the middle of the floor, and nine times he scattered around him a handful of salt, at each time exclaiming—

"Spirit arise!"

Then he struck thrice nine times with his hand on a chest that stood in the middle of the floor, and by its foot was the pale lamp, and at each blow he cried—

"Arise! spirit arise!"

When he had done these things, and cried twenty and seven times, the lid of the chest began to move, and a fearful figure with a red cap[12] on its head, and which resembled nothing in heaven above, or on earth below, rose, and with a hollow voice[13] inquired—

"What want ye Soulis!"

"Power!—spirit power!" he cried, "that mine eyes may have their desire, and that every weapon formed by man may fall skaithless on my body, as the spent light of a waning moon!"

"Thy wish is granted mortal!" groaned the fiend. "Tomorrow eve young Branxholm's bride will sit within your bower, and his sword return bent from your bosom as though he had dashed it against a rock. Farewell, invoke me not again for seven years, nor open the door of the vault, but then knock thrice upon the chest and I will answer you. Away! Follow your course of sin and prosper—*but beware of a coming wood!*"

With a loud and sudden noise the lid of the massive chest fell and the spirit disappeared, and from the floor of the vault issued a deep sound like the reverbing of thunder. Soulis took up the flickering lamp, and leaving the dying dog still howling in the corner whence he had driven it, he locked the iron door, and placed the huge key in his bosom.

In the morning his vassals came to him, and they prayed him on their bended knees that he would lessen the weight of their hard bondage; but he laughed at their

---

[12] Red-cap is a name given to spirits supposed to haunt castles.

[13] Wilson note: "In the proceedings regarding Sir George Maxwell, it is gravely set forth that the voice of evil spirits is 'rough and goustie;' and to crown all, Lilly in his Life and Times informs us that they speak Earse—and, he adds, 'when they do so it's like Irishmen, much in the throat!'"

prayers, and answered them with stripes. He oppressed the widow and persecuted the fatherless. He defied the powerful and trampled on the weak. His name spread terror wheresoever it was breathed, and there was not in all Scotland a man more feared than the wizard Soulis, the lord of Hermitage.

He rode forth in the morning with twenty of his chosen men behind him, and wheresoever they passed the castle or the cottage, where the occupier was the enemy of Soulis, or denied his right to the crown,[14] they fired the latter, destroyed the cattle around the former, or he sprinkled on them the dust of a dead man's hand, that a murrain[15] might come among them.

But as they rode by the side of the Teviot, he beheld fair Marion, the betrothed bride of young Walter, the heir of Branxholm, riding forth with her maidens, and pursuing the red deer.

"By this token, spirit," muttered Soulis joyously, "you have not lied—tonight young Branxholm's bride will sit within my bower."

He dashed the spur into the side of his fleet steed, and although Marion and her attendants forsook the chase and fled as they perceived him, yet as though his *familiar* gave speed to his horse's feet, in a few seconds he rode by the side of Marion and throwing out his arm, he lifted her from the saddle while her horse yet flew at its fastest speed, and continued its course without its fair rider.

She screamed aloud, she struggled wildly, but her attendants had fled afar off, and her strength was feeble as an insect's web in his terrible embrace. He held her on the saddle in front of him—

"Marion!—fair Marion!" said the wizard and ruffian lover, "scream not—struggle not—be calm and hear me. I love you!—Pretty one I love you!" and he rudely raised her lips to his. "Fate has decreed you will be mine, Marion— and no human power will take you from me. Weep not— strive not. Hear that I love you—love you fiercely, madly maiden, as a she-wolf does its cubs. As a river seeks out the sea, so have I sought you, Marion; and now you are

---

[14] Wilson note: "If legitimacy could have been proved on the part of the grandmother of Lord Soulis, he certainly was a nearer heir to the crown than either Bruce or Baliol."

[15] Infectious disease acquired by cattle

mine—Fate has given you unto me, and your fair cheek will rest on a manlier bosom than that of Branxholm's beardless heir."

Thus saying, and still grasping her before him, he again plunged his spurs into his horse's side, and he and his followers rode furiously towards Hermitage Castle. He locked the gentle Marion within a strong chamber, he

"Wooed her as the lion woos his bride."

And now she wept, she wrung her hands, she tore her raven hair before him, and it hung disheveled over her face and on her shoulders. She implored him to save her, to restore her to liberty; and again finding her tears wasted and her prayers in vain, she defied him. She invoked the vengeance of Heaven on his head; and at such moments the tyrant and the reputed sorcerer stood awed and stricken in her presence. For there is something in the majesty of virtue and holiness of innocence, as they flash from the eyes of an injured woman, which deprives guilt of its strength and defeats its purpose, as though Heaven lent its electricity to defend the weak.

But wearied with importunity, and finding his threats of no effect, on the third night that she had been within his castle, he clutched her in his arms, and while his vassals slept, he bore her to the haunted dungeon that the spirit might throw its spell over her and compel her to love him. He unlocked the massive door. The faint howls of the dog were still heard from a corner of the vault. He placed the lamp on the ground. He still held the gentle Marion to his side, and her terror had almost mastered her struggles. He struck his clenched hand on the huge chest—he cried aloud—"Spirit! Come forth!"

Thrice he repeated the blow,—thrice he uttered aloud his invocation. But the spirit arose not at his summons. Marion knew the tale of his sorcery—she knew and believed it, and terror deprived her of consciousness. On recovering she found herself again in the strong chamber where she had been confined, but Soulis was not with her. She strove to calm her fears, she knelt down and held her beads,[16] and begged that her Walter might be sent to her deliverance.

---

[16] Catholic Rosary beads

It was scarce daybreak when the young heir of Branxholm, whose bow no man could bend and whose sword was terrible in battle, with twice ten armed men, arrived before Hermitage Castle and demanded to speak with Lord Soulis. The warder blew his horn, and Soulis and his attendants came and looked over the battlement.

"What do you want, boy," inquired the wizard chief, "that ere the sun be risen you come to seek the lion in his den?"

"I come," replied young Walter boldly, "in the name of our good king, and by his authority, to demand that you give into my hands, safe and sound, my betrothed bride, lest vengeance come upon you."

"Vengeance! Beardling!" rejoined the sorcerer. "Who dares speak of vengeance on the house of Soulis?—or whom call you king? The crown is mine—your bride is mine, and you also will be mine, and a dog's death will you die for your morning's boasting."

"To arms!" he exclaimed, as he disappeared from the battlement, and within a few minutes a hundred men rushed from the gate.

Sir Walter's little band quailed as they beheld the superior force of their enemies, and they were in dread also of the sorcery of Soulis. But hope revived within them when they beheld the look of confidence on the countenance of their young leader and thought of the strength of his arm, and the terror which his sword spread.

As hungry tigers spring on their prey, so rushed Soulis and his vassals on Sir Walter and his followers. No man could stand before the sword of the sorcerer. Antagonists fell as impotent things before his giant strength. Even Walter marveled at the havoc he made, and he pressed forward to measure swords with him. But ere he could reach him, his few followers who had escaped the hand of Soulis and his host, fled and left him to maintain the battle singlehanded. Every vassal of the sorcerer, save three, pursued them, and against these three, and their charmed lord, young Walter was left to maintain the unequal strife. But as they pressed around him, "Back!" cried Soulis, trusting to his strength and to his charm. "From my hand alone must Branxholm's young boaster meet his doom. It is meant that I should give his head as a toy to my bride fair Marion."

"Your bride, fiend!" exclaimed Sir Walter. "Thine!—Now perish!" and he attacked him furiously.

"Ha! Ha!" cried Soulis, and laughed at the impetuosity of his antagonist, while he parried his thrusts. "Take rushes for your weapon, boy, steel falls feckless on me."

"Vile sorcerer!" continued Walter pressing on him more fiercely. "This sword will sever your enchantment."

Again Soulis laughed, but he found that his contempt availed him not, for the strength of his enemy was equal to his own, and in repelling his fierce assaults, he almost forgot the charm which rendered his body invulnerable. They fought long and desperately, when one of the followers of Soulis, suddenly and unobserved, thrust his spear into the side of Sir Walter's horse. It reared up, stumbled and fell, and brought him to the ground.

"An arrow-schot!"[17] exclaimed Soulis. "How, boy, did you presume to contend with me?" And suddenly springing from his horse, he pressed his iron heel on the breast of his foe, and turning also the point of his sword towards his throat—"You will not die yet," he said, and turning to the three attendants who had not followed in the pursuit, he added—"Here,—bind him fast and sure."

Then the three held him on the ground, and bound his hands and feet, while Soulis held his naked sword over him.

"Coward and wizard!" exclaimed Walter, as they dragged him within the gate. "You will rue this foul treachery."

"Ha! Ha! Vain boasting boy!" returned Soulis. "You indeed will rue your recklessness."

He caused his vassals to bear Walter into the strong chamber where fair Marion was confined, and grasping him by the neck while he held his sword to his breast, he dragged him towards her. He said sternly—"Consent now maiden to be mine, and this boy will live—refuse, and his head will roll before you on the floor as a plaything."

"Monster!" she exclaimed, and screamed aloud. "Would you harm my Walter?"

"Ha! My Marion!—Marion!" cried Walter, struggling to be free, and turning his eyes fiercely on Soulis. "Destroy me fiend," he added, "but harm her not."

---

[17] When cattle died suddenly, it was believed to be by an arrow-schot, that is, shot or struck down by the invisible arrow of a sorcerer.

"Think on it maiden," cried the sorcerer raising his sword. "The life of your bonny bridegroom hangs on your word. But you will have until midnight to reflect on it. Be mine then, and harm will not come on him or you; but a man will be your husband, and not the boy whom he has brought to you in bonds."

"Curse you vile sorcerer!" rejoined Walter. "Were my hands unbound, and unarmed as I am, I would force my way from your prison in spite of you and yours!"

Soulis laughed scornfully, and again added—"Think on it fair Marion."

Then he dragged her betrothed bridegroom to a corner of the chamber and ordering a strong chain to be brought, he fettered him against the wall. In the same manner he fastened her to the opposite side of the apartment, but the chains with which be bound her were of silver.

When they were left alone, "Mourn not sweet Marion," said Walter, "and think not of saving me—before tomorrow our friends will be here to your rescue, and though I fall victim to the vengeance of the sorcerer, still let me be the bridegroom of your memory."

Marion wept bitterly and said that she would die with him.

Throughout the day the spirit of Lord Soulis was troubled, and the fear of coming evil sat heavy on his heart. He wandered to and fro on the battlements of his castle, anxiously looking for the approach of his retainers who had followed in pursuit of the followers of Branxholm's heir. But the sun set, and the twilight drew on, and still they did not come. It was drawing towards midnight when a solitary horseman spurred his jaded steed towards the castle gate. Soulis admitted him with his own hand into the courtyard, and when the rider had dismounted, he asked him hastily and in a tone of apprehension—

"Where are the others, knave? And why do you come alone?"

"Pardon me my lord," said the horseman falteringly as he dismounted. "Your faithful bondsman is the bearer of evil tidings."

"Evil! Slave!" exclaimed Soulis striking him as he spoke. "Speak you of evil to me? What of it?—Where are the others?"

The man trembled, and added—"In pursuing the followers of Branxholm they sought refuge in the wilds of Tarras, and being ignorant of the winding paths through its bottomless morass, horses and men have been buried in it—they who sank not, fell beneath the swords of those they had pursued, and I only have escaped."

"And where did you escape, knave?" cried the fierce sorcerer—"Why did you live to remind me of the shame of the house of Soulis?" and as he spoke, he struck the trembling man again.

He hurried to the haunted dungeon and again performed his incantations, with impatience in his manner and fury in his looks. Thrice he violently struck the chest, and thrice he exclaimed impetuously—

"Spirit! Come forth!—Arise and speak with me!"

The lid was lifted and a deep and angry voice said—

"Mortal! Why have you summoned me before the time I commanded you? Was not your wish granted? Steel will not wound you,—cords bind you,—hemp hang you,—nor water drown you. Away!"

"Stay!" exclaimed Soulis, "Add, nor fire consume me!"

"Ha! Ha!" cried the spirit in a fit of horrid laughter that made even the sorcerer tremble—"*Beware of a coming wood!*" and with a loud clang the lid of the chest fell, and the noise, as of thunder beneath his feet, was repeated.

"Beware of a coming wood!" muttered Soulis to himself. "What does the fiend mean?"

He hastened from the dungeon without locking the door behind him, and as he hurried from it he drew the key from his chest and flung it over his left shoulder; crying, "Keep it spirit!"

He shut himself up in his chamber to ponder on the words of his *familiar*, and on the extirpation of his followers. He thought not of Marion and her bridegroom until daybreak, when with a troubled and a wrathful countenance he entered the apartment where they were fettered.

"Now fair maiden," he began, "have you considered well my words—will you be my willing bride and let young Branxholm live; or refuse, and look on his smooth face as his head adorns the point of my good spear?"

"Rather than see her be yours," exclaimed Walter, "I wish that you would hew me in pieces and fling my mangled body to your hounds."

"Troth! And 'tis no bad thought," said the sorcerer. "You may have your wish. Yet, boy, you think that I have no mercy. I will teach you that I have, and refined mercy too. Now tell me truly, were I in your power as you are in mine, what fate would you award to Soulis?"

"Then, truly," replied Walter, "I would hang you on the highest tree in Branxholm woods."

"Well spoken, young strong-bow," returned Soulis. "I will show you, though you think I have no mercy, that I am more merciful than you. You would choose for me the highest tree, but I will give you the choice of the tree from which you may prefer your body to hang, and from whose top the owl may sing its midnight song, and to which the ravens will gather for a feast. And you, pretty face," he added, turning to Marion. "You will not even be able to save him. Give me your hand. If I will not be your husband, I will be your priest and celebrate your marriage, for I will bind your hands together and you will hang on the branch next to him."

"For that I thank you," said the undaunted maiden.

He then called together his four remaining armed men, and placing halters round the necks of his intended victims, they were dragged into the woods around the Hermitage, where Walter was to choose the fatal tree.

Now a deep mist covered the face of the earth, and they could perceive any object at the distance of half a bow-shot before them—and when he had approached the wood where he was to carry his merciless project into execution—

"The wood comes toward us!" exclaimed one of his followers.

"What!—*The wood comes!*" cried Soulis, and his cheek became pale, and he thought of the words of the demon—"*Beware of a coming wood!*"—and for a time their remembrance, and the forest that seemed to advance before him, deprived his arm of strength and his mind of resolution, and before his heart recovered, the followers of the house of Branxholm, to the number of fourscore, each bearing a tall branch of the rown-tree in their hands,[18] as

---

[18] Wilson note: "It is probable that the legend of the 'coming wood' referred to in the tradition respecting Lord Soulis, is the same as that from which Shakespeare takes Macbeth's charm—'Till Birnam wood shall come to Dunsinane Hill.'"

a charm against his sorcery, perceived, and raising a loud shout, surrounded him.

The cords with which the arms of Marion and Walter were bound were instantly cut. But although the odds against him were as twenty to one, the daring Soulis defied them all. When his followers were overpowered, his single arm dealt death around. Now there was not a day passed that complaints were not brought to king Robert from those residing on the Borders against Lord Soulis for his lawless oppression, his cruelty, and his wizard-craft. And one day there came before the monarch, one after another, some complaining that he had brought diseases on their cattle, or destroyed their houses by fire, and a third that he had stolen away the fair bride of Branxholm's heir. They stood before the king and begged to know what should be done to him. Now the king was wearied with their importunities and complaints, and he exclaimed peevishly and unthinkingly—"Boil him if you please, but let me hear no more of him." But,

> "It is the curse of kings to be attended
> By slaves that take their humor for a warrant."

And when the enemies of Soulis heard these words from the lips of the king, they hastened away to put them in execution; and with them they took a wise man, one who was learned in breaking the spells of sorcery,[19] and with him he carried a scroll, on which was written the secret wisdom of Michael the wizard;[20] and they arrived before Hermitage Castle while its lord was contending single-handed against the retainers of Branxholm; and their swords were blunted on his buckler, and his body received no wounds. They struck him to the ground with their

---

[19] Wilson note: "Dr. Leyden represents this personage as being 'True Thomas, lord Eraylton;' but the Rymer was dead before the time fixed by tradition for the death of Lord Soulis, which took place in the reign of Robert the Bruce, who came to the crown in 1308, and the Rymer was dead before 1299, for in that year his son and heir granted a charter to the convent of Soltra, and in it he describes himself *Filius et hæres Thumæ Rymour de Erceldon.* (The son and heir of the remainder of Erceldon.)"

[20] Michael "the wizard" Scott of Balwearie (1255-1304) was believed to possess supernatural powers.

lances, and they endeavored to bind his hands and his feet with cords, but his spell snapped them as threads.

"Wrap him in lead," cried the wise man, "and boil him according to the command of the king, for water and hempen cords have no power over his sorcery."

Many ran towards the castle, and they tore the lead from the turrets, and they held down the sorcerer and rolled the sheets around him in many folds, till he was powerless as a child, and the foam fell from his lips in the impotency of his rage. Others procured a caldron in which it was said many of his incantations were performed, and the cry was raised—

"Boil him on the Nine-stane-rig!"[21]

And they bore him to where the stones of the druids are to be seen until this day, and the two stones are yet pointed out from which the caldron was suspended. They kindled piles of faggots beneath it, and they forced the living body of Soulis inside the lead, and thrust it into the caldron, and as the flames arose the flesh and the bones of the wizard were consumed in the boiling lead.—Such was the doom of Soulis.

The king sent messengers to prevent his hasty words being carried into execution, but they arrived too late.

In a few weeks there was mirth and music, and a marriage-feast in the bowers of Branxholm, and fair Marion was the bride.

---

[21] Stone circle near Harwick of nine stones placed by the Druids between 2000 B.C. and 1250 B.C.

Wilhelm Hauff
(1802-1827)

Wilhelm Hauff was the Keats and Shelley of early German fantasy writers in the sense that he was a nationally recognized poet and fiction writer who died at a very young age with a promising literary career in front of him.

Hauff was born in Stuttgart, Germany. He was the author of a number of outstanding fantasy stories during his brief life, including "The Severed Hand" found in *6a66le: The Best Horror Short Stories 1800-1849* and "The Spectral Ship," which rose to the level of tales in *Phantasmal: The Best Ghost Stories 1800-1849*. His classic fantasy short story is "*Der Zwerg Nase.*" All were published in his 1826 collection of short stories entitled "The Caravan."

Nineteenth century English translators ascribed various titles to "*Der Zwerg Nase*" such as "Nosey, the Dwarf," "The Dwarf Long Nose," and "The Dwarf Nosey." It is literally translated "The Dwarf Nose" and that is what I have used for this anthology.

Whatever the story is titled, it is more than simply a fantasy story about a dwarf with a long nose. Hauff appears to have added undertones that portray Frederick the Great (Frederick William II), king of Prussia, as the dwarf who was short in stature, slightly hunched over, had a pronounced nose, and long, slender fingers. In the story he is gone for seven years, just as Frederick the Great was preoccupied with the Seven Years' War from 1756-1763 where he fought in ten battles. He would reign over Prussia from 1740-1786, which was an amalgamation of many different areas of present day countries. As reflected in the story by the various food prepared by the dwarf, the areas of Prussia included parts of Germany ("red Hamburg dumplings") and Denmark ("Danish soup"). He also "ruled the under-cooks and scullions like a sovereign."

The old woman is a caricature of Empress Maria Theresa who ruled over Austria for a forty year period starting in 1740. The Seven Years' War began when Maria refused to hand over Silesia to Frederick the Great. Like the witch in the story, she had a long nose and Frederick the Great "had once insulted her" by going to war to gain power over the mineral-rich Silesia.

Then there's the fat goose who fits the bill (no pun intended) of Empress Catherine of Russia and the daughter of Peter the Great who teamed up with Prussia after being adverse for a number of years.

The food reference to "pie Souzeraine" in the story is a telling referral to the politics of suzerainty where one political area or state is subservient to another, a function of the many political states of Prussia at the time.

The year after "The Dwarf Nose" was published, in 1827, Hauff penned the fantasy novella "The Wine-Ghosts of Breman" and became editor of the respected *Stuttgart Morgenblatt* magazine. Later that year he would die of a high fever at the young age of twenty-four.

To this day Wilhelm Hauff is considered one of the best of the early modern German fantasy writers. This is no small feat given the company of writers that surrounded him not the least of which are Friedrich Heinrich Karl de la Motte and Ernst Theodor Amadeus Hoffmann.

THE DWARF NOSE
1827

O, MASTER! THOSE persons are much deceived, who believe that fairies and magicians have ceased to exist since the times of Haroun Al-Raschid,[1] sovereign of Bagdad, or who assert that those stories of the doings of genii, which one hears from storytellers in the marketplace, are all untrue. There are fairies in existence to this very day; and I myself was witness, not a great while since, of an incident in which genii manifestly had a hand, and which I will now relate to you.

Many years ago, in a considerable city of my dear native land, Germany, lived a cobbler and his wife. The cobbler sat daily at the corner of the street, mending shoes and slippers, and making new ones when any one would trust him with the commission. His wife sold herbs and fruits, which she cultivated in a little garden before her house; and many persons bought of her in preference to any other person, because her dress was always clean and neat, and she knew how to spread out and arrange her herbs in an attractive fashion.

This old couple had a son, of agreeable face and figure, and, for a lad of twelve years of age, well grown. He usually sat by the old lady in the marketplace, to carry home fruits and vegetables for the housewives who bought of his mother; and he rarely came back from such errands without some pretty flower, or bit of money, or some nice trifle to eat; for the masters and mistresses were always glad to see the boy's pleasant face at their houses and used to reward him handsomely.

The shoemaker's wife was sitting one day, as usual, in the market. Before her stood her baskets of herbs, cabbages, roots, and vegetables, and in a smaller one a choice lot of early pears, apples, and apricots.

---

[1] Ruled Bagdad as a caliph from 786-809 and established an intellectual court whose fictional exploits were featured in the collection of Arabic legends "One Thousand and One Nights"

Little Jacob was sitting near her, and calling the wares in his high, shrill voice: "Here, gentlemen, see what fine cabbages and elegant vegetables we have! Ladies, here are fresh picked pears, apples, and apricots! Who wants to buy? Who wants to buy? My mother sells very cheap."

While the boy was shouting his recommendations in this way, an old woman entered the market. Her clothes were tattered and shabby, and she had a little, pointed face, wrinkled with age, red eyes, and a sharp, hooked nose hanging down to her chin. She walked, leaning on a long cane, but it was hard to see how she managed to get along; for she hobbled and stumbled so much that it seemed as if she had sticks in her legs and would tumble down and scratch her long nose on the pavement every instant.[2]

The shoemaker's wife watched this old woman attentively. She had sat now for sixteen years in the marketplace every day and had never before seen so singular a figure; and she shrank involuntarily when the old creature hobbled up to her, and stopped before her baskets.

"Are you Hannah, who sells vegetables?" inquired the old woman, in a harsh, disagreeable voice, shaking her head incessantly.

"Yes," answered the shoemaker's wife. "Do you wish to buy some?"

"Perhaps so, perhaps so. Let me see your cabbages. You may have what I want," replied the old beldame, bending down over the baskets and feeling the vegetables with her brown, skinny hands. She picked out the nicely-spread cabbages with her long, spider-fingers, and, bringing them one after the other to her nose, smelled them.

The heart of the shoemaker's wife was in her mouth when she saw the old crone treating her delicate vegetables in this way, but she ventured no remark. For every buyer had a right to examine the goods, and she felt, moreover, a mysterious dread of the old creature.

After the latter had gone through the entire stock, she muttered: "Miserable trash! Wretched stuff! Nothing here

---

[2] Empress Maria Theresa (1717-1780) had a long nose and difficulty getting around in her later years due, perhaps, to having given birth to sixteen children.

to suit me! Things used to be a great deal better fifty years ago. Worthless stuff. Worthless stuff!"

Such criticisms disgusted little Jacob. "Hey! You are a shameless old woman," he cried angrily. "First you grope with your long fingers the beautiful vegetables, squeezing them out of shape, and then you hold them to your long, ugly nose, so that nobody who saw you will buy them. And, after all that, you call them miserable trash, though the duke's own cook always buys from us!"

The old hag leered at the angry boy, laughed a frightful laugh, and said, in a harsh voice:

"Sonny, sonny! So my nose displeases you, hey? My long, beautiful nose? Then you will have one yourself hanging down to your chin."

While speaking, she slipped along to the other basket, and, taking up one of the finest white cabbageheads in her hand, squeezed it together till you could hear it groan, and then, throwing it carelessly into the basket again, said, "Miserable trash! Miserable trash!"

"Don't wag your head about so frightfully," cried the little boy, in great anger. "Your neck is as thin as a cabbage-stalk, and may break off as easily, and then your head would fall into our basket. Who do you think would buy it then?"

"So you don't like my long, lean neck?" muttered the old woman, laughing. "Then you will have none at all. Your head will stick to your shoulders, so it cannot fall off from your little puny body."

"Don't talk like that to the little boy," said the shoemaker's wife, angry at the incessant inspecting, fingering, and smelling. "If you wish to buy something, hurry up. You are frightening away the rest of my customers."

"Very good. So be it, then," cried the old woman, with a savage glance. "I will take these six cabbageheads; but, you see, I must lean on my stick here, and can carry nothing, of course. Let your son carry them home for me, and I will pay him handsomely."

The boy felt little inclined to go, and began to cry, for he felt a horror from the hideous hag; but his mother sternly ordered him to do it, for she thought it a sin to impose such a burden on the feeble old creature. So, half crying, he obeyed her commands, and, collecting the cabbages into a basket, followed the beldame out of the market.

She moved along very slowly, and it was nearly three quarters of an hour before she halted at a small, tumbledown house in a remote quarter of the city. There she drew an old, rusty key from her pocket, and thrust it dexterously into a little hole in the door, which flew open, creaking loudly. But fancy little Jacob's astonishment when he entered the house!

The interior of the building was furnished magnificently. The walls and ceilings were of marble, the furniture of the finest ebony, inlaid with gold and precious stones, while the floors were of glass, and, withal, so polished and smooth that little Jacob slipped and fell on them several times.[3]

The old woman now drew from her pocket a little silver pipe, and blew a blast which sounded shrilly through the house. Several guinea-pigs rushed immediately upstairs, and Jacob was filled with profound astonishment at seeing that they walked upright on their hind legs, wore nutshells on their feet instead of shoes, and were dressed from head to tail in men's clothes.[4]

"Where are my slippers, you vile rabble?" cried the old lady, striking among them with her cane. "How long must I stand here in this condition?"

They ran hastily downstairs, and returned with a couple of cocoa-nut shells, lined with leather, which they put dexterously on the old woman's feet.

All her hobbling and slipping were at an end. Throwing her stick away, and taking Jacob's hand, she slid with great speed across the glass floor. At length she paused in a room bearing some resemblance to a kitchen, though the tables were made of polished mahogany, and the sofas, which were covered with rich damask,[5] would have better suited in a drawing-room.

---

[3] Schönbrun Palace in Austria was given to Empress Theresa as a wedding gift and was lavishly appointed with many chandeliers and marble walls.

[4] The guinea-pigs are perhaps a portrayal of Hungarians over which Empress Theresa ruled and who were known to keep guinea-pigs as pets they called *tengerimalac.*

[5] Fine woven material that usually includes a pattern

"Sit down," said the old witch very kindly, pushing him into the corner of a sofa, and shoving a table before him so that he could not escape. "Sit down. You have had a heavy load to carry. Men's heads are far from light, far from light."

"What are you talking so strangely for, ma'am?" cried the little fellow. "I am tired, I know, but it was the cabbages I carried which made me so. You bought them from my mother, remember?"

"Ha, ha, you are mistaken," laughed the old woman, uncovering the basket, and taking out a human head by a tuft of hair.[6]

The boy was beside himself with horror. He could not comprehend how such a thing had happened, and his thoughts reverted to his mother. *If any one were to hear of these human heads*, he thought to himself, *my mother would certainly be out of business.*

"I must give you some little present now, since you are so obliging," muttered the hag. "Wait a few moments, child, and I will get you a morsel to eat, which you will remember till the day of your death."

Saying this, she again blew her pipe. Several guinea-pigs instantly appeared, dressed in cooks' aprons, with ladles and carving-knives stuck in their girdles. These where followed by a troop of nimble squirrels, wearing wide Turkish trousers,[7] walking upright, and with caps of green velvet on their heads.[8] These last seemed to be the scullions of the establishment, for they clambered with great celerity up the walls, and bringing down pans, dishes, eggs and butter, and herbs and meal, carried them to the hearth. At the fireplace the old lady was bustling about very busily in her slippers of cocoa-nut shell, and

---

[6] When Frederick the Great (1712-1786) was eighteen, he tried to run away with his friend and lieutenant of the Prussian Army, Hans Hermann von Katte (1704-1730). They were caught and Katte was beheaded by Frederick the Great's father for treason, which had a deep and lasting effect.

[7] Pants with baggy legs, tight at the ankles. The squirrels dressed in Turkish clothing are a reference to the oriental clothing that was very popular in the court of Empress Theresa.

[8] In the 18th century Italians wore velvet hats in a burgundy or green color.

the boy saw that she was cooking some very nice treat for him.

The fire began to blaze, the pans steamed and boiled, a pleasant smell filled the room, and the old woman kept running up and down, with the guinea-pigs and squirrels at her heels, and, every time she came near the hearth, poking her long nose into the pot. At length the contents began to hiss and bubble, steam ascended from the pot, and froth flew out into the fire. She took it off the hearth, poured some of the contents into a silver saucer, and set it before little Jacob.

"There, little son," she said, "eat this nice porridge. You never tasted anything so nice in all your life. And you will be a skillful cook, lad, and be a famous man yet; but the cabbages,—no, you will never find the cabbages. Why hadn't your mother any cabbages in her basket?"

The little boy understood very little of what she said, but directed his whole energies on the porridge, which he found excellent. His mother had made him a great many nice titbits, but never any so good as this. The vapor of his herbs and cabbages rose to his nostrils and the porridge was very strong and thick. While he was supping up the last drops of the precious fluid, the guinea-pigs lighted some Arabian incense,[9] which floated in azure clouds through the room. Thicker and thicker grew the clouds, the vapor exercising a magic influence on the little boy.

Remind himself as often as he pleased that he ought to go back to his mother,—recover his consciousness as often as he might, he would sink back irresistibly into slumber again; and at length he lay sound asleep on the old woman's sofa. Strange dreams visited his slumbers. It seemed to him that the old woman had taken off his clothes, and dressed him instead in the skin of a squirrel.

He could now spring and climb like a squirrel, and serve his mistress about the house with the rest of the little animals, whom he found very sensible, intelligent creatures. At first he was employed merely as a shoeblack;[10] that is, he had to rub with oil and polish brightly the cocoa-nut shells that the old lady used for slippers. As he had often been engaged in this business at

---

[9] Another reference to the Turkish influence on Empress Theresa's court

[10] Shoe polisher

home, these duties came easily to his hand. At the end of a year he dreamed he was appointed to higher duties. With several other squirrels he was employed to gather atoms from the sunbeams, and, after collecting a sufficient quantity, sift them through the finest hair-sieves. The old woman prized these sun-atoms as precious esculents, and, being unable to bite for want of teeth, prepared her bread from these impalpable particles.

At the end of another year he was promoted to the office of collector of water for the old lady's drinking. Do not imagine that a cistern of this fluid stood ready in the garden, or that they resorted to a cask in the courtyard, placed there to collect the rain. Their duties were far more onerous. Jacob and the squirrels had to draw dew from roses, in shells of hazelnuts; and, this being the only drink used by their dainty mistress, and her thirst being excessive, the offices of these little water-carriers were far from relaxing.

Another year passed, and he was appointed to service within the house. It was now his duty to keep the floors unsoiled, and these being made of glass, which betrayed the faintest breath, his cares of office were extremely burdensome. He and his fellow laborers were compelled to brush them incessantly, and travel dexterously about the room with their feet wrapped in old rags.

After four years' service he was promoted to the kitchen; an honorable post, to be attained only after long preliminary training. There Jacob rose gradually from scullion to first pastry-maker, and acquired by degrees such extraordinary skill in everything appertaining to the art of cookery that he was often lost in wonder at his own accomplishments. The most difficult and delicate compounds,—pastry flavored with two hundred essences, herb-soups composed of all the vegetables of the earth,— all these he learned to prepare with the greatest skill and celerity.

Seven years[11] had thus passed in the service of the old woman, when one day, while she drew off her cocoa-nut shoes, and took her basket and cane to go out, she directed him to pluck a young chicken, stuff it with herbs, and roast it beautifully brown and crisp, for when she

---

[11] The Seven Years' War between Empress Theresa of Austria and Frederick the Great of Prussia lasted from 1756-1763

came back. He began according to all the rules of art. He twisted the chicken's neck, scalded it in hot water, skillfully drew out its feathers, and scraped its skin till it was smooth and soft. He then began to get together the herbs to make the stuffing.

While doing this, he discovered in the herb-room a cupboard, which he had never before noticed. Approaching it curiously to see what it contained, he saw, to his surprise, numerous little baskets standing inside, from which issued a strong and delightful odor. Opening one of them he found in it a plant of extraordinary shape and color. The stalks and leaves were of a bluish-green, and bore aloft a small flower of burning red, edged with yellow.[12]

While gazing thoughtfully at this flower, and smelling of it, the same strong odor streamed out which had ascended to his nostrils years ago from the broth which the old woman had cooked for him. The smell was so powerful that he began to sneeze, and the sneezing became more and more violent, till at last—he woke up.

He found himself lying on the old woman's sofa, and looked round him in bewilderment. "It is astonishing how vivid one's dreams are sometimes!" he said to himself. "I could have sworn just now that I was a filthy squirrel, a companion of guinea-pigs and other brutes, and that I had become a wonderful cook. How mother will laugh when I tell her the story! But I'm afraid she will scold me, too, for going to sleep in a strange house, instead of helping her in the market."

With these reflections he picked himself up to take his departure; but his limbs were still stiff from sleeping, and he found it impossible to turn his head, and he laughed heartily at his excessive sleepiness, too, for he was constantly thrusting his nose against a cupboard, or the wall, or striking it against the doorpost when he turned hastily round. The squirrels and guinea-pigs ran whining around him, as if they wanted to go away also, and he invited them to do so when he reached the threshold; but they ran swiftly back into the house on their nut-shell shoes, and he could hear them yelping in the far distance as he walked away.

---

[12] Reference to tiny Silesia, Poland with its core people favoring rule under the Prussians and extremities favoring that of Austria

It was a remote quarter of the city to which the old beldame had taken him and he could scarcely find his way out of the narrow lanes. There was a great throng of people in them besides, and the boy thought to himself that there must be a dwarf to be seen somewhere in the neighborhood, for he heard cries everywhere about him of, "Ho! See the ugly dwarf! Where does this dwarf come from? Ho, what a long nose he has! How his head sticks to his shoulders! See his hideous brown hands!"

At any other time he would have lingered to follow this creature, for he liked nothing so much in his life as to see giants and dwarfs, and similar monstrosities; but now he was in too great a hurry to get home to his mother.

He felt ready to cry when he came to the marketplace. His mother was still sitting where he had left her, with a good deal of fruit left in her baskets, so that he could not have slept a great while; and yet, it seemed to him, from the distance, as if she were looking very sad and unhappy, for she did not call to the passers-by to come and buy her wares, but was sitting silent, with her head supported in her hand; and, as he came nearer, the thought struck him that she seemed paler than usual.

He hesitated what to do, but he plucked up courage at last, and creeping behind her, laid his hand confidingly on her shoulder, and said, "Mother, what is the matter? Are you angry with me?"

The woman turned round to look at him, but started back with a cry of horror.

"What do you want with me, you frightful dwarf?" she shrieked. "Away with you! I will not bear such tom-foolery!"

"But, mother, what possesses you? Don't you know me?" asked little Jacob, terrified. "You are surely ill. Why do you drive your own son away from you?"

"I told you to be gone," answered Hannah, angrily. "You will get no money from me by such tricks, you frightful abortion!"

"Alas! God has taken away her understanding!" said Jacob, greatly alarmed. "What will I do to get her home? Dear mother, be reasonable a moment. Look at me. I am your son, your own Jacob."

"O, this is too shameless!" cried Hannah to her neighbors. "Look at this hideous dwarf. He stands here driving away all my customers, and dares to make a jest of my misfortunes. He calls himself my son, my own Jacob! The monster!"

At this her neighbors gathered round, and began to scold him with all their might,—and market-women, you know, understand that art perfectly,—and abused him for jesting at poor Hannah's unhappiness, who had had her pretty son stolen seven years before; and they threatened to fall upon him and tear him to pieces, unless he went away instantly.

Poor Jacob could not tell what to make of all this. He had come, as he believed, early this very morning, as usual, with his mother to the marketplace. He had helped to set out her fruit. Afterwards he had gone to the house of the old woman, and dropped asleep for a few hours; and now here he was back again, and yet his mother and the neighbors talked about seven years! and they called him a disgusting dwarf!

What, he thought, *can have happened to me?*

Seeing that his mother would have nothing to say to him, his eyes filled with tears, and he went sadly down the street to the shop where his father mended shoes during the day.

I will see, he thought to himself, *whether he refuses to know me too. I will stand at the door and speak to him.*

When he came to the shoemaker's shop, he stopped at the door and looked in. The shoemaker was so busy with his work that he did not see him at first; but casting accidentally a glance at the door, he dropped shoe, awl, and thread on the floor, and exclaimed in terror, "For God's sake, what is that! What is that!"

"Good evening, master," said the boy, coming into the shop. "How do you do?"

"Badly, badly, little gentleman," answered his father, to Jacob's great astonishment; for he too appeared not to recognize him. "Business comes in very slow. I am all alone, and growing old now, and yet I can't afford a salesman."

"But have you no son, who could be of assistance to you?" inquired the boy.

"I had a son once, named Jacob, who ought to be now a slim, strong lad of twenty, able to tuck me cleverly under his arm. Ah! What a clever fellow he would have been! When he was only twelve years old he was so intelligent, and skillful, and understood even then so many handy tricks, and was so pleasant and pretty! Ah! He would have drawn me customers, I'll be bound! I shouldn't have had to cobble much, I warrant. None but new shoes made here then! But so goes the world!"

"But where is your son?" Jacob asked, in a trembling voice.

"God only knows," he answered. "Seven years ago,—yes, full that,—he was stolen from the marketplace."

"Seven years ago!" cried Jacob, with horror.

"Yes, little gentleman, seven years ago. I can see my wife, as if it were today, come crying and shrieking home, saying that the child had been away the whole day, and that she had hunted for him everywhere and could not find him. I always expected it would be so. Jacob was a handsome boy, and my wife was very proud, and liked to hear people praise him, and often sent him with vegetables, and such like, to the great houses. That was all right. He was always handsomely tipped; but, I said, take care. The city is large. Many bad people live in it. Take care of little Jacob! And so it turned out. There comes, at last, an ugly old woman to the market, bargains for vegetables, and buys so much in the end that she can't carry it home. My wife, tender soul, sends the little boy with her, and—he has never been seen from that day to this."

"And that is now seven years, you say?"

"Seven years next spring. We sent the crier about. We went ourselves from house to house asking for him. Many persons knew the handsome boy, and liked him, and hunted with us. But all in vain; and nobody knew the woman who bought the fruit. But a decrepit old lady, ninety years old, said it might possibly have been the wicked fairy, Krauterweis, who comes out once every fifty years to make purchases."

While saying this, Jacob's father sat pounding his shoe bravely, and drawing out his threads with both fists. It was growing evident to the little lad that what he had gone through was no dream, and that he had actually served seven years as a squirrel with the wicked fairy. Anger and grief filled his heart almost to bursting. Seven years of his life the old hag had stolen from him, and what remuneration had he to show for it? He could polish slippers of cocoa-nut shell, and could clean chambers with floors of glass, and he had learned from the guinea-pigs the mysteries of cooking!

He stood thus a good while, thinking of his fate, and at last, his father asked him: "Would you like something of my manufacture, young gentleman? Perhaps a pair of slippers would suit you; or," he added, laughing, "perhaps a leather case for your nose?"

"Why do you refer to my nose?" inquired Jacob. "Why should I like a case for it?"

"Nay," answered the shoemaker, "every one to his taste; but I must say, if I had such a terrible nose I would have a case made for it at once of red shiny leather. Look, sir, I have a beautiful piece handy. You would require a yard of it at least. But, consider how well you would be protected. With a case, you might knock it against every doorpost. You might even let a cart run over it, and they would never hurt you."

The little fellow stood dumb with horror. He felt his nose, and found it thick, heavy, and two feet long! The old woman, then, had altered his shape! This was the reason why his mother did not know him, and why everybody called him a hideous dwarf!

"Master," he said, half crying, "have you a looking-glass at hand, in which I can look at myself?"

"Young gentleman," answered his father gravely, "you have no cause to be vain of the figure nature has given you, and no good reason to be looking all the time in the glass. Give up the habit, I advise you. In your case nothing can be more ridiculous."

"Alas! Please let me look in your looking-glass," cried the little fellow. "Believe me, it is not from vanity."

"Don't bother me, young gentleman. I have no such thing in the shop," replied the cobbler. "My wife has a little one, I believe, but I don't know where she hides it. If you must have a looking-glass, Urban, the barber, lives across the street, and he has one twice as big as your head. Go look into his shop; and now, good-morning."

With these words, his father pushed him gently out of the shop, and, shutting the door behind him, went back to his work. The boy went across the street, in a very miserable state of mind, to Urban, the barber's, whom he had known very well in former times.

"Good morning, Urban," he said to him. "I've come to beg as a favor that you will let me look a moment in your looking-glass."

"With all the pleasure in the world. There it is," cried the barber, laughing, and the customers waiting to be shaved laughed uproariously with him. "You are a pretty lad, I must confess; so slender and graceful, with a neck like a swan, hands like a queen, and a nose which I never saw equaled! You have some reason to be vain, to be sure. Take a good look, sir. Take a good look. Nobody will say I refused you permission out of envy of your beauty."

A rude horse-laugh filled the barber's shop, while the boy walked to the mirror and looked at his reflection. Tears streamed from his eyes as he gazed. "No wonder you did not recognize your little son Jacob, dear mother," he said to himself.

His eyes had grown small like a pig's. His nose was huge and hung down over his chin. His neck seemed to have disappeared, and his head was joined to his shoulders. It was with the greatest difficulty he could turn it from one side to the other. His body was of the same size as it had been seven years previously, when he was twelve years of age; but, while others grew in height from twelve to twenty, he had only increased in breadth, and his back and breast were curved like a bow, and looked like a little, well-filled sack. This extraordinary trunk was supported on a pair of small, weak legs, very ill-adapted to sustain the burthen, while the arms, which hung down at his sides, were as large as those of a well-grown man. His hands were yellow, and his fingers long and spidery, and, when he extended them to their full length, he could touch the ground without stopping. Such was little Jacob's appearance as he looked in the glass. He had been changed into a small, misshapen dwarf.

His thoughts went back to that morning when the old witch had examined his mother's baskets. Everything which he had then ridiculed,—the long nose, the hideous fingers,—she had now given to him. The long, trembling neck was the only thing she had omitted.

"Well, have you inspected yourself long enough, my prince?" said the barber, stepping up and looking him over with a laugh.[13] "Upon my word, if a man should attempt to

---

[13] Frederick the Great was still a prince while his father was alive.

dream such a figure, he could never imagine one so comical. Come, I will make you an offer, my little man. My barber's shop has a great deal of customers, of course, but, still, not so much as I should like. The reason is, my neighbor Lather, the barber, has picked up a giant somewhere, who draws customers.[14] Now, a giant is one thing, but a manikin like you is another. Come into my service, little chap. You will be given everything, lodging, eating, drinking, clothes, pocket-money. Your duty will be to stand at the door every morning and invite the people in, or make the lather, and hand napkins to the customers. Feel sure that both of us will make money by it,—I will get more customers than that fellow with the giant, and you will get pocket-money tips from everybody."

The boy felt, inwardly, outraged at the proposal that he should act as the barber's decoy-bird. But he was in no condition to resent the insult. So he quietly told the barber that he had no time to spend in such occupations, and left the shop.

Although the old harridan had changed his body, he felt a consciousness that she had failed to affect his mind, for he saw that his thoughts and feelings were no longer juvenile, as they had been seven years previously. He believed he had become much wiser and more intelligent. He did not mourn the loss of his departed beauty, nor sigh at the ugliness of his present figure.[15] His sole cause of unhappiness was that he had been hunted like a dog from his father's door.[16] He resolved to make another and final effort to convince his mother of his identity.

He went up to her, as she sat in the marketplace, and entreated her to listen patiently to his story. He reminded her of the day on which he had gone away with the old woman. He reminded her of all the little events of his childhood. He then told her that he had served seven

---

[14] After the Seven Years' War Britain aligned itself with the much smaller Prussia and Austria aligned itself with the much larger France.

[15] At the end of the Seven Years' War, Catherine the Great (1729-1796) of Russia, broke off her alliance with Prussia.

[16] Frederick the Great was hunted down by his father when he tried to escape Prussia with his friend Hans Hermann von Katte.

years with the fairy, as a squirrel, and that she had transformed him because he had once insulted her.[17]

The shoemaker's wife knew not what to think. Everything was true that he had told concerning his childhood, but when he added that he had been a squirrel for seven years, she said, "It is impossible, and there are no such things as fairies."

And when she looked at him she shuddered with disgust, and would not believe him to be her son. She decided, at last, that she had better consult with her husband. So she collected her baskets together and directed him to follow. They went to the shoemaker's shop together.

"Husband," she said, "see here. This man insists that he is our son Jacob. He has told me everything, how he was stolen seven years ago, and how he has been bewitched by a fairy."

"Indeed!" interrupted the cobbler, in a contemptuous tone. "Has he been telling you all this? The scoundrel! Why, I told him the whole story not an hour ago, and now he goes and makes a fool of you. So you have been bewitched, my man? Wait a minute, and I will exorcise you." Saying this, he took down a bundle of straps, which he had just cut, and, springing on the little pigmy, beat him over his crooked back and long arms, till the dwarf shrieked with pain and ran away crying.[18]

In that city, as everywhere else, there were very few compassionate souls, ready to assist an unfortunate person, whose misery rendered him also ridiculous. Hence it was, that our unhappy dwarf went the whole day without food or drink, and at night was forced to make his bed as best he might on the cold, hard steps of a church.

When the early beams of the rising sun awoke him the next morning from his slumbers, he considered seriously how he should earn his daily bread, since his father and mother had repudiated him. He had too much pride to act

---

[17] Seeking to own the mineral-rich Silesia, Frederick the Great threatened Empress Maria Theresa with war if she did not release it to him, and when she refused the Seven Years' War was started by Frederick the Great.

[18] Frederick William I (1688-1740), the father of Frederick the Great, was known to frequently measure out corporeal punishment on Frederick the Great.

as a barber's decoy-duck, and he was unwilling to work for a circus showman, and be exhibited for money. What was he to do? It occurred to his recollection, that, during his squirrel existence, he had made much progress in the science of cooking; and he believed, with good reason, that he might venture to back his skill against many a cook of high reputation. He resolved to avail himself of his accomplishments.

As soon as the streets grew busy, and the day had really begun, he entered the church and performed his devotions. He then set about the accomplishment of his plans. The duke of the county was a notorious glutton and gormandizer, fond of a good table, and hunting for skillful cooks in every quarter of the globe.[19] Our dwarf went to his palace.[20]

Coming to the outer gate, the sentries at the door demanded his business, and made him the butt of their brutal ridicule; but, undisturbed by their laughter, he inquired for the director of the kitchen. They conducted him through the courtyard into the palace, and, wherever he appeared, all the servants stopped in what they were about, stared after him, and, laughing uproariously, joined the procession, so that by degrees a large train of servants of every degree approached the palace stairs. The hostlers[21] threw down their currycombs, the runners ran, the carpet-cleaners forgot to beat their carpets. All crowded after the misshapen pigmy. There was an uproar as if an enemy were at the gates, and the air was filled with a universal cry of: "A dwarf! A dwarf! Have you seen the dwarf?"

At this moment the superintendent of the palace appeared at the door, with an angry look on his face, and a huge whip in his hand. "For heaven's sake, you hounds, why this noise? Do you forget that the duke is asleep?" And, swinging his whip round his head, he brought it down heavily on the backs of the hostlers and sentries.

"Sir! Sir!" they cried. "Don't you see? We are bringing a dwarf,—a dwarf, such as you never saw in your life."

---

[19] Duke Louis Philippe I, Duke of d'Orléans (1725-1785), known as "the fat," was a recognized "gourmand."

[20] Duke Louis Philippe I, Duke of d'Orléans was raised in the French Palace of Versailles.

[21] Stableman

The superintendent, with difficulty, suppressed a stentorian laugh when he caught sight of the diminutive lad; for he feared, by laughing, to injure his dignity. So, driving the rabble away with his whip, he led the boy into the palace and inquired of his business. When he heard that the latter desired to see the head cook, he replied: "You have made a mistake, my little fellow. You want to see me, the superintendent of the palace, I am sure. You want to be the duke's dwarf, do you not?"

"No, your honor," answered the dwarf. "I am a skillful cook, and learned in the composition of all rare delicacies for the table. Would you be so good as to take me to the chief cook? Perhaps he may find my services useful."

"Everyone to his taste, little man, but you are a foolish chap, and don't know your own good. The kitchen you want, is it? As the duke's dwarf you would have had no work to do, beautiful clothes to wear, and as much to eat and drink as your heart could wish. Your skill in cooking will hardly amount to what is needed for the duke's cook, and you are too good for a scullion in his kitchen. However, we shall see."

With these words, the superintendent took him by the hand, and led him into the pantry of the overseer of the kitchen.

"Excellent sir," said the dwarf to the overseer, bowing so low that he rubbed his long nose against the carpet, "Are you in want of a skillful cook?"

The director of the kitchen looked him all over from head to foot, and burst into a loud laugh. "You a cook! Do you think our ovens are low enough for a little fellow like you to look into without standing on tiptoe and stretching your head clean off your shoulders? You little jewel, whoever sent you to me for a cook has sent you on a fool's errand." Saying this, the director laughed heartily in chorus with the superintendent and all the servants who were in the room.

The dwarf, however, was not to be diverted from his purpose. "What matters an egg or two," he said, "and a little syrup and wine, with a little meal and spice in a house like this? Only give me some dainty trifle to prepare and find me the ingredients I need for it, and I will get it ready before your eyes, so that you will be compelled to say, 'He is a cook of science and genius.'" The dwarf continued to urge these and similar arguments, his eyes gleaming, his long nose twisting, and his spidery fingers working, as if emphasizing his words.

"Very well!" said the director, at length, taking the superintendent by the arm. "Very well, for the joke's sake, so be it. Come."

They passed through several halls and corridors, and came at last to the kitchen. This was a lofty, spacious apartment, nobly arranged and fitted. Huge fires burned on twenty hearths. A stream of clear water flowed down the middle of it with fresh fish. The provisions were stored in compartments of marble and costly woods, ever ready to the hand. On either side were ten store-rooms in which were gathered large quantities of whatever rare and choice delicacies can be found for man's palette in all Europe and the East. Servants of every grade were running to and fro, rattling and clattering among pots and pans; but the instant the director entered the kitchen everyone stood motionless, in whatever part of the room he chanced to be, and the only sounds to be heard in the apartment were the crackling of the fire and the rippling of the stream.

"What has the duke ordered for breakfast, this morning?" the director inquired of the chief breakfast-cook, an old and venerable man.

"My lord, he has ordered the Danish soup, and red Hamburg dumplings."[22]

"Good," said the director. "You heard the duke's orders, my little man? Do you think you can cook these difficult articles? You will certainly fail in the dumplings, because how they are made is a secret."

"Nothing easier," said the dwarf, to the general surprise of those present. He had often prepared these delicacies while a squirrel. "Nothing easier. Let me have, for the soup, such and such herbs, such and such spices, the feet of a wild pig, and greens and eggs. But for the dumplings," he said, in a lower tone, so that only the director and the breakfast cook might hear, "for the dumplings I need meat of four sorts, some duck's fat, a little ginger, and a certain herb called *Magentrost* (stomach-warmer)."

---

[22] Thick dumplings with a filling of meat, rice, minced onions and herbs. Hamburg, Germany and Denmark were both part of Prussia during the reign of Frederick the Great.

"Ho! by Saint Benedict![23] Of what magician have you learned your art?" cried the cook, in astonishment. "He has described the recipe to a hair; and the herb *Magentrost* we knew nothing about. Ay, that must be a vast improvement. O, you miracle among cooks!"

"I should never have thought it," said the superintendent. "However, let him give us proof of his skill. Give him the things he wants, utensils and all, and let him get together the breakfast."

The servants were told to obey his orders, and everything was placed in readiness on the hearth. But it was found that his nose scarcely reached the level of the fireplace. Two chairs were therefore set together, a block of marble placed on them, and the little prodigy invited to commence his demonstration. The cooks, scullions, and servants, stood round in a wide circle, and witnessed with astonishment the dexterity and nimbleness of his hands, and the delicacy and elegance of the results of his labors.

When he had completed all his preliminary arrangements, he directed that both the pots should be set on the fire and permitted to simmer till he should give the word. Then he began to count, one, two, three, and so on, till, exactly at five hundred, he cried out, "Halt!" The pots were taken off the fire, and the dwarf invited the director to taste.

The master-cook caused one of the scullions to bring him a golden spoon, and, washing it in the brook, handed it to the director. The latter stepped to the hearth with a solemn air, took up a little of the food in the spoon, and, tasting it, shut his eyes and smacked his lips with delight, exclaiming:

"Delicious! by the life of the duke, delicious! Would you like a spoon, superintendent?"

The latter bowed, took the spoon, and tasted. He was beside himself with delight. "With all respect for your great skill, breakfast-maker, I know you to be a very accomplished man. You have never made in all your life such admirable soup, and such delicious Hamburg dumplings as these."

The cook now tasted in his turn, and, shaking the dwarf with reverence by the hand, said to him, "Pigmy,

---

[23] Also, Benedict of Nursia (480-547), was the patron Saint of Europe under Catholicism

you are a master of your profession! That *Magentrost* does indeed impart a unique and miraculous flavor to the entire compound."

At this moment the duke's groom of the chambers entered the kitchen, and said that his grace was inquiring for his breakfast. The soup and dumplings were straightway served on silver dishes and sent to the duke. The director of the kitchen meanwhile took the little wonder into his private room to converse with him. They had been there hardly as long as it takes to recite a paternoster (which is a sort of prayer of the Franks, my lord, not half as long as the prayers of true believers), when a message came, summoning the director into the duke's presence.[24] He put on a dress-suit as rapidly as he could, and followed the messenger.

The duke's countenance wore an expression of extreme satisfaction. He had swallowed the whole contents of the silver dishes, and was wiping his beard as the director entered.

"Look, director," said the duke, "I have been invariably delighted with your cooks. Tell me who it was that cooked my breakfast this morning. It was never so delicious since I mounted the throne of my ancestors. Tell me the name of the cook, that I may send him a token of my gratitude."

"Please your highness, it's a wonderful story," answered the director of the kitchen, and told him how, early that morning, a dwarf had been brought to him who insisted on being a cook, and how everything had turned out. The duke, greatly surprised, called the dwarf into his presence and asked him who he was and from where he came. Of course little Jacob could not tell the duke that he had been bewitched and had been serving hitherto in the capacity of a squirrel. Still, he adhered to the truth when he stated that he was without father or mother, and had studied his art with an old woman.[25] The duke inquired no further, but made merry over the extraordinary figure of his new cook.

---

[24] The Franks were an early set of Germanic tribes that practiced paganism. The Franks occupied parts of Rhineland were organized under Prussia in 1822.

[25] Frederick William I, father of Frederick the Great, died in 1740 and his mother, Sophia Dorothea of Hanover, died seventeen years later in 1757.

"If you will stay in my service," he said, "your wages will be fifty ducats a year, besides a suit of clothes and two extra pairs of trousers. In return, you must cook my breakfast every day with your own hands, look after the preparation of my dinner, and take general charge of my kitchen. As everyone in my palace receives his name from me, your name will be Nosey, and you will hold the rank of sub-kitchen-inspector."

Nosey fell at the feet of the mighty duke, and, kissing his shoes, swore to serve him faithfully.

Thus, at length, was the little fellow well provided for; and his subsequent efforts covered his office with glory. It can be safely asserted that the duke was a different man during Nosey's administration. Hitherto he had often been pleased to throw the dishes and plates at his cook's head; nay, he once struck the director himself so violently on the head with a baked calf's foot, which he declared was too tough, that he fell senseless to the ground and was obliged to lie in bed three days.

To be sure, the duke repaired whatever damages his anger inflicted, by the gift of handfuls of ducats; but, notwithstanding, his cooks never entered his highness' presence without fear and trembling. Since the arrival of the dwarf, however, everything seemed magically changed. The duke now took five instead of three meals every day, so as to get the full benefit of his diminutive servant's skill, and never showed the faintest indication of discontent. On the contrary, everything the dwarf prepared he declared to be original and excellent. He became amiable and condescending, and grew fatter every day.

He frequently summoned the kitchen-director and Nosey into his presence while dining, and, seating one on his right hand and the other on his left, would shove bits of the choicest delicacies into their mouths with his own fingers, an honor which both well knew how to appreciate.

The dwarf was the wonder of the city. People raved of the kitchen-director, with tears in their eyes, to be permitted to see the sub-inspector cook, and some of the most distinguished men of the dukedom obtained permission to send their servants to the royal kitchen to take lessons from Nosey by the hour. The lessons brought him in no little money, for each paid a half ducat daily. To keep the other cooks in goodhumor and prevent any feeling of jealousy, Nosey resigned to them all the money which the gentlemen paid for the instruction of their servants.

In this way Nosey passed two years in extreme comfort and honor; and the only reflection causing him a pang was the memory of his parents. Thus he lived, with nothing remarkable to disturb the even tenor of his way, till the following event occurred. Being exceedingly skillful and fortunate in his purchases, he went in person, as often as time permitted him, to the market, to procure poultry and fruit for the duke's table. He went one morning to the goose-market and made inquiries for fat geese, of which his highness was extremely fond. His appearance, so far from exciting laughter and ridicule, inspired the greatest respect and veneration, for he was well known as the duke's famous master-cook, and every market woman felt herself fortunate if he so much as turned his nose in her direction.

He saw at length a woman sitting in a corner, at the extreme end of the row, who had geese for sale like the rest, but who did not, like them, commend her wares or shout to buyers to come and purchase. He went up to her and examined and weighed her geese. They proved to be such as he wanted, and, buying three, with the cage containing them, hoisted them on his broad shoulders and trudged back to the palace. It struck him as singular that only two of the geese gamboled and screamed like common birds, while the third sat perfectly silent and absorbed, heaving deep sighs, and groaning like a human being.

"This one is sick," he said to himself. "I must make haste to kill and dress her."

The goose answered, in a perfectly distinct and audible voice:

> "One movement of thy murd'rous knife,
>   And instant snaps thy thread of life!
> By fear, if not by love, be stayed;
>   Then, stranger, spare, O, spare thy blade!"

Nosey the dwarf, much terrified, set down his cage on the ground and the goose, sighing profoundly, gazed at him with her beautiful, intelligent eyes. "The deuce!" cried Nosey. "So you can talk, Miss Goose? I should never have thought it. Nay, never be so down-hearted. Men are no fools and no one would put an end to so rare a bird. But I lay a wager, you have not always worn feathers. I myself was once a filthy squirrel."

"You are right," answered the goose. "I was not born to this ignominious body.[26] Alas! It was not sung to me in my cradle, that Mimi, the daughter of the great Wetterbock, was to be slain in the kitchen of a duke."[27]

"Make your mind easy, my dear Miss Mimi," said the dwarf, consolingly. "As surely as I am an honest fellow, and sub-kitchen-inspector to his highness the duke, no one will touch a hair of your head. I will give you a coop in my private room. You will have food in abundance and I will devote all my leisure time to your entertainment. I will tell the rest of the kitchen gentlemen that I am fattening a goose for the duke with a variety of choice herbs; and, as soon as I find a good opportunity, I will set you at liberty."

The goose thanked him with tears in her eyes, and the dwarf fulfilled his promise to the letter. He slaughtered the two other geese, but built for Mimi a private coop in his own chamber, and gave out that he was fattening her for the duke's especial eating. He did not furnish her the food usually given to geese, but supplied her with pastry and sweetmeats.

All his spare time he spent in conversing with and consoling her. In return she told him her story. Nosey learned in this way that the goose was the daughter of the wizard Wetterbock, who lived on the island of Gothland;[28] that he had a quarrel with an old fairy, who had vanquished him by fraud and artifice, and changed her into a goose by way of revenge. The old fairy had taken her a great distance from her native country.

When Nosey had told her his story, also, she said: "I have some experience in such matters. My father has

---

[26] Empress Elizabeth Petrovna (1709-1762) of Russia grew rotund later in life.

[27] Peter the Great (1672-1725) was the father of Empress Elizabeth of Russia.

[28] Modern day St. Petersburg, the capitol of Russia, was an island founded by Peter the Great in 1703, on which he built a palace in 1725 called Perterhof.

given me and my sisters[29] as much insight into them as he dared to communicate. Your account of the dispute over the vegetable baskets, your sudden transformation on smelling of that herb, and those words by the old woman, which you repeated, all convince me that you are under the magical influence of some plant; and, if you can find the herb which the old fairy used for your enchantment, you can be released."

Little consolation was all this for our diminutive hero, for where was he to find the required herb? But he expressed his thanks for the information, and began to cherish some little hope.

About this time the duke received a visit from a neighboring prince, his friend. He summoned Nosey the dwarf, before him, and said, "The time has now arrived when you must show yourself a faithful servant, as well as a master of your profession. This prince, who is now making us a visit, is, next to me, the most distinguished gourmand living. Be careful, therefore, that my table is so attended to that he will be thrown into profounder admiration every day. With this view, you must never, under fear of my displeasure, produce the same dish twice. You can obtain from my treasurer whatever sums you need. And, if you find yourself obliged to cook diamonds and gold, do so without hesitation. I prefer being impoverished to blushing before my guest."

So spake the duke, and the dwarf answered with a respectful bow: "It will be as you say, your highness. God willing, everything I make will be suited precisely to the taste of this prince of good-livers."

The little cook now summoned to his aid all the resources of his art. He had no mercy on the duke's treasury, and was still less lenient on himself. He was seen the whole day long enveloped in a cloud of fire and smoke, and his voice sounded incessantly through the arches of the kitchen. He ruled the under-cooks and scullions like a sovereign.

The foreign prince had already stayed a fortnight with the duke, and feasted royally. They devoured not less than five meals a day, and the duke was well satisfied with his

---

[29] Although Peter the Great and his wife, Catherine I, had seven daughters, only two survived: Elizabeth and Anna; so the reference to a plurality of sisters by Wilhelm Hauff may have been a mistake.

cook's efforts, for he saw contentment in the features of his guest. On the fifteenth day, however, it happened that his highness called the dwarf into his presence, and, presenting him to the prince, asked him if his dwarf had pleased him.

"You are a wonderful cook," answered the foreign prince. "During the whole time I have been here, you have not repeated a single dish and everything has been cooked sublimely. But, pray explain why you have delayed so long in producing that queen of delicacies, the pie Souzeraine?"[30]

The dwarf was much startled, for he had never heard of this queen of pastries; but, summoning his presence of mind, he answered: "May it please your highness, I was in hopes that your presence might still long illuminate this court, and for this reason I delayed this sovereign dish. For with what should your slave testify his veneration at your departure, if not with the pie Souzeraine?"

"So," answered the duke, laughing, "in my case you intended to wait till the day of my death before testifying your veneration. For, I remember, you have never sent up to me this wonderful pastry. But you must devise some other testimonial, for tomorrow you must furnish us with the pie Souzeraine."

"Your will is law, your highness," answered the dwarf, and withdrew. His mind was much agitated, for the day of his disgrace was at hand. He could not imagine the composition of this pie, and retired to his private room, weeping over his unhappy fate. While thus engaged, Mimi the goose, who had the run of his chamber, inquired the cause of his lamentations.

"Dry your tears," she said when she had heard of the pie Souzeraine. "This dish came often to my father's table, and I know nearly all its ingredients. You take this and that, so much and so much; and, even supposing these are not all that are necessary, the tastes of your master and his friend are not delicate enough to discover the deficiencies."[31]

---

[30] Reference to the politics of suzerainty where one political area or state is subservient to another, a function of the many political states of Prussia

[31] Reference to suzerainty under Peter the Great of Russia

At these words of Mimi, the dwarf sprang up delighted, and, blessing the day on which he had bought the goose, set at once about preparing the queen of pies. He made a little at first by way of experiment, and its flavor was so delicious that the director of the kitchen department, to whom he gave a little to taste, again glorified his inimitable genius.

Next day he prepared a similar pie, of larger size, and sent it to the royal table, warm from the oven, and decorated with wreaths of flowers. He himself slipped on his best court-suit, and took his post in the dining hall. At the moment he entered, the head carver was cutting up the pie and handing it to the duke and his guest on silver plates. The duke swallowed a huge mouthful, and, casting his eyes up to the ceiling, said, after gulping it down: "Ah! ah! ah! This pie is justly called the queen of pastries; and my cook is no less the pastry-king. Is he not, my friend?"

His guest took a small piece on his plate, and, having tasted it with great attention, burst into a scornful laugh. "This thing is well made," he answered, pushing away his plate, "but it is not quite up to the Souzeraine I expected."

The duke wrinkled his forehead with rage, and blushed with mortification. "Hound of a dwarf!" he cried, "How dare you play this trick on your master? Must I have your big head chopped off as a punishment for your infamous cookery?"[32]

"Alas! my lord, I swear to heaven I cooked the dish by all the rules of art. Failure is impossible," replied the dwarf, in an agony of terror.

"It is a lie, you knave!" shouted the duke, kicking him from one end of the room to the other. "Do you think the prince would say so, if it were not? I will have you chopped to pieces and baked in a pie yourself!"

"Have mercy!" cried the pigmy, falling on his knees, and embracing the prince's feet. "Say, sire, what is wanting in this pastry to render it acceptable to your palate? Suffer me not to die for a handful of meat and flour!"

"It will be useless to tell you, my dear Nosey," answered the stranger with a laugh. "I was thinking all

---

[32] Another reference to the friend of Frederick the Great and lieutenant of the Prussian Army, Hans Hermann von Katte who was beheaded by Frederick the Great's father for treason

yesterday that you could not make this pie like my cook. But, if you must know, it needs an herb, unknown to anyone in this country, called Sneeze-with-pleasure. Without this the pie is without flavor, and your master will never eat it as I do."

The duke was boiling with rage. "But I will eat it," he cried, his eyes sparkling with fury. "For I swear by my princely honor, either I will show it to you tomorrow as you want it, or the head of this scoundrel here will disfigure the gate of my palace. Go, dog! I give you four-and-twenty hours' time to reprieve yourself."

The dwarf repaired to his chamber and told the goose with many tears that his death was near, for he had never heard of the herb Sneeze-with-pleasure.

"Is that all?" she said. "Then I can soon help you, for my father taught me every herb that grows. At any other time your death would be certain, but fortunately tonight is the new moon, and at this time the plant is flowering. Tell me, are there any old chestnut trees near the palace?"

"Yes, indeed," answered the dwarf with reviving courage. "A large group of them stands on the lakeshore, not two hundred paces from the house. But why do you ask?"

"This herb grows only at the foot of old chestnut trees," said Mimi. "Let us lose no time, but seek for it at once. Take me under your arm and set me down when you get into the open air. I will help you hunt for it."

He did as she directed, and went with her to the palace gate. But the sentinel there held out his musket, saying, "My dear Nosey, you are in trouble. I have specific orders not to let you leave the palace."

"But surely I can go into the garden?" answered the dwarf. "Be obliging now. Send one of your comrades to the superintendent and ask him whether I may not go into the garden and hunt for herbs."

The sentinel assented, and permission was given; for the garden had high walls, and escape from it was inconceivable. As soon as the dwarf reached the open air, he set Mimi carefully down, and she went before him rapidly to the lakeshore, where stood the chestnut trees. He followed her with a beating heart, for it was his last and only hope. Should she fail to find the herb, his resolve was taken unalterably to throw himself into the water, rather than submit to be beheaded. The goose sought everywhere in vain, wandering about under the chestnut trees, and turning over every tuft of grass with her bill. The herb was nowhere to be found and she began to cry with compassion and anguish; for the evening was growing darker, and the plants were becoming more and more difficult to recognize.

The dwarf's eyes were turned to the opposite shore of the lake, and he suddenly cried: "See, see, there is a large, old tree on the other side! Let's go there and search. Perhaps the herb is growing there."

The goose hopped and flew to the spot, and he ran after, as fast as his little legs would let him. The chestnut tree cast a vast shadow, and it was so dark in its vicinity that scarcely anything could be discerned. But the goose suddenly came to a halt, and, clapping her wings with joy, thrust her head into the tall grass and plucked out something that she gave in her bill to the astonished dwarf with great caution, saying: "This is your herb, and a great abundance of it is growing here; so it will never fail you in the future."

The dwarf gazed at the plant in deep thought. A sweet odor was streaming from it, which reminded him involuntarily of the scene of his transformation. The stalk and leaves were a bluish-green, and supported a crimson flower with a yellow edge.

"God be praised!" he cried, after a pause. "A miracle! Do you know, Mimi, I think this is the same plant that changed me from a squirrel into this hideous shape? Will I make the trial?"[33]

"Not yet," entreated the goose. "Take a handful of this herb with you, go with me to your room, collect your money and the rest of your property, and then we will try the power of this plant."

Obedient to her directions, the dwarf carried her back to his chamber, his heart beating audibly from excessive anxiety. After tying about fifty ducats, the amount of his savings, with some clothes and shoes into a bundle, he said: "Please God, I will now get rid of my burden." And, thrusting his nose deep into the flower, he took a long, strong sniff of the fragrance.

---

[33] Again, a reference to Silesia, Poland that Frederick the Great started the Seven Years' War over

He instantly felt a snapping in all his limbs, and was conscious that his head was rising from his shoulders. He took a look at his nose, and saw that it was growing smaller and smaller. His back and chest began to straighten, and his legs grew longer and bigger.

The goose gazed in astonishment at all these changes. "Ha! How large, how handsome you are!" she exclaimed. "God be praised! There is not a particle left of what you were a moment ago."

Jacob was rejoiced beyond measure, and in the abundance of his gratitude folded his hands and prayed. But his joy did not cause him to forget the extent of his obligations to Mimi. His heart impelled him to fly at once to his parents, but he repressed the impulse, and said to his invaluable ally: "Whom have I to thank but you that I am restored again to myself? Without you I should never have found this herb. Without you I should have retained forever this frightful figure, or perhaps have died under the headsman's axe. Come! I will requite you. I will take you to your father. He, who is so skillful in all the arts of magic, will be able to disenchant you without difficulty."

The goose shed tears of pleasure and accepted his proposal. Jacob passed unrecognized out of the palace, and set forth on the road to the sea-coast to find Mimi's home.

What more can I say, except that they accomplished their journey successfully; that the wizard Wetterbock disenchanted his daughter, and dismissed Jacob, laden with splendid presents; that he returned to his native land and his parents recognized with delight their long-lost son; that he purchased a shop with the gifts which he had received from Wetterbock, and that he became a rich, happy and successful man?

I will only add that a tremendous excitement took place at the palace after the dwarf's flight; for when, on the following day, the duke made ready to perform his oath, and gave orders to strike off the dwarf's head if he had not procured the required herb, he was, of course, nowhere to be found; and the foreign prince, suspecting that the duke had secretly removed the culprit, in order to avoid depriving himself of his best cook, accused him of being faithless to his pledge.

As a necessary result, a great war arose between the two princes, well known in history by the name of "The

Vegetable War." Many battles were fought, and much injury inflicted on either side; but, in the end, a peace was made, which Europeans call "The Pastry Peace,"[34] because, at the feast given in honor of the reconciliation of the two nations, the prince's cook was sent for, for the express purpose of providing the Souzeraine, the queen of pies, for the royal table, where the duke devoured it with intense satisfaction.

Thus, as you see, the greatest results often flow from the smallest causes; and this is the history of Nosey, the dwarf.

------

[34] Reference to the Treaty of Hubertusburg, also called The Hubertusburg Peace, signed February 15, 1763, among Saxony, Austria and Prussia; which in combination with the Treaty of Paris marked the end of the Seven Years' War

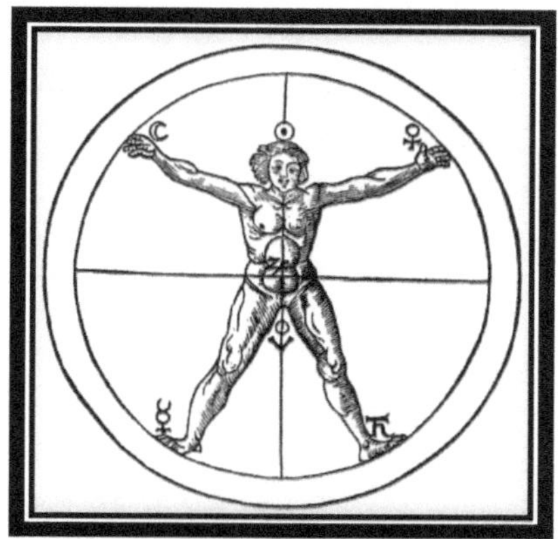

"Seddik Ben Saad, the Magician" is one of the best wizard stories to come out of the first half of the nineteenth century; yet it was only published once and then disappeared. *Poof!* As if by the wave of a wizard's wand, the story vanished and does not appear to have been republished in nearly 175 years.

The first publication was 1832 in *The Imperial Magazine; and, Monthly Record of Religious, Philosophical, Historical, Biographical, Topographical, and General Knowledge; Embracing Literature, Science and Art* of London. The full title was the rather cumbersome "Seddik Ben Saad, the Magician, and the Earl of Essex." The fantasy short story was nestle among the usual political diatribes, tales of wonders found by brave adventurers exploring South America, and random poetry.

The author was identified only by the initials D.C. and the date of the fantasy story was given as February 1829.

Long before there was a boy named Harry Potter training to be a wizard at Hogwarts School of Witchcraft and Wizardry, Seddik Ben Saad was conjured by an excellent writer who sadly chose to remain anonymous. Just like the spirit in the story, "Seddik Ben Saad, the Magician" made an unexpected entrance and then vanished from our literature just as quickly.

Poof!

It is time to resurrect him and it comes at the hands of a wizard named *Seddick ben Saad.*

SEDDIK BEN SAAD, THE MAGICIAN
1829

"But 'tis strange;
And oftentimes, to win us to our harm,
The instruments of darkness tell us truly."
Macbeth.[1]

THE ZEALOUS ANTIQUARY, or the observant citizen of London, whose memory carried him back for a period of fifty years, may remember an old low-browed house, which formerly stood on the north side of Towerhill, on the site of the gardens, which once belonged to the ancient monastery of the Crutched-friars; though its name was successively changed, as the royal grant allotted it in the first instance to Sir Thomas Wyat, and at a later period to Sir Thomas Savage:—the last designation it still retains, though modem alterations and improvements have at length done away with this long-surviving relic of old days, and the spot where it stood is now undistinguished from the surrounding neighborhood.[2]

The peculiar style of gothic architecture which characterized this building, had, even so far back as the reign of queen Elizabeth,[3] rendered it remarkable for its

---

[1] *The Tragedy of Macbeth*, William Shakespeare, 1611

[2] "Adjoining is Savage Gardens, at part of the possessions of the dissolved Monastery of the Brothers of the Holy Cross, or Crutched Friars. Henry VIII giving this ground to Thomas Wyatt the elder, he erected a mansion on the spot, afterwards possessed by John Lord Lumley, who distinguished himself in the battle of Flodden Field. Its next inhabitant was Sir Thomas Savage, afterwards Lord Savage, and Earl Rivers in the reigns of James and Charles I; from the latter nobleman the estate took its name of Savage Gardens." *London: Being a Complete Guide to the British Capital*, Third Edition, 1810, p. 587

[3] Queen Elizabeth I of England (1533-1603) reigned from November 1558 to March 1603.

antiquity, and sufficiently attested the early period of its construction. The front of the house was low, and consisted of only one story, which, projecting far into the street, completely cast the lower part into shade. The roof rose high and conical, and terminated at the top in a grotesque device of carved oak, representing what might pass for an angel in the eyes of the pious, or a fiend in those of the less scrupulous.

Many subordinate deities were freely sculptured at the extremities of the beams which formed the framework of the large lattice, and supported the cross timber of the upper story;—the doorposts also were enriched with the same minute and labored ornaments. The portal itself was low and wide, and the thick oaken planks of the door were profusely and irregularly studded with small iron knobs, bearing no very remote resemblance to those ancient inscriptions which Orientalists have termed the Babylonian characters.[4]

The window above, though large, and extending along the whole front of the house, was yet so obscured by the garniture of woodwork which surrounded it, as to make it difficult for the light of day to penetrate far into the gloomy recesses of the chamber. In addition to this, the house stood not alone, but situated in a narrow street, with loftier buildings in front and around, which seemed inclined to topple upon their lowly neighbor, and effectually precluded the sun's rays, even on the brightest days, from enlightening the dusky mansion. Such was the appearance of this edifice in the year 1584, when it became the residence of a being as singularly distinguished from the rest of the human race, as the tenement he occupied would now appear beside the palaces of our modern Vitruvii.[5]

Of his birth, and even of his country, nothing was precisely known,—but from the observations, which the inquisitiveness of his neighbors prompted them to make, it was conjectured that he was of Arabian origin. His appearance in this quarter of the world was sudden; but it

---

[4] Cuneiform characters used by ancient Babylonian scholars, many of which excelled in astronomy

[5] Reference to Marcus Vitruvius Pollio (80 B.C. – 15 A.D.), was a Roman engineer and architect who wrote "The Ten Books on Architecture" that defined classical Roman architecture for this period.

was rumored that he had found his way to England in the suite of a foreign ambassador, as the previous occurrences of his life rendered such a mode of travelling necessary to his safety.

Though he never mixed voluntarily with his neighbors, his doors were always open to such as crossed his threshold; but the number of his visitors was few. He neither invited nor repelled observation; but there was that about him, which was far from stimulating the superstitious and unenlightened people, in the midst of whom he dwelt, to a renewal of their visit. Such as had once entered within the precincts of his dwelling, returned impressed with a degree of awe, which gradually communicated itself to all in the vicinity; so that, in a short time, without any real cause for dislike, be was marked, feared, and generally avoided.

The report went abroad that his knowledge in the occult sciences was unbounded, and those who had seen the interior of his abode gave marvelous descriptions of the wonders which attracted their astonished gaze on all sides. Philosophical instruments, and others whose uses were more imperfectly imagined,—strange garments,— weapons of peculiar form,—crucibles and retorts,— mounted animals of various kinds, and one or two living ones unknown in Europe, together with numerous emblems of mortality, alike fitted for the contemplation of the moralizing philosopher, or the mystic appendages of the magician, were all to be seen in the apartment of him who had insensibly acquired the reputation of one of the magicians of old. Though it was probable he was only another link of the long chain of those who labored in the advancement of what was generally termed the grand magisterium, or secret,—the discovery of the philosopher's stone, with all its mysterious accompaniments.

The personal appearance of this individual was as remarkable as the furniture of his dwelling. His dress was usually a long violet-colored robe (the mourning garment of the East), confined round the middle by a broad leather belt on which were inscribed the signs of the zodiac,[6] and various unknown characters. He wore a high conical cap made of dark fur, such as seen on Armenians, Persians, and other inhabitants of Asia. His feet were shod with

---

[6] Twelve astrological signs defined by star configurations

sandals and from his waist depended a small case of
writing materials. A scroll of parchment only partially
concealed in the folds of his ample robe, and a long ebony
staff, which he invariably carried abroad, completed his
external appearance.

In form he was tall, though somewhat bent,—either
from age, or the habit of meditation, which fixed his gaze
almost constantly upon the earth, save when he was
about to speak. His head was then raised, and discovered
a set of features, the expression of which was strikingly
fine and noble. The forehead was high and expansive, the
eyes dark and piercing, the mouth grave and well-formed;
and a long beard, of snowy whiteness, falling on his
breast, gave an air of venerable solemnity to his whole
countenance, which could not fail to impress the
beholders with respect, if not with awe. The name by
which he was known was that of *Seddick ben Saad.*

In the daytime he was rarely seen, but in the evening
when the dim haze of twilight began to wrap every object
in obscurity, he might be observed issuing forth, and
pacing with majestic step towards the open country which
skirted this part of the town, or descending to the banks of
the river, along the margin of which it was his wont to
walk sometimes for several hours together. The night
appeared not to be allotted by him to the purpose of rest,
for the faint twinkle of the solitary lamp which flamed
from the upper chamber, indicated that his studies were
unremitting, whatever might be their object.

He seemed above the natural wants of mankind, for
his diet consisted only of bread and herbs, which were
bought in very small quantities, and at long intervals
between; less, it would seem, from a habit of parsimony,
than a principle of abstemiousness. Though no one could
judge of his means by the very slight expenses which he
incurred, it was nevertheless imagined that he possessed
great riches, and this belief continually gained ground.

It has been observed that Ben Saad was more
shunned than sought;—there were times, however, when
this prejudice gave way, before the necessities of those
who came with humble looks to implore his assistance;
their health, their undertakings, and their fortunes, were
by turns the theme of solicitation, and to all he lent an
attentive ear. His medical skill restored their former
strength. His prescience afforded them wise rules for their

future guidance, if it did not absolutely predict the course of events; and his liberality often relieved, in a more tangible manner, the wants of such as were not undeserving of his kindness.

The fame of Seddik ben Saad soon spread far and wide; and upon the last mentioned circumstance, the conjectures of his wealth were more ostensibly founded.

It was a chill and wintry night at the latter end of the month of October, when a boat, pulled by four stout rowers, was rapidly urged along the river, as it returned from the royal residence at Greenwich, to London. Though the moon was at the full, her light was obscured by heavy masses of dark clouds, which drifted before her, and cast a fitful gloom over the face of nature. The wind whistled shrilly, and, sweeping in sudden gusts across the stream, curled up the surface of the waters, and dashed the cold spray over the boatmen, as they sped the light and bounding bark. A young man sat in the stem of the boat, wrapped in a large cloak, which completely concealed his figure.

He seemed absorbed in a profound reverie, though constant habit gave him the power to guide the helm mechanically, and avoid the many impediments which obstructed the channel. The boat was now fast approaching the city, and the frowning battlements of the ancient Tower of London were at intervals perceptible, when the moon for a moment struggled through the dark veil which obscured her brightness. On a sudden, the young man started from the musing attitude in which he had been reclining and commanded the boatmen to rest on their oars while he bent himself forward to listen for a repetition of the sound which he said had originally disturbed him.

It was then that all on board distinctly heard the voices of men on shore loud in altercation, and, as it seemed, engaged in some desperate act of violence. In this opinion they were confirmed by hearing the cry of *murder* several times repeated. The young man already mentioned directed the rowers to pull towards the shore as fast as they could, and with as little noise as possible. Favored by the darkness of the night, and the turbulent state of the waters, which concealed their approach, they had almost gained the bank of the river, at the spot from whence the sounds proceeded, when their purpose was discovered. A violent but brief struggle ensued, and then a heavy plunge into the stream, accompanied by a deep execration, announced that all was over.

The moon at the same moment burst through the clouds which obscured her, and by her light two men were seen for an instant at gaze, as they reconnoitered the party in the boat, and then were speedily lost from the view. The boatmen shipped their oars, and the bark glided swiftly forward to the bank, where, vainly grasping at the slippery surface which it presented, a figure was descried, striving manfully to regain the shore. His efforts would, however, have been unsuccessful, had not the leader of the party, which had come so opportunely to his rescue, leaned over the side of the boat, and supported him in the stream, till, by the assistance of his men, he was safely raised from the water and placed on dry land.

On examining the person of him whom they had rescued, the young stranger observed that his garb was Oriental, and the first words he uttered, when sufficiently recovered from the state of exhaustion which his violent efforts had caused, were in an unknown tongue. "Mashallah," was his oft-repeated exclamation, as with uplifted hands he raised his eyes towards heaven—then, turning to those who surrounded him, he addressed himself in English to him who was evidently their chief.

"Stranger," he said, "you have saved my life; and, if you wish to add to the good work you have begun, you will send an escort to my dwelling, for I much fear, that, in my protracted absence, the villains with whom I was engaged may effect a part of their design; and the strength of threescore and ten avails little after so severe a struggle. "Just Allah," he exclaimed, interjectionally, "when my your trusting servant pass through his Goal trial and become the type of thine own Omnipotence below!"—then, turning again, be added, "Deny not my request, it will profit you much. I have that which can amply satisfy your utmost wishes, and your reward will not be wanting."

"There needs none, reverend father," replied the young stranger, with the frankness of youth. "I myself will be your escort, and fear not that I can sufficiently defend you. I have used my sword in a good cause too often, to dread the result, should we be attacked by a score of such craven fellows as we just now scared. I return not with you, Walter," he said, speaking to the foremost boatman. "It may be that I will stay for tonight in the neighborhood."

The man to whom he spoke replied only by an obedient gesture, and the party withdrew to the boat, leaving their leader and the old man alone together.

A slight pause ensued, which was broken by the former, who demanded to know if his companion were able to renew his journey homewards. Receiving an assent, they slowly left the shore, and, in a short time, reached the inhabited precincts of the town. The old man led the way through several narrow and obscure streets, and at length stopped opposite the low portal of a house which has already been described. He then eagerly searched his clothing and produced a small master key, which he applied to the lock, and the door stood open before them.

"Enter, my son," said Seddick Ben Saad, for he it was. "There is nothing now to dread—the ascendancy of the evil planet has past and good fortune predominates. It has decreed that you should this night be my guest, though not even *I* could have divined the means. What says the holy Koran, 'No man shall see death, till the time arrives which is fixed by the immutable decree of Allah.' Follow me, then, my son, and believe that the events of this night have been long foredoomed to happen."

He entered, as he spoke, into a low vaulted room, where a solitary lamp sent forth a flickering light, and only half-illumined the dusky chamber. The stranger followed him and Ben Saad cautiously closed the door. He then crossed the vault, and, taking up the lamp, beckoned his companion to ascend with him a narrow, gloomy staircase, the first steps of which were just visible as the light fell faintly on a dark recess. The stranger hesitated for an instant, and then, as if reflecting that he had gone too far to recede, and that he was armed and alone, with a defenseless old man who owed him his life, felt ashamed of his momentary apprehension and advanced towards Al Seddik. The latter seemed to guess what was passing his mind.

"I come," he said, "from a land where inhospitality and ingratitude are unknown. I owe you the reverse of both. A *robber,* even my country, respects the sacred character of his guest."

They ascended the narrow stairs, and, assisted more by touch than eyesight, at length gained the summit, where the stranger found himself in a spacious apartment.

Ben Saad trimmed his lamp, and invited his guest to rest while he procured him some refreshment. In the meantime, the latter was occupied in examining the chamber of which he was so unexpectedly the tenant. The walls of the room were wainscoted, and, as well as the ceiling, were composed of dark oak, which was much blackened by time and smoke. From the center of the ceiling was suspended a heavy silver chain to which hung a lamp of the same metal, in the shape of a globe, with four long branches, fantastically trimmed. As the old man traversed the apartment, light flashed on the walls, where numerous steel weapons were arranged in peculiar devices; and between each group of arms was suspended a human skull, a skeleton, or some other ghastly emblem of mortality.

Strange figures were also chalked onto the wainscot, exhibiting many of the mystical signs which are inscribed on the tombs of the ancient Pharaohs. Among these were others which, more regularly mathematical, were more intelligible. Various scrolls of parchment, covered with hieroglyphics, glass-cases containing the sacred ibis,[7] the swathed mummy from the pyramids, the embryo crocodile of the Nile; and numerous other fragments of Egyptian antiquity, were scattered round the room. In the further corner was a deep recess in which appeared many of the instruments proper for a chemist's laboratory. A small fire of charcoal was also burning steadily beneath a large alembic.[8] All these signs were sufficient to assure the stranger that he was in the dwelling of one of those sages whom subsequent times have stigmatized as astrologers and visionary enthusiasts.

Ben Saad now placed some provisions on a small table, and set them before his guest. "They are not," he said, "such as you are doubtless accustomed to, but who, in traversing the sandy desert, can look to behold the delightful valleys of Yemen? The juice of the grape you know is forbidden to all who profess the true belief, since

---

[7] Long beaked bird from Africa

[8] Two containers joined by a tube, used for chemistry experiments

our holy prophet denounced it the *Omen Alkhabdt,* or mother of destruction."

"Father," replied the youth, "I know so much of the rites of Eastern hospitality, as to partake gratefully of that which is cheerfully offered. These dried fruits and this delicious beverage are a greater luxury than the costliest viands and the brightest wines. Will you not comply with your native custom, so far as to eat the bread and salt with me?"

"I may not," answered Seddik. "Indulge in the sensual delights of appetite. Long and severe fasting can alone free the mind from earthly desires and raise it to the state of perfection which is needful for him who toils after the light of truth; nevertheless, to remove your scruples, a few dates and a cup of sherbet will assure me as truly your friend as if I had sworn by *Al Corsi,* the brightest of the thrones of Allah."[9]

Their repast was soon finished and the stranger now demanded of Ben Saad the particulars of the accident which had caused his interference. They were briefly explained.

It appeared that, pursuing his accustomed path by the riverside, and immersed in deep thought, he had suddenly been stopped by two ruffians, who, aware of his usual habits and influenced probably by the general report, sought to steal from him given his supposed wealth. He had nothing on his person except the key for his house, which was carefully concealed; but the robbers, disbelieving his assertions, proceeded to acts of violence. He defended himself as well as he could, but they had just succeeded in mastering his weapon at the very crisis when the boat appeared in sight; and, in revenge for the loss of their prize, they had hurled Al Seddik into the river.

"I knew," continued Ben Saad, "for the stars had predicted it, that danger was near me. The conjunction of opposing planets spoke only too plainly; but I knew, also, that a more favorable influence was predominant, and such it has proved. Tell me, then, my son, in which way Seddik, the humble recluse, can show his gratitude to his preserver."

"My father," replied the stranger, "I doubt not that the book of knowledge lies open to your skill, or does it exceed

---

[9] *Ayat Al-Kursi* or the verse of Allah's throne in the Qur'an

the limits of your art to predict the future destinies of a nameless man; if not, I would entreat that my fate may be revealed to me."

"And is it even so," exclaimed Ben Saad. "Old and young, rich and poor, all seek after futurity. Believe me that the knowledge is often fatal. Ask for some other gratification which may be more easily attained, and less dangerous when possessed."

"Nay," replied the youth. "Deny not my request. I am indifferent to the danger, and can wish for no higher gratification. Trust me, I have framed my mind to endure my fortune, be it of good or evil. To know it, cannot make me unhappier than I have been. It may have a better effect on the days which are in store."

"Be it so, then," said Al Seddik. "Remember it is the voice of heaven that speaks. Give me your hand." The young man extended his palm in obedience to the sage's direction. After a long and attentive perusal of the interesting lines, Ben Saad spoke.

"This hand," he said, "is a mysterious intelligencer of the decrees of fate. I see in it the course of an eventful life. Ay," he exclaimed, rather as it were in communion with his own thoughts, than addressing his companion, "a long and slender palm, and taper fingers. Yet spirit and enterprise are clearly developed, as well as their consequence, honors and dignities, in these ruddy nails; and the line of life, ay, that indeed, 'tis strongly and boldly marked, but see where it suddenly terminates. Though bright and successful is your career, the end appears abrupt and violent—a sharp and sudden death must close thy mortal span!"

"So be it," said the youth, "I would rather gleam like a meteor through the midair, than twinkle obscurely, however steadily, where none would heed my light; but tell me more, Seddik. What of my particular fortunes, and how are they to be attained?"

"My son," replied the astrologer, "as yet I see but dimly into the events of futurity, if you wish to learn all that may betide, as far as human skill can point it out, it will be done, but not now. I must make some necessary preparations and observe the favorable hour. You, yourself, must give me the precise indications which are necessary for setting your horoscope. Then all will be made known to you. Your hand, again," he said,—he once more looked on it with attention. "Success and power are, indeed, distinctly marked, but friendship is wanting throughout; and all things portend a violent death. Don't you see the brevity of the mensal line,[10] and the upward-turning branches of the line of life? Enough for the present. In eight-and-forty hours we will speak further on this matter. And now, my son, you doubtless stand in need of rest. Tonight, you are my guest, if you can sleep in a dwelling so dreary."

"The prospect of the future," he replied, "will not at any rate mar my present slumbers; and sleep will seal my eyes as readily here as elsewhere."

"Arise, then, and follow me," said Ben Saad; and, opening a small door, he led the way down a narrow passage, at the extremity of which was a small chamber, covered with the skins of various animals, and spread out so as to form a luxurious couch.

"Here," said the astrologer, "is my bed. Rest here till daylight. For myself, I must be a watcher till the stars shed their latest ray. In the morning, when you wish to depart, seek me not, but descend the staircase, which leads into the lower apartment. Remember to close the portal, and fail not to present yourself here when the sun has set on the second day from hence. Forget not, also, to note the precise hour and period of your birth. And now may the star of the sleeping eagle[11] shed its influence over your couch!"

The old man withdrew at these words. His companion stretched himself upon the soft bed of furs which was prepared; and, despite the novelty of his situation, and the imperfect prophecies he had heard relative to his own fate, which haunted his imagination, in a short time he slept soundly. He was stirring at early dawn. And, obedient to the sage's injunction, departed as silently as he arrived. That day passed away, and the second was sinking fast with the shades of night, when he returned to the dwelling of the astrologer, prepared, though with a beating heart and anxious mind, to encounter his fate with firmness, whatever the stars might predict.

---

[10] Palmists refer to this line as the hear line, while a short mensal line means a short lifespan

[11] *Nasr al Vaké* as called by the Arabs

At the period of which we speak, a belief in judicial astrology was generally entertained; and even some of the master-spirits of the age owned, in a slight degree, their partial belief in the science. It has been said that the queen herself, on one occasion, allowed her judgment to be influenced by the predictions of an astrologer. At least such is the assertion of the acute and entertaining Italian, whose history of her reign is in most respects a faithful one. A further proof may be deduced from the proceedings against witchcraft which characterized the reign of her successors, as well as from the numerous memoirs, public and private, which tend to illustrate the fact.

Though liberally educated, travelled, and abundantly endowed with the gifts of nature and the acquirements of art, the mind of the young man had not in this respect risen superior to that of the multitude; or, if so, it was but with a slight shade of difference, arising from the effect of education, which corrected, though it could not eradicate, the early impressions of superstition.

Arrived at the sage's dwelling, he knocked, and was presently admitted. The old man stood before him, and accosted him with the Eastern salutation of peace. "*Saam Aleikum,*" was his greeting, as he bent his head, and once more welcomed the stranger to his abode. They ascended in silence into the upper chambers, where a great difference was now perceptible in the apartment, as well as in the dress, of the astrologer. The red-colored garment which Al Seddik usually wore, was exchanged for a robe of pure white. The sleeves and hem of which were bordered by deep rows of Oriental writing, representing the ninety and nine mysterious names of Allah.

His cap was high and conical, and of the same color; and a verse from the Koran was inscribed around it; the same that is applied to the "wondrous night,"[12] which all Mussulmen hold in the deepest veneration. The purport ran thus: "May peace be upon this night, till the light will dawn from the east!"

His waist was encircled by the black and white skin of the serpent Arkam, known for its wisdom and venomous

---

[12] Reference to Bellerophon, the poet, who road with the prophet Mohammed on his night journey on horseback to the Seven Heavens of Islam. Bellerophon fell off his horse, but Mohammed continued on through the Seven Heavens.

qualities in the province of Turquestan; and on his breast he wore a triangular ornament of gold, the emblem of perfectibility. In his right hand he held an ebony wand, which was chased with a serpentine wreath of silver, from one extremity to the other.

The chamber was now brilliantly illuminated by long tapers of camphor,[13] but the splendor of the light was not visible from without, owing to several thick folds of dark cloth which were suspended across the room, in front of the window, the lattice of which was also closed by heavy oaken shutters. The middle of the apartment was the center of a large circle, accurately traced in chalk, and regularly divided according to the twelve signs of the zodiac, which marked the several houses. A small peeled wand was also laid at each division of the circle, composed alternately of the elm and aspen branches. The interior of the circle presented a barrier of a more formidable nature, being formed of skulls and bones, together with divers other more inexplicable objects.

"Behold, my son," said Al Seddik, "these relics of mortality. They are the bones of the wise, who, like me, have toiled long and suffered much, to discover the grand secret of nature. Each fragment which you see there, was once an animated portion of the living frame of the sages who inhabited the city of *Ain al Schams,*—the fountain of the sun, once the capital of Egypt and of the world. Alas for the wreck of time!—The city is desolate and the bones of the wisest who dwelt within its walls, alone attest the past existence of that which was once the renowned among nations.

"These shining relics," he continued, pointing with his wand as he spoke, "were formerly among the gems which adorned the crown of *Zein Algaman,* the mighty founder of the city of Auberabad, in the isles of the Indian ocean.

"In the same circle, you may mark the various stones which possess the strongest power in conjunction with the planetary signs; from the pearl of the sea of Oman and the amber of Chaldea, to the turquoise of Istakhar, and that stone, more precious than all, which is found in the eyes

---

[13] Obtained from cinnamon tree, camphor is a whitish, waxy material used in candles

of the stag, whose food is of serpents in the sandy deserts of Thibet[14] and Cathay.

"Nor are these alone sufficient to counteract the malignant influence of the planets which are in opposition to this night's work. I name them to you, my son, that you may see that the productions of the earth, the holiest, the most rare, and some the most ordinary, are alike needful to success. 'A wise man,' says the Hâkim *Lokman,*[15] 'neglecteth not the aid of the meanest of the creatures of Allah.' Observe this vase of alabaster. It contains the crystallized tears of the dove of the sultan *Mahmoud ben Sebekteghim,* a holy bird, sent by the prophet to his faithful servant from the river *Kautser,* in the garden of Eden, whose shores are of pure gold, and the sands of its shining bed are pearls and rubies. These crystal drops have power to disperse the noxious qualities of poison, and of all things hurtful to man.

"It needs not to describe more of the precious fragments which have been collected, to heighten the force of the charm I am about to assay; nor is it needful to inquire how all these powerful auxiliaries have been procured, enough, that a long life of toil and pain have enabled me to discover their mysterious attributes. Soon I trust to lead to the accomplishment of the grand object of existence, the attainment of knowledge and powers beyond that of *Soliman ben Daoud,* whose slaves were the genii of the elements.

"Before, however, we enter within the limits of the circle, to invoke the presence of the spirits of the elements to embrace your demands, first tell me the precise hour and minute of your birth that I may complete the horoscope I have already prepared."

As he spoke, *Al Seddik* drew from his chest a broad sheet of parchment on which was accurately depicted the table of the twelve houses of life. Receiving the required document, he examined it attentively, and seated himself on the floor while he proceeded to make the necessary calculations. His companion observed him with interest. In a short time the old man spoke:

---

[14] Tibet

[15] Wise man of the Qur'an after which Surat Luqman, the thirty-first chapter of the Qur'an is titled

"My son," he said, "I was not deceived. The stars are the willing interpreters of the decrees of fate. The lines of your hand agree but too well with the destiny which is inscribed in the heavenly spheres. In the first house, which is that of *Life,* I see where Jupiter enters direct into the sign of *Al Gedi,* or the ram. Believe me, that ere long the bright course of your fortunes will begin. They will be brilliant and successful; still further in the same planet, predominant in the eleventh house, where dignities, and the favors of princes are profusely strewed; but, again being retrograde in Taurus, it is clear that the house of life is endangered, in the midst of the highest sweep of fortune. Your career will be eminently prosperous, but its end will assuredly be sudden!

"Behold where the planet Zohair, which is Venus, enters into the balance with the sun in the ascendant; as surely does it betoken the love of woman and the dangerous favors which she bestows. Bear then in mind the words of the poet Dahban,[16] to mistrust four things— 'the friendship of princes, the caresses of women, the smiles of enemies, and the warmth of winter, for none of these things endure.' Rely on this saying, for that which follows assures its truth.

"The Sun being retrograde in Taurus, denotes, that, though the prospect of marriage may seem to offer the surest means of happiness, it will never be successful. In the tenth house, Mars entering direct into Cancer, repeats the prediction of danger and violent death; and Venus being in conjunction, declares, that from woman will the danger ensue.

"There are three occurrences which will mark your future life, all in themselves productive of honor, but linked to a fatal termination—the first will speedily arrive, and open the road to fame and fortune. The second will be occasioned by the death of a dear friend, whose end you will yourself accelerate, and almost gain the topmost round of ambition's ladder. The third will go near to raise you to the pinnacle of human greatness, but your opposing fate will quickly reverse the picture. The horoscope tells me no more; and more if you wish to know, must be demanded of agency no longer mortal."

---

[16] Abû Muhammad Al-Dahbán, who was more an Arabic philosopher than a poet

"I cannot pause," the young man replied, "in the acquisition of knowledge which holds out such splendid lures, though accompanied by terms which might appall a less resolute querist. I need not repeat, Ben Saad, that I seek to know all that can be told, and I care not what may be the means employed."

"Propose, then, your questions in writing, before we enter into the circle, where, by the uninitiated, neither must word be uttered nor sign made."

The stranger mused for a moment, then rapidly wrote down a series of questions, which he gave to the astrologer.

"It is well," he said. "Approach, then, and bare your feet, for the dust whereon you are about to tread is sacred—'tis the sand of the island of Gezirat, far, far away beyond the giant mountain of Caf, where reigned the pre-adamite sultans before this nether world was created. Take, also, this mantle, once worn by the wise *Abou Maascher*,[17] and cast it over your own garments, before you enter this mystic circle, the true emblem of eternity."

The stranger obeyed implicitly the mandates of the sage; for, though his own faith taught him to doubt much the efficacy of all the relics which were thus arrayed, yet, impressed with the idea of the learning and skill of the Eastern magi, he gave involuntary credit to much that was said, from the imposing manner in which the old man uttered his words, and the peculiarities of time and place which surrounded him.

They entered the circle together, and Al Seddik carefully retraced the outline over which they had passed. He then proceeded with the mystic ceremony. He first prostrated himself towards the east, and remained for a few minutes apparently absorbed in prayer; then, rising, he drew from his vest the magical volume that was written by the celebrated Bazur,[18] containing all the rites and ceremonies necessary to be observed in the progress of the incantation. He then slowly paced the circle, following the direction of the sun, and pausing at each of the twelve divisions, to repeat the formula of adjuration.

---

[17] Abū Ma'shar (787-886) was a great astrologer and Islamic philosopher of his day.

[18] In the Iranian epic poem "Shahnameh" by the poet Ferdowsi, Bazur is the Turanian wizard.

When the circle was encompassed, he took a small crucible, and, pouring into it a dark liquid, he lit a taper, and bent it downwards to the vessel, the contents of which instantly ignited, and a bright flame sparkled far and wide. Ben Saad next produced an Oriental drug reduced to powder, which he scattered over the flame, and a dark vapor arose, as gloomy as that which floats perpetually above the well of Heodskar. The mist gradually extended itself throughout the chamber and the lights were well-nigh extinguished, all but the flame from the crucible, which still burnt fiercely, and cast a red glare over the persons of the astrologer and his neophyte.

This action was accompanied by a solemn invocation to the terrific powers of darkness; and presently was heard a rushing noise, like the sound of the deadly blast as it sweeps over the sands of Egypt. A dusky form was then descried, pacing with impatient gestures the circumference of the magic ring. Al Seddik gazed fixedly on the apparition. The stranger shuddered with an undefined sensation of dread as he endeavored to discern the imperfect form and features of the shadow, which seemed alike impalpable and ever-changing.

The old man was the first to break the appalling silence: "Slave of Eblis, dark spirit of futurity," he exclaimed, "pause in thy circling flight, and obey the power of him whose spell has called you from the realms of Ginnistan[19] to the regions of upper air."

The figure remained in one spot, while, with expanded wings, it still seemed hovering as a bird before it rests itself on earth. A deep harsh voice was heard.

"What wouldst thou?" was the question. "Speak, and be brief."

"*Demrouset Nere,*" said the sage, "for such I know you now. Hearken to the words of one as potent as *Tahmuras*[20] of yore, and reply with the voice of truth to that which I shall demand of thee."

"What fate awaits the querist whose foot is even now on the threshold of life?"

"His fortunes will prosper till his age is doubled," was the corresponding reply.

---

[19] Fictional dreamland, usually brought on by deep sleep

[20] In Ferdowski's epic poem "Shahnameh," Tahmuras is the third shah of the world.

"Will he experience happiness in his career?"

"Mortals toil eagerly in pursuit of *pleasure* and *ambition,*—he will have enough of both."

"Will he be successful in love?"

"It will raise him to the pinnacle of greatness,—will hurl him from the giddy height,—will betray him while living, and mourn over him when dead."

"Who will prove his greatest foe?"

"His fairest friend."

"When will he die, and how?"

"Four hours have not elapsed since he saw the spot where he will yield up his last breath,—let him beware the axe."

"What shall occasion his death?"

"The treachery of woman."

"What is the name of her whose destiny is linked with his?" A pause ensued,—the spirit appeared moody, and unwilling to answer further.

"Speak, foul spirit," cried Al Seddik, "I conjure you by the powerful seal of Noe, in the name of the mighty *Senkiduh* I command you!"

"Seek for the name beneath the sign *Sunbulah,*" replied the voice. "I may not tell you more."

"*Sunbulah,*" exclaimed Ben Saad. "'Tis the sign of the *Virgin;* perchance a regal one. I say, once more, will this favored son of fortune ever wear a kingly crown?"

"*His sway shall be that of royalty,*" was the final answer of the voice, as the figure became more and more indistinct amid the thickening vapor.

"Enough," said the astrologer to his companion. "More it profits not to inquire."

In a few moments the apartment was again clear, and the lights burned brightly as before.

"What think you, my son," said Al Seddik. "Are you satisfied with the prospect of your future lot?"

"It is more than the fondest dreams of my imagination could have pictured," replied the youth. "How will I thank you, my father, how express my gratitude?"

"Reserve it, my son, till you have better learned to appreciate the nature of what you have just heard. A time may come when your thoughts may change,—meanwhile live well and wisely. Forget not, that though the stars rule the destinies of men, they themselves are but the agents of the all powerful Allah. Live then so as to deserve the fortune which fate has prepared; and when Azrael, the angel of death, shall summon you, may you be prepared to accompany him! Farewell then, Robert Devereux; and, in the days of your prosperity, remember the words of *Seddik ben Saad.*

•••••

Who is there to whom the prosperous career and unhappy fate of the unfortunate Earl of Essex, the favorite of Queen Elizabeth, are unknown! They are recorded in the pages of history, and inseparably connected with the annals of the maiden queen. Yet there are few, perhaps, who are aware that the predictions of which we have spoken were actually made, and that they came to pass almost according to the letter.

In the year 1585, he accompanied the Earl of Leicester to Holland, where he obtained the rank of general (though so young, being barely eighteen); and where he behaved with distinguished bravery at the memorable battle of Zutphen. On his return from the Low Countries, he made his first appearance at court, where he immediately attracted the notice of the queen, who in an incredibly short time loaded him with dignities and rewards; conferring upon him the office of Master of the Household, Grand Marshal, and Chancellor of the University of Cambridge. Her personal regard, also, accompanied these high honors, being permitted to wear in his hat a glove from her right hand; "a favor," says a contemporary historian, "the greatest that a mistress could bestow on an accepted lover."

The influence of Leicester, whose friend he was, was not at once eclipsed. They continued to divide the favors and councils of Elizabeth, till by degrees the star of Leicester sank before that of his more youthful rival, who forgot the ties of friendship in the lures of ambition; and eventually became the concealed enemy of his former friend, whose death has by some been ascribed to poison, and by others to a broken heart, owing to his having lost the friendship of the queen; which circumstance it is well known, was caused by the intrigues of Essex.

On Leicester's death, he became lord paramount, and bore the title, at court, of "*The EARL." Par excellence.* The vice royalty of Ireland, while it kept the word of promise to his ear, yet broke it to his hope; and though it put into his hands the possession of an authority in every respect that of a king, was yet, through the treachery of his friends, the final cause of his disgrace.

The last act of his power was his desperate attempt to secure the person of the queen, which, so fatally for his fortunes, was unsuccessful. From that period, till his final condemnation, the transition was most rapid; and when, in the last extremity, be transmitted Elizabeth's ring by the faithless countess of Nottingham, and awoke the remorse of Elizabeth, whose spirit bowed beneath it till she sunk in the grave, the terra of prophetic events was completed, which verified the predictions of the astrologer.

Elizabeth F. Ellet
(1818-1877)

"Elizabeth ("Lummis") Ellet was the daughter of Dr. William A. Lummis, a man honorably distinguished in his profession. She was born at Sodus, a small town on the shores of Lake Ontario, in the state of New York. Her mother was the daughter of General Maxwell, an officer in the American Revolutionary War; and thus the subject of this memoir was in childhood imbued with patriotic feelings, which, next to the religious, are sure to nourish in the female mind the seeds of genius.

"Miss Lummis was early distinguished for vivacity of intellect and a thirst for learning, which her subsequent life has shown was no evanescent fancy, but the natural stamp of her earnest mind. She was married, before she was seventeen, to Dr. William H. Ellet, an accomplished scholar and then Professor of Chemistry in Columbia College, New York City, whither he removed his youthful bride. There she had such advantages of study as she had never before enjoyed, and her proficiency was rapid. She soon began to write for the periodicals. Her first piece, a poem, appeared in 1833 in the "American Ladies' Magazine," published at Boston. Her articles were favorably noticed, and the name of Mrs. Ellet became known among literary circles.

"In 1834 appeared her translation of "Euphemia of Messina," one of the most admired productions of Silvio Pelico; and in the following year, an original tragedy from her pen, "Teresa Contarini," was successfully represented in New York and also in some of the western cities. In the same year, 1835, she published her "Poems —Translated and Original." For several succeeding years, Mrs. Ellet wrote chiefly for periodicals. To the *American Review* she contributed "Papers on Italian Tragedy," "Italian Poets," "Lamartine's Poems," "Andreini's Adam," etc.

"Dr. Ellet, receiving the appointment of Professor of Chemistry and Natural Philosophy in the college at Columbia, South Carolina, moved there and Mrs. Ellet found herself among new scenery and new friends, but her old love of literature remained unchanged. Besides contributing to the *North American Review*, *Southern Quarterly Review*, *The Lady's Book*, and other periodicals, in 1841 she produced "The Characters of Schiller," an analysis and criticism of the principal persons in Schiller's plays, with an essay on Schiller's genius, and translated extracts from his writings. "Joanna of Sicily" was her next work; soon followed by "Country Rambles," a spirited description of the scenery she has observed in her journeyings through the United States.

"In the autumn of 1848, her most elaborate, as well as important work, was published in New York, "The Women of the American Revolution," in two volumes, to which she has since added a third. This contribution to American history, and the ability with which it was executed, has, deservedly, given Mrs. Ellet a high place among female writers. In 1850, she published "Domestic History of the American Revolution," in one volume, designed to exhibit the spirit of that period, to portray, as far as possible, the social and domestic condition of the colonists, and the state of feeling among the people during the war. Another work of hers, "Pictures from Bible History," was also published in 1850.

"Mrs. Ellet has tried nearly all varieties of literature, original and translation—poetry, essay, criticism, tragedy, biography, fiction, history, and stories for children; to say, as we truly can, that she has not failed in any, is sufficient praise. Still she has not, probably, done her best in any one department. The concentration of genius is one of the conditions of its perfect development. She is yet young, hopeful, and studious. Nor are her accomplishments confined to the merely literary. In music and drawing she also excels; and in the graces that adorn society, and make the charm of social and domestic intercourse, she is eminently gifted. Her residence is now fixed in the city of New York."[1]

In 1857, Elizabeth F. Ellet began editing the Evening Express magazine in New York. Two years later her husband died. She continued to write for the next thirty years later, dying in 1877.

Originality was always the Achilles heel of Ellet in her fictional works. That's why it is not surprising she admits in the preamble to "The Witch Caprusche," her best fantasy story, that it is not of her own creation. She attributes it to a "household tale" of Denmark.

Ellet is, perhaps, best known today for the *scandal* she brought in relation to Edgar Allan Poe's rumored affair with Frances Sargent Osgood while both were married to other people. That is never a good sign for an author. Ellet tried all forms and variations of writing, ultimately becoming best known for a non-fiction work: "The Women of the American Revolution," published in 1848, three years after she published "The Witch Caprusche."

Seeking revenge for the scandal Ellet brought into his life, Edgar Allan Poe references the "wholesale plagiarism" for which Ellet had been charged. Though refusing to believe it, the mere reference by Poe caused the damage. Poe admits that he has little interest in her works and closed the piece by referring to her as short and fat.

"Mrs. ELLETT, or ELLET, has been long before the public as an author. Having contributed largely to the newspapers and other periodicals in her youth, she first made her *debût* on a more comprehensive scale, as the writer of "Teresa Contarini," in a five-act tragedy, which had considerable merit, but was withdrawn after its first night of representation at the Park. This occurred at some period previous to the year 1834; the precise date I am unable to remember. The ill success of the play had little effect in repressing the ardor of the poetess, who has since furnished numerous papers to the Magazines. Her articles are, for the most part, in the *rifacimento* way, and,

---

[1] *A Cyclopeadia of Female Biography*, edited by Henry Gardiner Adams, 1857, pgs. 269-270

although no doubt composed in good faith, have the disadvantage of *looking* as if hashed up for just so much money as they will bring. The charge of wholesale plagiarism which has been adduced against Mrs. Ellett, I confess that I have not felt sufficient interest in her works, to investigate—and am therefore bound to believe it unfounded. In person, short and much included to *embonpoint*."[2]

True originality aside, Ellet penned one of the best witch stories for the first half of the nineteenth century in "The Witch Caprusche." It is a short tale, but full of good characters that must be attributed to Ellet. She published the fantasy story in *The Columbian Lady's and Gentlemen's Magazine* during August of 1845 where her name was listed as "Mrs. E. F. Ellett." *The Tribune* newspaper of New York called the story "a singularly wild and beautiful legend."[3] Five years later Ellet would republish the story in the collection she edited, *Popular Legends; or, Evenings at Woodlawn.*

---

[2] *Literary America*, Edgar Allan Poe, 1848, Manuscript
[3] *The Tribune*, August 15, 1845

THE WITCH CAPRUSCHE
1845

"Toke Jarl" has been call the Danish "Macbeth;"[1] and indeed resembles, in his ambition and evil fate, the king whom Shakespeare has immortalized. In other respects, the story is different. The following is the legend as it is current throughout Denmark; familiar as a household tale among the people, though never recorded in any lasting work.

IN THE DARK ages, when Paganism[2] ruled over the land and the light even of civilization but faintly shone, there lived a king in Denmark whose name has not descended to later times. Yet he governed a fair country and possessed much power. At the period of this story he was in the decline of life and had been twenty years a widower. His only child was a daughter, the beautiful Ruscha, whose mother had died in giving her birth.

In all of the neighboring kingdoms the fame of princess Ruscha's beauty was widely spread; and many were the noble suitors for her hand. But the princess was proud and imperious as fair. She rejected every proposal of marriage and treated her lovers with so much scorn that almost all were incited to hate and speak ill of her. She thus raised up enemies on every side.

The old king was much incensed at this conduct and sharply reproved his daughter. "Was it not enough," he said—"that you would not choose of one of your suitors—but they must be repulsed with such bitter contempt? Your haughty bearing and evil tongue have converted these friends into foes. Murmur not, therefore, at what I will do. I am old and feeble. A few years—and I must depart from this earth to take my place among the heroes of Valhalla[3] and drink the mead[4] of Odin.[5] You are young,

---

[1] *The Tragedy of Macbeth* by William Shakespeare, 1611
[2] Religious practices based strongly on nature and things of the earth
[3] A great hall that paid homage to Norse warriors in Norse mythology
[4] Wine made from honey

and a woman. Who will shield you when I am gone from the powerful warriors—your enemies? By the hammer of Thor[6] do I swear, you will choose a husband—who may be your protector and king in my place. If you still refuse to do this I swear by Odin's golden horn, out of which heroes drink, I will name me a successor! I will not suffer you, ungrateful girl, to rule my people according to your own capricious will!"

When the king had spoken, he went out leaving the princess alone. Her face was crimson with anger, and her blue eyes flashed resentment. She paced the room for some time with unquiet steps; for the thought that the sovereignty might be wrested from her was too painful for her to bear. At length she threw herself into a seat and sat long with her fair head drooped on her hands. Then starting up, as if she had suddenly formed a resolution, she retired to her own apartment.

For many days after the old king showed much severity toward his daughter and his harsh rebukes were frequent. At length she informed him she was willing to choose a consort.

"Let all the neighboring princes and nobles and those who have sought me in marriage," she said, "be invited to the court—that I may make choice among them."

But her father answered, "Not so, by Odin and Frela![7] The princes and nobles of the neighboring countries have no longer any pleasure in you! I counsel you to choose one of your own kinsmen. What about Bue, the stout, or Eric—or Swed, the squinter?"

The princess curled her haughty lip in scorn and answered not. But after some days she signified her choice. The person she selected was not among her rejected suitors. It was Toke Jarl, surnamed the slender. He was of princely descent, possessed a large patrimony of land and was moreover distinguished for courage and manly beauty. He was richer than Ruscha's own kinsmen, so that the old king made no objections to his becoming the husband of his daughter and his declared successor. He dispatched messengers to Toke Jarl to announce to him his good fortune. Toke was well pleased with the

---

[5] God Odin in Norse mythology
[6] God in Norse mythology who wields a large hammer
[7] Goddess of Norse mythology who represents love and fertility

intelligence and praised the blue eyes and the ripe judgment of the princess. He ordered some of his best horses and his finest oxen to be led as a present to the king, with thanks for the honor done him; and announced that he would the next day present himself as a suitor before the beautiful Ruscha, who should never have reason to repent her choice.

The marriage was celebrated with due splendor at the king's castle, where Toke Jarl proved himself a veritable hero; for he drank not only his father-in-law under the table, but also his cousins Bue, the stout, Eric, and Swed, the squinter without showing himself the slightest symptom of inebriation. After this achievement he took the fair bride from her maidens and led her to the nuptial chamber.

Ruscha was not happy even after her union with the object of her choice. Ambition was her ruling passion; and she longed to feel the golden circlet of royalty on her brows, even before it could lawfully become hers by the death of her father. An evil spirit possessed her, and she hated the good old king from the day he had so harshly reproved her and proposed a marriage with one of her cousins.

She knew that Toke Jarl loved her passionately and resolved to make him her instrument for the gratification of her wicked desires. She assumed a deep melancholy—and a grief-worn aspect—as if she shed many tears in secret. "What ails you, Ruscha?" he would ask, and she would not reply. Then Toke would swear by Thor and Odin that if anyone had vexed her he would die.

The cunning princess wept more bitterly, and whispered, "Could you take away the life of the king, my father, and escape the infamy of being called his murderer?"

Toke Jarl started and looked earnestly and gloomily on his wife.

"It is the king," she continued, "who torments me day by day. I must die if he is suffered to live. Know also, Toke, that he is about to disinherit me and you, and to declare Eric his successor."

The brow of Toke Jarl grew black. "You have said it!" he exclaimed. "It will be done!" And he went out hastily.

The same day one of his slaves, a Finlander by birth, stole from the armory of Eric an arrow marked with his name. Toke Jarl went forth into the woods with this arrow, where the king was accustomed to hunt.

At evening when the monarch did not return, men were dispatched in search of him. They found his corpse in the wood, the arrow buried in his side. The body was brought back with loud lamentations. The people ran tumultuously to the palace gates. Every one recognized the arrow, and the cry was, "Eric, the bloody Eric, has slain our good king! Death to the murderer!"

Toke Jarl dispatched officers to arrest his wife's cousin and had his head stricken off in the sight of all. Then he was proclaimed king and solemnly crowned, with Ruscha his wife.

The guilty pair were now at the height they had longed to reach; but happiness came not with power. On the contrary, both grew every day more gloomy and dejected, and each distrusted the other. *If the queen had no scruples to doom her own father to death*, thought Toke Jarl, *much less would she hesitate to foster my destruction!* And Ruscha reflected with equal reason, that he who had basely taken away an old man's life at her prompting, would as readily sacrifice her whenever his love should be transferred to another. They looked on each other therefore with suspicion; the king watching closely every word and action of his consort, and jealously preventing her from any interference in the concerns of the kingdom, lest she should win from him the hearts of the people.

The queen hated her husband more and more every day and would gladly have rid herself of him but that she feared to undertake any deed of violence. The people loved their young sovereign who ruled them wisely though he was severe even to cruelty in matters of punishment.

Ruscha, however, was deceitful and cunning, and pondered day and night on the means of accomplishing her wishes without drawing suspicion on herself. One day she wandered alone in the forest, in the depths of which dwelt an old woman, whom common rumor accused of dealings with evil spirits of the wood. The virtuous feared and shunned her, but the queen now sought her out and was not long in finding her. The old woman was picking up sticks. She looked up as she saw her fair young visitor and a smile curled her withered lips.

"I am the queen," said Ruscha coming at once to the object of her visit. "I seek your aid against Toke Jarl, my husband."

"What has he done?" asked the witch.

"He practices treason against my life. I would he be dead before I band with him."

The old woman dropped her bundle of sticks, and stood upright, looking full into the eyes of the queen. "I can do nothing for you," she said "till you form a compact with me and those with whom I am leagued. You must sign the compact and give me your blood. Then will your veins be filled with the fire that animates immortal spirits and you will never taste of death."

"Will you promise me then, revenge on Toke Jarl?" Ruscha asked, her blue eyes flashing fire.

The old woman nodded.

"Then I will comply with your conditions," said the queen; and the wood-witch led the way to a cave hidden from sight by very thick bushes and foliage that shut out the beams of sun even at noon-day.

Within the recesses of this cave the deep darkness was rendered more horrible by hideous shapes that flashed like tongues of flame before the eyes, and by the sullen glare of the fire over which hung the caldron of infernal preparations. When the queen reappeared from that den of demons, a change had taken place in her looks. Her skin before so delicately fair, had a strange dazzling glow, as if tinged with the reflection of sunset. Her eyes were much darker and flashed with almost intolerable brightness. With a light step and joy in her face she returned to the city and the palace, having promised before she parted with the witch to visit her on the seventeenth day of every month to renew the league into which they had entered.

From that hour king Toke Jarl was attacked with illness. During the day he suffered not, but as soon as night came, the most agonizing pains tortured him in all his limbs. It seemed to him as if molten metal, instead of blood, flowed through his veins. The anguish was so intense that it threatened to destroy him. He grew every day more emaciated, and wandered like a spectre about his palace. All the science of his physicians availed nothing.

The little Finnish slave, hopeless of relief for his master from ordinary means, determined on a desperate remedy. He went through the woods, and reaching the mountains, gathered herbs in the moonlight from which he prepared a drink and administered it to the king, who lay helpless on his couch and knew not what was done to him. After a while the pain abated. Toke Jarl rose up in bed and looked around him. "What has been done to me?" he asked.

The Finnish slave threw himself on his knees before the king. "My gracious lord," he cried, "I know now what is your malady! I have sought the most poisonous herbs impregnated by the moonbeams and banned by evil spirits and distilled them into a drink of which you have taken. The potion has done you no harm, but driven away your pains. This would not have happened had your malady been a natural one. Now I know that my lord the king is bewitched and I know moreover that if he had not means to break the spell, his life will have been sacrificed and the land will have to seek another ruler."

Toke Jarl sprang in horror from his couch. "By Thor's hammer and the horn of Odin I swear," he cried, "if you will help me discover who has done me this evil turn, from that hour you will be free, and the highest noble at my court!"

But the boy quietly seated himself on the footstool by the royal couch and answered, "My lord and master, I would always remain your slave and servant, and receive from your hands my wheat bread and honey, and cured bear's flesh and as much old mead as I can drink. May this be, I will speak my whole mind."

Toke Jarl nodded, and the boy went on: "Consider, my lord, how long it is since this bad demon had power over you! Was it not from that very night when my royal lady the queen was missing all day from the palace and returned late, saying she had lost herself in the wood? Has she not three times since wandered in the same wood, and been lost, and returned at night? By all your gods, my king, and their horns and their hammers, of which I know nothing, I do believe that my lady, the queen, knows but too well the way to the dwelling of the old witch Runna, who can conjure all the wood spirits, and has for a servant, a dark looking elf, a little demon with red tongue always hanging out of his mouth!"

The king grew paler and paler while his servant was speaking. Then he seated himself on the side of the bed and mused awhile. At length he said, "You are right! Yes, I do believe you are right! May all good and evil spirits help me to take vengeance on my faithless wife! Tell me, boy, have you observed when the day returns?"

"The day after tomorrow, my lord."

"It is well; and the hour, do you know it?"

"I do, my lord! We will follow the queen and hear what she will say to old Runna."

"Well said, boy. Now give me another draught of your poison drink that I may go to sleep. That golden horn over there is full of excellent mead. Drink to my health."

Griep administered to the king another draught of the medicine and the monarch fell into a slumber, while the boy crouched on the low stool, sipped the mead from the golden horn and pleased himself with the prospect of abundance of honey, wheat bread and bear's flesh.

The next day and the following, queen Ruscha observed that the king gained strength visibly in spite of the power of her spell. The poison draught of the little Griep had restored him.

Her dismay was excessive. She longed impatiently for the seventh hour of the evening, and as soon as the West was crimson with sunset she departed, attired in a plain dress and her face concealed by a veil. She left the city and with steps trembling from eagerness hastened into the forest.

Griep led the king also by a secret and shorter path through the wood close to the old witch's cave. There, hidden among the bushes but near enough to hear all that was said, they awaited the arrival of the queen.

Ruscha came at length, stood before the cave and called, "Runna!" three times. At the third call a sullen rumbling noise was heard within the cavern. The iron door, which had been closed, opened slowly and the old witch appeared. "What do you want?" she asked.

"Help!" cried Ruscha. "Your spell has no longer any effect. For the last three days Toke Jarl has been on the recovery. In vain every night, by your direction, I have strewed coals around his waxen image and enveloped it in poisonous vapors. He has seemed yesterday and today stronger than ever!"

The hag knit her brows. "If it be as you say, there must be a counter spell at work more potent than mine. If this avails not, you must deprive the king of life at once."

"And lose the pleasure of tormenting him?" cried the evil queen. "But how can it be done?"

The witch laughed bitterly, for she was piqued at the failure of her magic in the first instance. "Were he a hero as mighty as the great Thor himself," she said, "he must yield to the word of power which I will give you."

Ruscha's eyes sparkled. "Oh, give it to me, good Runna!" she exclaimed.

Runna pronounced the word of power. The king listened breathlessly "When you meet Toke Jarl," continued the witch, "fix your eyes steadily upon his. Utter the word and call him by name. He will fall instantly, struck down by its magic. Now, fare-thee-well! My spirits summon me!"

The witch vanished and Ruscha turned from the cave on her way homewards. At the entrance of the wood she suddenly encountered the king standing in a threatening attitude, with his drawn sword uplifted. She started back with a scream of terror; but with scornful mockery he shouted the word given her by Runna, adding her own name and at the same time dealt her a furious blow with the sword, which cleft her head. Ruscha sank to the ground.

Toke Jarl fled to his castle, wiping the blood from his sword with his hand. Then he returned it to its sheath. Soon his hand began to burn, as if scorched with fire. In vain he plunged it into water and moist earth. The horrible burning extended to his arm, gradually spreading over his whole body, and before many hours elapsed he expired in dreadful torments.

Ruscha could not die, as the witch had assured her, nor could she live like the other inhabitants of earth. To this day it is said she wanders about her native country, a being who belongs neither to the living nor the dead. Many persons have averred that she has been seen wandering at night, in white fluttering garments, with face beautiful but ghastly pale, her veil red with blood that continually flows from the gaping wound in her head.

Old and young in Denmark believe in her existence, and that she sometimes appears. From the circumstance that the "word of power" given her by Runna, was supposed to sound like "Cap" that has become the popular prefix to her name and she is universally known as the fair but evil witch *Caprusche*.

George Soane
(1790-1860)

At a young age George Soane proved adept at translating foreign works into English and writing original dramas and excellent fiction. He thought much of the fantasy genre, too, penning dramas titled *The Dwarf of Naples* in 1819; *Faustus, or the Demon of Drachenfels* in 1825; and *Aladdin, a Fairy Opera* in 1826. Nearly a decade later George Soane wrote the fantasy short story "The Chamber of the Pale Lady," which had a brief run in the British magazines.

His originality of concept shone through in 1843 when he published the "Three Spirits" in his excellent short story collection *The Last Ball and Other Tales*. When Charles Dickens published "A Christmas Carol" on December 14, 1843, some thought Soane had plagiarized Boz though the "Three Spirits" was published months before "A Christmas Carol" and Soane claimed to have written it years before. In the "Three Spirits" a Dutchman clock falls in a house and from its shattered remains emerges three spirits—the ghosts of present, past and future. Soane's story is not nearly as developed as that of Dickens's "A Christmas Carol," but could have given Boz the genesis of his idea for the most famous Christmas story outside of the Bible.

It is unfortunate that George Soane is primarily known today (if know at all) as the rogue younger son of John Soane, the famous English architect, who spurned the Soane family's lucrative profession for an impoverished one in the written word. The similarities to Edgar Allan Poe in this regard—and so many other writers—come to mind.

"Sir John Soane, the architect, died, possessed of great wealth, in 1837, having founded at an expense of £120,000, the Soane Museum, in Lincoln's Inn Fields, which he bequeathed in trust for national purposes, and the gratification of the public. To his son, George he showed an animosity only equaled by that which Dr. Johnson has so eloquently recorded, of the Countess of Macclesfield to her offspring, the poet Savage.

"Sir John left to this son George Soane, whom he had caused to be educated at the University of Cambridge, and brought up with suitable expectations, forty pounds a year! George Soane, who was a man of ability and learning, endeavored to support himself and his family by the exercise of his pen and became a dramatic author of some celebrity. But ill-luck tracked him in all his efforts, and when old age crept on, and the hand that guided his pen became feeble, his case was truly pitiable. At times he was reduced to absolute want. On one occasion, when all else failed him, he was recommended to apply for the office of Librarian or Custodian of his father's Collection, which office was endowed with a few hundred pounds a year; but here again, Sir John Soane's Will was against him. It prohibited his son's appointment.

"Poor Soane is now dead and whatever may have been the errors and follies of his early career, he made atonement by thirty or forty years of the bitterest suffering. Not very long before his earthly miseries ended, he printed a piece of autobiography, entitled "Facts connected with the Life of George Soane, A.B." It is a sad memorial of the sorrow and wretchedness the unrestricted power of a testator may inflict on his own child. George Soane's autobiography thus concludes:—"I write not in malice, not in revenge for the wrongs of a whole life, but in my own defense, and in justice to my children—*Suum cuique tribuito.* * * * My father's rancor has been the deadly

Upas-tree, spreading its noxious shade over me, and blighting every prospect, every effort I have made for the benefit of those who are in nature nearest and dearest to me. I must once more take leave to ask, will this great nation do nothing for the family whose natural inheritance it is enjoying? Will it leave the immediate descendants of Sir John Soane to starve, while it quietly devours the food of those descendants? I believe that the wrong only requires to be known, and it will be redressed; in which conviction I throw myself upon the justice, the liberality, and the Christian spirit of my countrymen; reminding them only that if ten times more could with truth be brought against me than really pan, yet 'Joy shall be in heaven over one sinner that repenteth, more than over ninety and nine just persons.'"[1]

---

[1] *Vicissitudes of Families*, edited by John Bernard Burke, 1883, pgs. 403-405

THE CHAMBER OF THE PALE LADY
1837

EVERY OLD MANSION of any size or repute, that stands away from cities and has the good luck to outlast a few generations, is sure to have its legends. They gather and grow about the original truth, like ivy about ruins, till they have completely hidden the substance that supports them. Some of these relics of past ages have their haunted chambers. Others have their warning spirits to announce the approaching death of the lord of the mansion[1] and not a few retain the dim lustre of chivalrous daring and warlike achievement.

My father's hall, had its chamber of the Pale Lady, a name given to a particular room from the presence of a certain portrait painted on a panel of the oaken wainscot. The lady in question was of a very small figure, and, though beautiful, had a complexion of singular paleness, while there was a startling wildness about her large black eyes,—at least, all those said so, who saw the portrait after having heard her story. For myself, I perfectly well remember that she had inspired me, when a boy, with so much awe, that I never ventured into the room occupied by her portrait, except in broad daylight, and then I always took good care to have a companion.

Even now, when time has destroyed all other youthful fancies, mercilessly banning and banishing the spirits, black, white, and grey, that once delighted while they terrified me, I feel a sort of lingering veneration for the Pale Lady, and find a pleasure—childish, perhaps, but still a pleasure—in gazing at the old picture when the moon shines full upon it. Then is the hour for such a tale; shorn of those circumstances of time and place, which have made it so striking to my imagination, I fear its shadows will become as substantial, and as little apt to awe, as the

---

[1] Reference to banshees, old female spirits who wail outside the widow of a person about to die

ghost of Banquo upon the modern stage,[2] represented, as he always is, by some portly feeder, who seems sent to vouch for the good living of folks in the other world. But, not to draw out the grace much longer than the meal, thus runs the legend.

Queen Mary[3] had been on the throne of England almost twelve months and had already begun that career of blood, which has given an odious celebrity to her name. Thus encouraged by the royal example, the zeal of the Catholics grew hotter and hotter every day at the fires they had kindled for the spiritual benefit of their Protestant brethren, till at last there was little safety for the heretic in their neighborhood.

Much, however, in the more distant counties depended on the characters of the leading individuals professing the predominant faith. If they chanced to be tolerant, there was comparative impunity for the Protestant, who, if he did not make too intrusive a display of his principles, might then hope to pass unnoticed. Luckily for the neighborhood of Ivy Hall, Sir Hugh Trevor, though in other respects a good Catholic, was of this better class of spirits, so that the wood had not yet been kindled within the circle of his influence.

But to no one, not even to the father confessor of the family, did this tolerant disposition give so much displeasure, as to his own lady mother; so deadly was her hatred of the heretics that had she loved her son a grain less than she actually did, it was an even chance she had used her influence with Bonner,[4] to warm his zeal by the help of the stake and the wood. As it was, Dame Margaret contented herself with attributing his lukewarmness to the bad example of an early friend, a certain Sir Robert Lonsdale, who had latterly abandoned his faith for the uncourtly and dangerous creed of the reformers. On him, therefore, who was many years older than Sir Hugh, she poured down all her wrath, and he in a great measure served as a sort of conductor to carry off its lightnings from the head of the near offender.

---

[2] Macbeth has Lord Banquo murdered in *The Tragedy of Macbeth* by William Shakespeare, and he reappears in Act 3, Scene 4 as a ghost
[3] Queen Mary I of England (1516-1558)
[4] Edmund Bonner (1500-1569) was an English bishop who burned unbelievers at the stake and was known as "Bloody Bonner."

Such was the state of affairs at Ivy Hall, when one night, just as the mother and son were about to leave the supper table for their respective bedrooms, a loud and hasty ringing was heard at the great gatebell.

"*Sancte Maria!*" exclaimed the old lady, crossing herself in much trepidation, and sinking back again into the armchair, from which she had just risen. "What unhallowed thing is abroad at this hour?"

"There is no occasion for any alarm," said Sir Hugh. "If the visitor be a friend, he is welcome, late as the hour is. If an enemy, we are strong enough, I hope, to protect ourselves."

"Against such an enemy the arm of the flesh is all too weak," replied Dame Margaret, her head shaking as much from her fear as from the effects of a slight blow of palsy.

Again the bell rang, and yet more violently than at first, its shrill clamors seeming to be blown about the house by the wind as it howled in fierce and fitful eddies.

"A plague upon the coward knaves!" exclaimed Sir Hugh. "Tall fellows, and stout are they in the broad day; but at night, a shadow would start the best of them. Not one, I'll be sworn for it, will leave the hall-fire, unless I drive him from the ingle-corner."

"They believe in a devil," solemnly observed Dame Margaret, in whom even her extreme terror could not for a single instant tame the fierceness of her bigotry.

Sir Hugh made no reply, but seizing a candle, hurried out to enquire into the cause of this nocturnal visit, while the old lady, left alone with her terrors, mumbled prayer upon prayer, and invoked all the saints in the calendar to her assistance. Perhaps, the good folks listened to so fervent a votare, for it was not long before her fears were silenced by the return of her son who half supported, half carried, into the room a beautiful little female about sixteen years of age, apparently exhausted by the fatigues of a long journey.

At the first glance, Dame Margaret was much scandalized in seeing such service rendered by the Lord of Ivy Hall, and the inheritor of so many broad acres, to one, apparently so humble. For the maiden wore the garb of a wandering minstrel, and carried a lute suspended at her back by a plain, green ribbon. Nor was this feeling much diminished, when in a few hurried words, Sir Hugh committed the damsel to her own immediate care, begging, and it might be almost said commanding that she should receive every attention her situation required.

"She is noble, I hope," said the old lady, "or at least of such gentle blood as may warrant the service of your mother."

A faint smile passed over the pale features of the stranger, and Sir Hugh answered hastily, if not harshly,— "The daughter of a friend—of a near and dear friend."

"And her name?" asked Dame Margaret.

"Tomorrow, mother," replied Sir Hugh,—"tomorrow you will know all—all, at least, that is beseeming for you to know."

There was something in the tone of this qualified promise, that awed the querist into an unwilling silence. Never before had she seen her son in so uncompromising a mood, and the very novelty of the occurrence vouched for the occasion being of no ordinary a nature.

But days elapsed after this eventful night and still there appeared no signs of the promised tomorrow. The utmost amount of information that her pertinacity could extract was only this—the stranger's name was Emmeline. To add to her discomfort, as the character of the little damsel unfolded itself, which it did not fail to do in a very short time, she saw reason to fear that an *esprit follet*[5] had taken up its residence in her orthodox domicile.

The Pale Lady, as she now began to be called from the extreme fairness of her complexion, was no less capricious in her movements than Will-o'-the-Wisp[6] himself, and took the same delight in leading those, who followed her into trouble. Hence, it was no wonder if the servants, who were often the subjects of these pranks, became convinced that they had got a fairy, or some elementary spirit, for an inmate—a conviction which, when the first sentiment of fear had worn off, did not make the stranger less welcome to them. She became to their fancy a sort of household spirit, a freakish elf, such as Robin Goodfellow[7] had been to the cotters of yet earlier times, full of humorous pranks indeed, but friendly in temper, and never mischievously

---

[5] Elf spirit

[6] Playful fairy of light

[7] Also called "Puck" in English folklore, Robin Goodfellow was a woodland spirit who led people into the woods and got them lost.

disposed except when provoked by the ill-will or thwartings of her mortal companions.

When once the little maiden grew conscious of this belief in her supernatural nature, she seemed rather to delight in it than to wish to conceal her fairy origin. The milk was often found churned and the hearth swept, without the help of human hands, or at least of those hands whose proper occupation it would have been, and a silver sixpence would occasionally be dropped into the shoe of the careful housemaid. Then too her dress, however it might vary in the fashion of its shape, was invariably green, the traditional color of the fairies.

But the most decided proof, and there were more than one who could swear to it, was that her figure threw no shadow in the sunlight and received no reflection from any mirror. This strange tale, which she did not fail to encourage, at last reached the ears of Dame Margaret, who, with mingled feelings of horror and curiosity, determined to put the truth of it to the test. For this purpose she summoned the Pale Lady to a meeting in her private chamber where stood the only mirror in the house; a looking-glass not being so common a thing in those days, as it has since grown to be with us. But to no mandate of the kind could the little damsel be brought to lend an ear, word it as the messengers would, either in the way of threat or of gentle invitation. She was, it seemed, in one of her most dogged moods, or else suspected the cause of the summons and had no mind to submit herself to the ordeal.

"My lady begs you will come directly," said the Abigail, repeating her unnoticed message for the third time.

Emmeline gave no reply, but opened her large black eyes to their utmost extent and stared at the ambassadress in a way that made her feel anything but comfortable.

"Heaven bless us!" muttered the alarmed Abigail. "I have often heard of the Evil Eye, and, if ever there was such a thing, it is upon me now. I wish I were safely out of the room—Miss Emmeline!"—this was in a louder key—"Miss Emmeline, will it please you to come? My mistress loves contradiction as little as any lady in Christendom."

Here the elfin damsel burst into a long, unearthly laugh, that with every moment grew wilder and wilder, till it well-nigh reached a shriek. There was no standing for this. The *soubrette* uttered as loud a scream as her lungs would admit and fled, banging the door to, as a sort of barrier between herself and the laughing goblin.

It may be easily imagined with what feelings Dame Margaret received this account. There was something of fear, and more of irritation mingled with excited curiosity, in her voice as she dispatched a second message by Annette, her favorite maid, who was specially employed about her own person. This renewed summons was full of authority, and dignified resentment, proportioned to the confidential character of the person bearing it.

"Tell the young woman," she said, "that Dame Margaret Trevor, the lady of this mansion, requires the immediate presence of her nameless guest. If she have no respect for the hostess, who affords her an unwilling asylum, she at least owes the duty of youth to my grey hairs."

Annette had no great fancy for this mission, which, as it implied offence to the object of it, might not be altogether without peril to herself. But there was no choice, and besides she had naturally more courage, though not less superstition, than her companions. Down, therefore, she went, when, if she found nothing to try her boldness of spirit, she saw quite enough to astonish her, with all her previous experience of the little damsel's vagaries. Was the Pale Lady sad for the past, or doubtful of the future? Neither the one nor the other. She was dancing away as if the spirit of some frantic marabout[8] had possessed her, at every bound almost touching the ceiling, and whirling round like the little motes that dance in the sunbeams.

Nothing that Annette could say availed to stop her even for a moment; and when, as a last resource, she seized the hand of the emphatic dancer, so far from being able to stay her flight, she was herself borne along in the same giddy round, much after the manner of a straw caught up and tossed about by a whirlwind. In the midst of all this hurly-burly entered Dame Margaret, whose impatience could no longer endure the delay opposed to her curiosity. Her presence gave a new turn to the scene. A stranger would have fancied that he saw a merry schoolgirl detected in some forbidden game of romps by

---

[8] A dervish animal in Muslim Africa thought to have special powers

the unexpected appearance of her mistress; so suddenly did the Pale Lady break off the dance, and so motionless did she stand, after having dropt a profound courtesy to Dame Margaret. In the meanwhile, the unlucky Annette, released from the supporting hold of her companion, plumped down at once upon the floor, where she sat with her clothes carefully drawn over her feet, the very image of comical despair.

"What is the meaning of these witch Saturnalia!"[9] said the old lady, her angry glances wandering from the one to the other of the delinquents. "Are we all mad, I ask?"

"It is the full of the moon," replied the little damsel, with malicious gravity. "Yet I would fain hope for the best. You feel not giddier than you are wont, dear lady?"

"I sent to request your presence," said Dame Margaret, not perceiving, or not choosing to notice, the lurking malice of this tender inquiry. "Perhaps, now that the dancing mood is over, you will be pleased to follow me to my chamber, where we may have some private conference on matters that touch your repute as a Christian maiden."

"It is too late," said the Pale Lady, laughing.

"Too late?" exclaimed the elder dame.

"Too late," repeated the Pale Lady—and then sang, or rather chanted, with a look of peculiar archness,—

The word has been spoken,
  The magical token!
And the mirror is broken.
  Hoo! har, bar!—hoo!

The repetition of this familiar witch burthen sounded to the orthodox ears of Lady Margaret little better than actual blasphemy. She was perfectly confounded, and, before she could find either breath or sense to reply, in rushed the Abigail who had been left in the chamber of the mirror, wringing her hands and exclaiming in a voice of terror, "Oh, my lady! My lady!—it's not my fault—pray be not angry with me—it's not my fault."

"What is not your fault?" said Dame Margaret. "Speak out plainly, child—or has the madness seized you too, who used to be so reasonable?"

---

[9] In Roman mythology, Saturn was a deity who was celebrated with wild parties.

"The mirror, my lady!—The mirror! It is broken—dashed into a thousand pieces, and not a piece so large as a silver groat."

"How strange!" exclaimed the little damsel in a tone of earnestness, by no means usual with her. "I was only joking when I hinted that the glass was broken, and, lo now!—Cassandra herself could not have prophesied to better purpose. Rightly says the proverb,."

There was something in the glance of her eye strangely at variance with her words and with the tone in which they were uttered. It jarred most unpleasantly on the nerves of Dame Margaret. And now it would have been naturally supposed that the old lady, bigoted and fearful as she was, would have taken measures without delay for ridding the house of so ambiguous a being. And such, indeed, for a while seemed to be her purpose. The servants were ordered to quit the room, and, as their curiosity still kept them listeners at the door, they could hear her voice loud in anger, though the thick oak would not allow them to distinguish the precise import of every word.

Then, as usual, came the sound of the lute, the little damsel's weapon of defense against all assaults, and which by half the household was supposed to be a talisman, no less powerful in charming men's ears than the Syren's voice of old.[10] In a very few minutes its melody had so effectually lulled the storm, that, on peeping through the keyhole, they saw her seated on a low stool, her head in the lap of dame Margaret, who looked down on her with a smile of unwonted benevolence, while the withered hands played tremblingly with her dark ringlets, and smoothed their cluster from a brow and temples that shone more dazzlingly white than ever.

"Now the saints defend us!" exclaimed the peeping Abigail. "If ever fairy danced by moonlight, there's one hid in the body of that lute this blessed moment."

"I ever said so," replied the other.

And away they both hurried, partly in the fear lest a longer stay might betray them as listeners, and not less, it may be presumed, from a liberal spirit of communication, that could not remain satisfied till the rest of the

---

[10] Reference to the mythical sea siren who would lure sailors to their deaths on the rocks by the beauty of her singing

household were as well acquainted with the whole story as themselves.

It will be asked what had become of Sir Hugh while Ivy Hall was thus being turned topsy turvy by the frolics of his nameless protégé. At first he had treated her as a child, seeming to take no little delight in her wild pranks; but it was soon evident that the child had grown into a woman to his imagination, and in his altered manners towards her a shrewd spectator might have inferred that the Hall was likely ere long to have a new mistress.

This passion, as sudden as it was vehement, was attributed to the magic influence of the lute, though it seemed that Sir Hugh had been equally able to captivate the Pale Lady without any such advantage. She loved him with no less ardor; and, what might not have been so easily anticipated, made little scruple of showing it after her own wayward fashion, teasing and pleasing him in about an equal measure. Often it would happen that she exceeded even the endurance of a lover, and his wrath would settle down into a sullen mood that predicted a determined rupture. On such occasions she always had recourse to her lute, which never failed to do its work, the shadows flying from his brow like mists before the sun when it breaks out from the clouds of April.

It will hardly be supposed that so keen-sighted a personage as Dame Margaret was all this time ignorant of a love-affair passing immediately under her eyes. How indeed should she be, when one of the parties at least took so little pains to conceal it? But her wrath smoldered quietly enough among the embers while there was a chance that it might end, like half the affairs of this kind, in vapor, for she was too prudent to provoke a different catastrophe by unseasonable opposition. "Say nothing,"— thus would she argue it in her own mind,—"say nothing, and this little spark will go out of itself, when a puff of breath from me would kindle it into a flame. I must be silent?"

Silent she was accordingly, refraining from words good or evil, though, as might be expected, such an excess of discretion cost her much heartburn, 'till one day Sir Hugh gave her notice in due form that it was his intention to marry the little damsel. Then indeed she made herself ample amends for all her past forbearance, and poured forth such a storm of wrath on the devoted head of Sir

Hugh that might well have excused him had he deviated from his purpose. But all in vain. It is so easy to maintain a resolution when it happens to be in perfect consonance with our own desires. Women, however, do not so lightly give up any scheme it may once please them to take into their heads, even when it does not come recommended, as in the present instance, by the semblance at least of sound policy. Finding her son inflexible, to a degree that baffled all her powers of persuasion, she could only attribute an obstinacy so unusual with him, to the influence of magical practices. It was clear that the Pale Lady had cast a spell over him, and where could the secret source of the charm be better sought for than in the lute, the potency of which had been made apparent to every one of the household?

To destroy the instrument then was to take the fang from the adder, and accordingly it was in her own mind doomed to destruction with the first opportunity. When this would offer itself was another question, for the lute was the little maiden's constant companion, at home and abroad, on foot and on horseback, nor was she ever observed to set it down except on one particular occasion that recurred but once a month. This was on the full of the moon, when she never failed to find some pretense for walking alone in the neighboring forest. At such times it was always remarked that she grew sadder and sadder as the day declined. Her eyes would fill with tears, and she would gaze on Sir Hugh, when she thought herself unnoticed, with the anxious looks of one who was about to part from a near and dear friend forever.

The motives for these nightly wanderings none could discover, though there was no want of curiosity on the part of the inmates of Ivy Hall, who, to do them justice, had to the utmost extent of their courage exerted themselves to learn the secret. One or two of the boldest went so far, more than once, as to visit her supposed haunts on the following morning, when they found, or said they found, the print of feet, exactly corresponding to hers, in a certain plananguare, or round as it is sometimes called, a relic from the times of the Druids.

Here, they had no doubt, she had been to meet the queen of the fairies and obtain leave of absence for another month to dwell amongst the human mortals. In confirmation of this opinion, they remarked the wild joy she always evinced on her return, and the liberality with which she scattered silver,—fairy silver no doubt,—among the servants. But the more popular belief was that she went to worship the moon, from whom she received her power; and an altar, standing in an open part of the forest, was pointed out as the altar where she laid her monthly offerings. These offerings were supposed to be of an innocent nature given the fashion of the altar. It consisted, according to the usual form of such monuments, of an upright stone and a second mass placed on it horizontally, the latter having a cross rudely cut into it; and hence it was inferred that sylph, or fairy, or whatever else the little maiden might be, she could not belong to the evil spirits, since she was so familiar with the holy symbol.

The moon had now come to the full for the twelfth time since the eventful night that opened our tale, when Dame Margaret finally set about breaking the spell, as she deemed it, which had enthralled her son. By a coincidence, not perhaps very wonderful, seeing that kindred wits will jump together, Annette, the waiting-maid already mentioned, had her own plans of discovery reserved for this same evening. Having been more than once baffled by her fears when attempting to follow the Pale Lady into the forest, she magnanimously resolved, while yet the daylight lasted, to take up a secret position near the altar, thus flinging herself at once upon the peril that she was afraid to meet coolly.

It was a close autumnal evening, and the thick sultry air hung heavily on the leaves and flowers, that seemed to droop despondingly beneath its weight, the gnats and water-flies swarmed on the still face of the pools and there was uneasiness as well as listlessness in the motions of the cattle.

At times a pale flash of lightning would show itself far off in the horizon and the thunder would mutter at distant intervals, but not a drop of rain fell, and not a blade of grass stirred. It would seem that even the Pale Lady, goblin or fairy as she was supposed to be, yet felt the influence of the hour, for, as she threaded the dingles and green alleys of the forest, there was none of the usual wild gaiety either in her subdued step or saddened features. The smile, that so seldom left her lips, was now absent. Her wonted song was hushed, her looks expressed extreme anxiety, and ever and anon she would stop and lean against a broad-trunked oak, evidently not from weariness, but from reluctance to meet some dreaded object, to which she was of necessity advancing.

But linger as she might, she at length reached the open glade, in the middle of which stood the altar where a flood of yellow light poured down on it, as if the Druid stone had some secret power of attraction that drew the moonbeams to itself, while the sward about it lay in shadow. The heart of the fairy-wanderer, if fairy she was, beat fast as she neared the rugged pile, and her colorless cheek was tinted with that passing flush which hope lends when struggling for the mastery with fear. Again she paused, apparently to muster up resolution for the fated task, and then slowly resumed her onward march towards the altar. Annette, who saw everything from her hiding place behind a clump of trees, always vowed, in telling the tale, that she neither ran nor walked, but skimmed over the grass that waved beneath her feet as if it had been swept by the passing wind—"It was a strange sight," she would say, "to see the grass rippling in one narrow stripe, just like the sea when a squall walks over it, darkening and agitating its surface while all beyond the immediate influence of the fitful breeze remains unruffled."

No sooner had the Pale Lady reached the altar than she became sensible of a branch of mistletoe lying on the horizontal, upper stone. If not a subject of surprise, it was evidently unwelcome to her, for in the moment of perceiving it she uttered a faint scream, and sank against the monument, trembling and exhausted, like one who has received a sudden shock. With reluctant hand, after a brief pause, she took up the branch, her tears dropping fast on it, hesitated awhile, then broke the stem in two and flung it from her as if it had been a serpent.

It would seem that the storm, which had been so long gathering, had reserved itself to this particular moment. A loud peal of thunder, rolling from one end of the heavens to the other, gave the signal, when down it came in all its fury, the rain pouring, the blast howling, and the lightning wrapping the earth for many seconds together in one continued blaze. Then followed a longer, sharper crash, like the groan of convulsed nature, and in the next instant a thunderbolt hurtled through the air and shivered the altar into a thousand pieces.

Annette wanted to see no more. With a speed proportioned to her terror, she ran back to Ivy Hall, dashed by the astonished household, and hurried into the presence of her mistress for protection. But Dame Margaret had in the meantime met with her own proper causes of alarm, and to all appearance was as much in need of comfort as her terrified dependent. She stood gazing on the broken lute, her usually pale face yet paler from the workings of fear, her eyes dilated, and her aged limbs shaking in every joint. The ejaculations of Annette, neither low nor few, failed for a time to withdraw her attention from the ruins of the supposed talisman, and, when she did become sensible of the handmaiden's presence, it was only to give way to those feelings which had hitherto held her speechless.

"Dreadful!" was her first exclamation. "Surely it was from the fiend himself! *Beata Maria, ora pro nobis—ora pro nobis!*[11]—And she crossed herself repeatedly and fervently.

"Now, all the saints be good unto us!" re-echoed Annette, her own previous terror visibly augmented by the fears of her mistress, though she was unable to guess the precise cause of them.—"The saints be good unto us!"

"They have been," cried Dame Margaret. "They have been. But get me a chair. This shock has rudely shaken my old limbs and I can stand no longer. The holy Virgin—blessed be her name!—was with me, or I must have died on the spot. Awful times, Annette—awful times. The world grows worse as it grows older, and heaven alone knows what it all will end in. But whatever it may be, thank God I will not live to see it. I will be safe in that home where the wicked cease to trouble."

"In the name of all that's terrible, what has happened?" exclaimed Annette.

"What indeed, girl! Oh, it was an awful moment when I dashed the accursed lute to pieces, and, with uplifted cross and counted beads, adjured him to fly—him, the unholy one, who had so long housed within it. Was it you, child, who it was that lent the strings their melody, witching all ears and hearts, that none of us were the masters of our own will?—Apollyon,[12] child—Apollyon! Ah!

---

[11] The blessed Mary, pray for us—pray for us!
[12] Another name for Satan

it is a wonder that my brain and sight still hold, and that my tongue can tell it to you."

Dame Margaret placed her hands to her forehead, as if she thought to still the inward pain by their pressure. The sympathizing Annette, forgetting at the moment her own immediate cause of terror in anxiety for her mistress, burst into tears.

"My dear lady!" she cried. "My dear lady, you are ill. Let me go for help. Should I call the servants?—Should I call Sir Hugh?"

"Heed it not, my good Annette. It is a passing pang only, and, with the blessing of the saints, will soon be over.— Mother in heaven! What now?"

This last exclamation was provoked by the loud yell of many voices from the rooms below, announcing some general cause of terror.

"Run, girl," continued the old lady. "Learn what new mischance has happened to excite this fearful outcry."

But Annette had no occasion to leave the room to gain this knowledge. A single glance through the window, which opened on the fields between the house and the Severn,[13] was sufficient to show the cause of the uproar.

"Merciful powers!" she said, or rather shrieked. "See! See!—how the sparkles fly from his hoofs! How the flames stream from the creature's red nostrils!"

"Who? What?" exclaimed the old lady.

"How they fly!—and the lightning flies after them, flash upon flash—it's aimed at them—only at them—and passes over the trees without scorching a single leaf."

"Who? What?" reiterated Dame Margaret in the very agony of fear. "Speak out, girl. Tell me all—tell me at once, for I feel my senses are fast leaving me."

"Apollyon! The great fiend!—He rides off with the Pale Lady—there's not a speck of white on the black horse that carries them."

With that irresistible impulse, which often compels our attention to objects of dread or loathing, Dame Margaret tottered forward to the window and beheld the Pale Lady flying, or carried off, her clothes drenched with rain, and her loose hair streaming to the tempest. The speed of the coal-black horse outstripped the wind and the rider, who bestrode him, appeared in the uncertain light to be of

---

[13] The Severn River is the longest river in the United Kingdom.

colossal stature. Their course lay for a few seconds along the banks of the Severn, but suddenly, amidst the renewed rattling of thunder and the howling of wind, one long continued flash of the broadest and reddest lightning blazed about them, and in the next moment the horse was seen with his riders in the midst of the boiling waters. Then came a loud shriek of agony from the maiden, followed by a yell so fierce and unearthly, that both the watchers instinctively closed their eyes in terror. It was an instant—only an instant—and, when they again looked out, nothing was visible on the river but the white foam of the angry billows.

Such is the accredited tradition of the Pale Lady, as I received it from the old servants of the family, and as it had been handed down to them from father to son through many generations. I must not, however, conceal the fact of there having been another version of the story, less allied to the marvelous, yet, perhaps, not a whit more real. According to this gloss, Sir Robert Lonsdale was the midnight visitor, who, being compelled to fly from England by the tyranny of Queen Mary, could find no better way of disposing of his daughter than by entrusting her to the care of his young friend, Sir Hugh Trevor. That this gentleman professed the Roman Catholic faith was rather an advantage than otherwise, inasmuch as it ensured the sanctity of the asylum, while his well-known spirit of toleration gave promise of his being a warm and efficient protector. The little damsel, thus unceremoniously introduced into Ivy Hall, was of a lively, if not a wayward, temper, and from the habits of a spoiled childhood, as well as from natural inclination, apt to indulge in whatever might happen to be the caprice of the moment. With such a disposition, the general belief of the household in her supernatural qualities delighted her beyond measure, as affording ample scope for the enacting of those wild pranks, in which she ever found too much gratification.

As to her lute and song, there was indeed a magic in them, but it was the natural magic belonging to matchless skill, and a voice of such extraordinary sweetness as rarely to have been equaled. Her monthly visits to the altar were, if this version might be believed, the result of a previous compact with her father, who, when he had taken the requisite order abroad for her commodious home there, was to signify his return by depositing a branch of mistletoe on the Druid stone. The circumstance of the black horse plunging into the Severn, in which both steed and riders were lost, might be sufficiently accounted for by supposing that the sudden fury of the storm had startled the animal from his course, and urged him towards the Severn, which was at the time rendered as wild as any sea by a sudden hygre, or eagre, a name given in that county to designate the meeting of the sea-tide with the freshwater current.

Those, who like this explanation, may adopt it. For my part I stick to my old nurse's legend, and am ready to die on it, that the Pale Lady was either a sylph or a fairy.

FANTASY SHORT STORIES
CONSIDERED

Anonymous

    1804 Artless Love
    1816 The Tomb of Amestris; a Persian Tale
    1821 The Haunted Ships
    1822 The Lady Sprite; an Old Tale
    1825 The Irish Witch and the Rebel's Wife
    1825 The Dwarf; or, the Deformed Transformed
    1825 The Four Brothers
    1825 The Gnome of the Hartz Mountains
    1826 Amorassan; or, the Spirit of the Frozen Ocean!
    1826 The Chase of King Waldemar, the Dane
    1826 The Dwarfs of the Nine Mountains of Rambin
    1826 The Elf with the Featureless Head
    1826 Elphin Irving, the Fairies' Cupbearer
    1826 The Gnome King, or the Magic Sceptre
    1826 The Lepreghaun, or Gold Goblin
    1826 The Magic Dollar
    1826 Maredata and Giulio; or, the Ocean Spirit
    1826 Peter of Stauffenburg
    1826 The Sprite of the Glen
    1826 The Treasure Seeker
    1826 The Unknown!, or the Knight of the Blood-Red
Plume
    1827 The King of the Hartz
    1828 The Legend of Number Nip
    1828 The Philosopher's Stone
    1830 Almanzor; or, the Reward of Virtue
    1830 Emma at the Woodman's Hut
    1830 Fairy Gifts; or, the Happy Choice
    1830 Florimond; or the Magic Ring
    1830 The Little Black Bag; or, the Fairy Gem
    1830 Marmosetta; or, the Power of Gratitude
    1830 Pernoella and the Old Queen
    1830 Prince Pironette; or, the Reward of Virtue
    1832 The Mine of Saint Margaret. A Story of
Falkenstein.
    1833 The Boarwolf
    1835 The Mermaid; A Reverie

1835 The Witch
1836 The Sea-sprite; or, a Voice from the Deep
1837 Legendary Lore. The Palace of Morgana
1837 The Pirates Retreat
1838 Sylph Etherege
1839 The Fairy Shoe
1839 The Gnome King
1839 The Kelpie Rock
1839 The Linn of the Caldron
1841 The Water Kelpie's Bridle and the Mermaid's Stone
1845 The Magician and the Favorite
1847 The Story of Bellina (Fairies)
1849 Tragical Effects of Jealousy

F. A.
1844 The Wizard's Cave. A Tale of Italy.

J. Y. A____N
1829 Will O' the Wisp. A Fairy Tale.

A. Apel
1810 Der Freischutz; or, the Seven Magic Bullets

M. L. B.
1831 Fairy Favours. A Vision of Fairy Land.

Mark Bancroft
1836 Lydia Ashbaugh, The Witch

N. C. Brooks
1836 Obadiah Leatherby; or, the Tight Shoe

S. J. Burr
1844 The Philosopher's Stone

D. C.
1829 Seddeck Ben Saad the Magician

E. S. C.
1826 The Wizard's Revenge

M. Corbett
1827 Legends of Number Nip

Alfred Crowquill
    1828 The Sea Sprite

Allan Cunningham
    1822 Elphin Irving, The Fairies' Cupbearer

George Darley
    1824 Lilian of the Vale

Charles Dickens
    1836 The Story of the Goblins Who Stole a Sexton

Alexander Dumas
    1840s The Enchanted Whistle

Elizabeth F. Ellett
    1845 The Witch Caprusche

Joseph von Eichendorff
    1808-1809 Autumn Sorcery

T. F.
    1831 The Story of Welzheim, the Charcoal Burner

Baron Friedrich Heinrich Karl De la Motte Fouquâe
    1820 The Field of Terror
    1823 The Magic Dollar
    1825 The Magic Ring; a Romance

Theophile Gautier
    1840 The Mummy's Foot

Robert Pearse Gilles
    1826 Nikkur Holl

Nikolai Gogol
    1832 A Terrible Vengeance
    1832 A Bewitched Place
    1835 Viy

William Child Green
    1819 Secrets of Cabalism, or Ravenstone and Alice of
Huntington

John Hamilton
    1844 Oriana and Vesperella; or, The City of Pearls; Chapter II

John M. Harney
    1816 Crystalina, A Fairy Tale.

Wilhelm Hauff
    1827 The Dwarf Nose
    1827 The Prophecy of the Silver Florin
    1828 The Fortunes of Said
    1828 The Cavern of Steenfoll

Nathaniel Hawthorne
    1835 Young Goodman Brown
    1837 Dr. Heidegger's Experiment
    1846 The Hall of Fantasy

R. Haworth
    1825 The Talisman

Charles F. Hoffman
    1843 Ko-rea-ran-neh-neh; or, The Flying Head

Earnest Theodore Hoffmann
    1817 A New Year's Eve Adventure
    1826 The First of May, or Wallburga's Night

James Hogg
    1827 The Brownie of the Black Haggs
    1837 The Witches of Traquair

W. Hughes
    1847 The Blind Ogre

Washington Irving
    1819 Rip van Winkle

Prosper Mérimée
    1837 *La Vénus d'Ille*

Charles Nordhoff
    1808 Once Upon a Time
    1808 How Rubezahl Got His Nickname

Francis Lathorn
    1800-1830 The Water Spectre

Sir Thomas Dick Lauder
    1841 The Water Kelpie's Bridle and The Mermaid's Stone

John MacKay Wilson
    1835 The Doom of Soulis

Gérard de Nerval
    1832 The Enchanted Hand

Edgar Allan Poe
    1831 Bon-Bon
    1836 Four Beasts in One
    1841 The Island of the Fay
    1844 The Angel of the Odd
    1845 Some Words with a Mummy

Thomas Peckett Prest
    1833 The Demon of the Hartz

Thomas De Quincey
    1823 The Magic Dice

Edwin F. Roberts
    1848 The Rosicrician

Alois Wilhelm Schreiber
    1822 The Devil's Ladder, or the Gnomes of the Redrich

Sir Walter Scott
    1828 The Tale of the Mysterious Mirror

J. D. Shaw
    1831 The Demon Ship

Mary Shelley
    1830 Transformation

Joseph Snowe
    1839 Ursel. The Water-Wolf

George Soane
    1841 The Legend of Narwarth Castle
    1841 Friar Bacon's Key
    1841 The Singular Trial of Francis Ormiston
    1841 The Chamber of the Pale Lady
    1841 A Legend of Knole, or Knowle Park

Sternberg
    1845 Green and Black Tea

Ludwig Tieck
    1811 Elphin-Land
    1823 The Sorcerers

G. H. W.
    1846 My Grandmother's Tale

OTHER TITLES BY ANDREW BARGER

<u>BlooDeath</u>
<u>The Best Vampire Short Stories 1800-1849</u>

Unearthed from long forgotten journals and magazines, Andrew Barger has found the very best vampire short stories from the first half of the 19th century, which are collected for the first time in this award-winning book on the origins of vampire lore. The cradle of all vampire short stories in the English language is the first half of the 19th century. Andrew combed forgotten journals and mysterious texts to collect the very best vintage vampire stories from this crucial period in vampire literature. In doing so, Andrew unearthed the second and third vampire stories originally published in the English language, neither printed since their first publication nearly 200 years ago.

Also included is the first vampire story originally written in English by John Polidori after a dare with Lord Byron and Mary Shelley. The groundbreaking book contains the first vampire short story by an American who happened to be a graduate of Columbia Law School. The book further containes the first vampire stories by an Englishman and German, including the only vampire stories by such renowned authors as Alexander Dumas, Théophile Gautier and Joseph le Fanu. As readers have come to expect from Andrew, he has added his scholarly touch to this collection by including annotations, story backgrounds, author photos and a foreword titled "With Teeth."

<u>Shifters</u>
<u>The Best Werewolf Short Stories 1800-1849</u>
Andrew has compiled the best tales from the period when werewolf short stories were first unleashed. The stories are "Hugues the Wer-Wolf: A Kentish Legend of the Middle

Ages," "The Man-Wolf," "A Story of a Weir-Wolf," "The Wehr-Wolf: A Legend of the Limousin," and "The White Wolf of the Hartz Mountains." It is believed that two of these stories have never been republished in over 150 years since their original printing. Read *Shifters: The Best Werewolf Short Stories 1800-1849* by the light of a full moon.

A seminal work of impressive scholarship, "The Best Werewolf Short Stories 1800-1849: A Classic Werewolf Anthology" is highly recommended reading for fantasy fans, and a valued addition to academic library Literary Studies reference collections. – **MIDWEST BOOK REVIEW**

Mesaerion
The Best Science Fiction Short Stories 1800-1849

Looking for sci-fi stories that defined a genre? How about what is possibly the first science fiction story by a female or the first steampunk short story? There is the first voyage to the moon and a meeting with a lunar alien— Zuloc! What about a darkness machine and the first robotic insect? There is also the first story that deals with cryogenic freezing and reanimation. Andrew has searched two-hundred-year-old magazines and journals to find the very best science fiction stories from the period when the genre came to life, some of which are published for the first time in nearly 200 years.

More than just a simple anthology, 'Mesaerion: The Best Science Fiction Stories 1800-1849' significantly benefits modern readers with the editor's story back ground commentaries, annotations, author photos, and in informative foreword. – **MIDWEST BOOK REVIEW**

Phantasmal
The Best Ghost Short Stories 1800-1849

Ghost short stories became very popular in the first half of the nineteenth century and this collection by Andrew Barger contains the very scariest of them all. Some stories thought too horrific were published anonymously like "A Night in a Haunted House" and "The Deaf and Dumb Girl," with the later being anthologized for the first time since its original publication in 1839.

The other ghost short stories in this fine collection are by famous authors. "The Mask of the Red Death," is by Edgar Allan Poe; "A Chapter in the History of a Tyrone Family," by Joseph Sheridan le Fanu; "The Spectral Ship," by Wilhelm Hauff; "The Old Maid in the Winding Sheet," by Nathaniel Hawthorne; "The Adventure of the German Student," and "The Legend of Sleepy Hollow," by Washington Irving; as well as "The Tapestried Chamber," by Sir Walter Scott. Andrew Barger has added his familiar scholarly touch to this collection by including annotations, story backgrounds, author photos and a foreword titled "All Ghosts Are Gray."

[A] unique perspective on this dawn of horror's early roots and their connections to our modern day. "The Best Ghost Stories 1800-1849" is a choice pick with stories from many legendary authors such as Edgar Allan Poe and Washington Irving, very much recommended reading. **—MIDWEST BOOK REVIEW**

<u>The Divine Dantes</u>
<u>Squirt Gun in Hades (Infernal Trilogy #1)</u>

An Indie Book Awards best second novel finalist, the first book in *The Divine Dantes* trilogy finds young rocker Edward T. Nad down on his luck after the other member of his two-person band (and girlfriend—Beatrice) leaves their small town for Europe. Once there, Beatrice has second thoughts about the breakup and asks their erstwhile manager cum travel agent, Virgil, to bring Edward to her without him knowing it. This sparks off the hilarious intercontinental journey of the staid, nerdy manager and the young rocker with an active and opinionated mind who struggles with the basics, like settling on a name for the band: "Grain of Sand and the Clams" versus "The Beelzebubbas." The novel contains the characters of "The Inferno" and tracks their movements through Hades in modern times. *Dante's Infernos: Squirt Guns in Hades* is the first in a trilogy of novels that parallel "The Inferno," "The Purgatorio," and "The

Paradiso" of Dante's *The Divine Comedy* through modern times. Read the first chapter at the end of this book.

[A] lively and good-natured work . . .. **—PUBLISHER'S WEEKLY REVIEWER**

[R]eminds me a little of the fun I find in Carl Hiaasen or Christopher Moore, but he definitely has his own vibe . . .. **—AMZ BREAKTHROUGH NOVEL AWARD EXPERT REVIEWER**

<u>Coffee with Poe</u>
<u>A Novel of Edgar Allan Poe's Life</u>

Coffee with Poe brings Edgar Allan Poe to life within its pages as never before. The book is filled with actual letters from his many romances and literary contemporaries. Orphaned at the age of two, Poe is raised by John Allan—his abusive foster father—who refuses to adopt him until he becomes straight-laced and businesslike. Poe, however, fancies poetry and young women. The contentious relationship culminates in a violent altercation, which causes Poe to leave his wealthy foster father's home to make it as a writer. Poe tries desperately to get established as a writer but is ridiculed by the "Literati of New York."

The Raven gains Poe renown in America yet he slips deeper into poverty, only making $15 off the poem's entire publication history. Desperate for a motherly figure in his life, Poe marries his first cousin who is only thirteen. Poe lives his last years in abject poverty while suffering through the deaths of his foster mother, grandmother, and young wife. In a cemetery he becomes engaged to Helen Whitman, a dark poet who is addicted to ether, wears a small coffin about her neck, and conducts séances in her home. The engagement is soon broken off because of Poe's drinking. In his final months his health is in a downward spiral. Poe disappears on a trip and is later found delirious and wearing another person's clothes. He dies a few days later, whispering his final words: "God help my poor soul."

*To give us a historical fiction look at Edgar Allan Poe is great. The start where we are at his mom's funeral gives a little insight into why he may write the way he does. It is very interesting the ideas the author has put into the story about Poe. I like the idea of detailing the life of Edgar Allan Poe into a historical fiction novel. . . . A great idea to give us some insight into why Poe may be the way he is. —**AMZ BREAKTHROUGH NOVEL AWARD EXPERT REVIEWER***

<u>Edgar Allan Poe</u>
<u>Annotated and Illustrated Entire Stories and Poems</u>
For the first time in one compilation are background information for Poe's stories and poems, annotations, foreign word translations, photographs of individuals Poe wrote about, and poetry to Poe from his many romantic interests. Here is a sampling of the tales and poems included: "Annabel Lee," "The Bells," "The Black Cat," "[The Bloodhounds]," "The Cask of Amontillado," "The Conqueror Worm," "A Descent into the Maelstrom," "The Fall of the House of Usher," "The Gold-Bug," "The Haunted Palace," "Lenore," "The Masque of the Red Death," "MS. Found in a Bottle," "Murders in the Rue Morgue," "The Oblong Box," "The Pit and the Pendulum," "The Premature Burial," "The Purloined Letter," "[The Rats of Park Theatre]," "The Raven," "Some Words with a Mummy," "The Swiss Bell-Ringers," "The System of Doctor Tarr and Professor Fether," "The Tell-Tale Heart," and "Thou Art the Man." The classic illustrations are by Gustave Dore and Harry Clarke, with a great introduction by Andrew Barger.

This is an ambitious work and one that immediately becomes the scholar's gold standard for research on this major writer of mystery and thrills. If for no other reason than to have a solid selection of the works of Poe on the shelf, this beautifully designed and handsomely printed book will serve that intent. But once the reader thumbs through this book, pausing to re-read favorites such as 'The Fall of the House of Usher', 'The Murders in the Rue Morgue', 'The Pit and the Pendulum', and 'The Raven', there are many little known gems of short stories, articles, essays, and poems in addition to the stories that are less familiar to the larger audience to discover.

Barger adds 'guidance' to his method of presenting these works by such devices as listing all of the poems under the subheadings of 'Women in Edgar Allan Poe's Life', 'Miscellaneous Poetry both Before and After Age 25', 'Autobiographical', and 'Men in Edgar Allen Poe's Life.' These may seem like minor adjustments to the collections, but in Barger's hands the divisions add meaning and context to the works.

This is simply a splendid book, handsomely written and produced, and a fine tribute to the literature of Poe - and to the scholarship of Andrew Barger! Highly Recommended. — **AMZ TOP TEN REVIEWER**

<u>Mailboxes – Mansions – Memphistophels</u>
<u>A Collection of Dark Tales</u>

A finalist in the International Book Awards anthology category, Andrew Barger's first short story collection unleashes a blend of character-driven dark tales, which are sure to be remembered. In the collection Andrew unleashes a blend of character-driven dark tales, which are sure to be remembered. In "Azra'eil & Fudgie" a little girl visits a team of marines in Afghanistan and they quickly learn she is more than she seems. "The Mailbox War" is a deadly tale of a weekend hobby taken to extremes while "The Brownie of the Alabaster Mansion" sees a Scottish monster of antiquity brought back to life. "Memphistopheles" contains a tale of the devil, Memphis, barbeque and a wannabe poet. "The Serpent and the Sepulcher" is a prose poem that will be cherished by all who experience it. "The Gëbult Mansion" recounts a literary hoax played by Andrew on his unsuspecting social networking friends that involves a female vampire. Last, "Stain" is an unforgettable horror story about a stain that will not go away.

<u>6a66le</u>
<u>The Best Horror Short Stories 1800-1849</u>

The Best Horror Short Stories 1800-1849 is a book for anyone who loves a classic horror story.

Thanks to Edgar Allan Poe, Honoré de Balzac, Nathaniel Hawthorne and others, the first half of the nineteenth century is the cradle of all modern horror short stories. Andrew Barger, the editor, read over 300 horror short stories and compiled the dozen best. A few have never been republished since they were first published in leading periodicals of the day such as *Blackwood's* and *Atkinson's Casket*. At the back of the book Andrew includes a list of all short stories he considered along with their dates of publication and the author, when available. He even includes background for each of the stories, author photos and annotations for difficult terminology.

'The Best Horror Short Stories 1800-1849' will likely become a best seller . . . What makes this collection (of truly terrifying tales!) so satisfying is the presence of a brief introduction before each story, sharing some comments about the writer and elements of the tale. Barger has once again whetted our appetites for fright, spent countless hours making these twelve stories accessible and available, and has provided in one book the best of the best of horror short stories. It is a winner. —**AMZ TOP TEN REVIEWER**

Through his introduction and footnotes, Barger aims for readers both scholarly and casual, ensuring that the authors get their due while making the work accessible overall to the mainstream. —**BOOKGASM**

A top to bottom pick for anyone who appreciates where the best of horror came from. —**MIDWEST BOOK REVIEW**

ABOUT ANDREW

Andrew Barger is the award winning author of *Coffee with Poe: A Novel of Edgar Allan Poe's Life,* and a short story collection: *Mailboxes – Mansions – Memphistopheles.* His most recent fiction is *The Divine Dantes* trilogy that follows the characters of *The Divine Comedy* through a messed up (and funny) modern world. Andrew is also the editor of a number of classic anthologies in the fantasy genre including, *Mesaerion: The Best Science Fiction Stories 1800-1849, Shifters: The Best Werewolf Short Stories 1800-1849* and *Phantasmal: The Best Ghost Stories 1800-1849.*

CONNECT WITH ANDREW ONLINE

AndrewBarger.com

Blog:
AndrewBarger.blogspot.com

Facebook:
facebook.com/AuthorAndrewBarger

Goodreads:
goodreads.com/author/show/1362598.Andrew_Barger

Twitter:
@AndrewBarger

9 781933 747538